Praise for *The Do*

When country music star Trina Pott
ham, Texas, she finds herself caught up in a mystery that makes everyone look like a suspect. Her high school rival Bitsy is about to divorce her hairdresser husband and gets a tad jealous of Trina being back and getting cozy with lawyer Wyatt Chastain. Because Trina is worried about her mother and her niece Mari, who runs the local animal rescue shelter, she decides to buy land in Brenham and let Mari have a building to renovate and use for the Second Chance Ranch rescue clinic. And there is Blue Bell ice cream. Soon, strange things start happening--pipe bombs, her dog getting hurt, the BBQ obsessed neighbor threatening to shoot first and ask questions later, and she's falling for Wyatt. How can she keep up when her record company wants her to stay in Nashville. This book has all the feels--Texas, ice cream, dogs, and a fun family, all wrapped up in quirky small town package. You'll woof you way through this one. It's fun!!

–Lenora Worth, *New York Times* bestselling
author of *The X-Mas Club*

Y'Barbo takes you on a fun visit to small town Texas where you can practically smell the barbeque cooking (and the apple pie). She creates a cast of characters that shine, each with their own wonderful personalities. As you read, you wonder *'who done it?'* right up until the very end. Steller writing, fun characters, and a caper so good you just can't put it down!

–Kari Trumbo, *USA Today* bestselling author

Kathleen Y'Barbo's *The Dog Days of Summer* is a fun tale set in little Brenham, Texas. Dog-loving, country-music-star heroine, Trina Potter's first-person narration gives the story an authentic Texas twang to go along with all the mystery, sweet romance, and small-town schemes a reader could want.

–Julianna Deering, author of the Drew Farthering Mysteries

Kathleen has done it again! Steller writing, relatable characters, twisty plot, and rescue dogs. . .who could want anything more? You don't want to miss Dog Days of Summer.

–Robin Caroll, author of the Darkwater Inn series

Oh, my goodness, I loved this story! Take a plucky yet compassionate song-singing heroine. Add a swoon-worthy hero, secondary characters who provide spice and mischief, and a whole cast of lovable canines. Place them in a small-town atmosphere and then stir in an intriguing mystery wrapped around doggy-rescue. End result? A must-turn-one-more-page story from beginning to end. I've loved every Y'Barbo book I've ever read, but *Dog Days of Summer* is at the top of the list. Treat yourself to this entertaining, heart-touching, soul-impacting tale of healing old wounds and crafting new beginnings.

–Kim Vogel Sawyer, bestselling author of *Freedom's Song*

DOG DAYS of SUMMER

KATHLEEN Y'BARBO

The Dog Days of Summer ©2022 by Kathleen Y'Barbo

Print ISBN 978-1-63609-394-9

Adobe Digital Edition (.epub) 978-1-63609-395-6

This book is a work of fiction. Names, characters, places, and incidents are either products of the author's imagination or used fictitiously. Any similarity to actual people, organizations, and/or events is purely coincidental.

Cover Design: Kirk DouPonce, DogEared Design

Published by Barbour Publishing, Inc., 1810 Barbour Drive, Uhrichsville, Ohio 44683, www.barbourbooks.com

Our mission is to inspire the world with the life-changing message of the Bible.

ecpa Member of the Evangelical Christian Publishers Association

Printed in the United States of America.

DEDICATION

For as long as I can remember, I have dreamed of moving to Washington County, Texas, and living close to the bluebonnets, my favorite restaurant and pie shop (Royer's Café and Royer's Pie Haven in Round Top), the rolling hills, the Junk Gypsy Company store (also in Round Top), the twice yearly Antiques Weeks shopping extravaganza, and well. . .you get the idea.

I love that place!

However, my feet are firmly planted some sixty or so miles away from my version of heaven on earth.

For now.

But someday. . .

In the meantime, this book is dedicated to my favorite Washington County, Texas, women authors, creatives, and entrepreneurs:

Tara "the Pie Queen" Royer Steele, author of *Eat, Pie, Love* and the owner of Royer's Pie Haven and All Things Acres;

Amie and Jolie Sykes (aka the Junk Gypsies), authors of *Junk Gypsy: Designing a Life at the Crossroads of Wonder & Wander*;

and

because she's my inspiration for Trina Potter, Miranda Lambert, who with her mom, Bev Lambert, founded MuttNation Foundation in 2009 to ensure that as many dogs as possible would have a safe and happy place to call home.

Also, I write this in memory of my sweet English springer spaniel, Bandit, who is gone but definitely not forgotten, especially when I eat popcorn. He was the bestest boy.

And finally, I give all the glory to God and all the thanks to Janice Thompson for coming to me with the brilliant idea of writing about dogs.

CHAPTER 1

A few minutes before 6:00 p.m.
on the first Saturday in December

The Brenham, Texas,
Annual Lighted Christmas Parade

When I told Mama that I was fine with whatever Christmas plans she had, I had no idea I would arrive in my hometown of Brenham, Texas, to discover I'd been named grand marshal of the annual Lighted Christmas Parade. And I certainly didn't expect I'd end up on a glow-in-the-dark float made from a flatbed trailer loaned for the occasion from Bubba's Haul-It-Fast, Inc.

But there I sat, shivering on a cold December evening and wondering how in the world a woman of my age with a long list of hit records and Miranda Lambert's personal cell number on speed dial got herself into this situation.

Of course the answer was simple. My mother had always had a way of talking me into things. And my niece Marigold Evans, known by everyone as Mari, had inherited that talent.

I glanced around at my motley crew of companions on the light-covered float—a half dozen adorable, barking mutts in elf suits—and couldn't help but smile. Every one of them was rescued by Mari and her volunteers and dressed by my mother.

Yes, my mother makes dog clothes. Trust me, I encourage this every chance I get. If I don't, I'm afraid she will go back to insisting on making my stage costumes, and nobody wants that.

It was bad enough that Mama made a Christmas vest for me complete with lights spelling the words *Merry Christmas* that flash on and off. It was my fault though. I told her I absolutely refused to wear an outfit she made, and I may have let her think that I was contractually obligated to wear something chosen by my manager.

I mean, it's probably written into the contract somewhere. Who reads the fine print on those things? So Mama made the vest—which she pointed out was technically not an outfit—skirting around the rules to find a loophole yet again.

In the middle of the Christmas-themed chaos, my niece sat cross-legged with a smile as big as Texas and a headband with lighted candy canes. Mari might be able to talk me into just about anything, thanks to my mama, but she got her love of animals from me and her mama.

Mari had made a career out of this by working as a vet tech at Lone Star Veterinary Clinic in Brenham. That evening, both veterinarians and the rest of the staff had lined up to greet me as I climbed aboard the float emblazoned with the words GIVE A PET A SECOND CHANCE on a lighted sign at the front and LONE STAR VET CLINIC—BRENHAM'S BEST, JUST ASK YOUR PET! on the back.

Mari's description of that hunky vet Dr. Tyler Durham was not an exaggeration. He really is that handsome. And Dr. Keller—I'm supposed to call her Kristin—is sweet as pie.

And the vet tech who follows Mari around like a lost puppy? Parker something-or-other? I'll never forget those gorgeous blue eyes or the way he looks at my niece.

And the way she returns that look.

I had met the others, but I am terrible with names. I sure hoped they'd all be wearing name tags at the clinic Christmas party after the parade.

Oh, but the fur babies? I knew all their names and would have taken every one of them home if I could have gotten away with it.

Bucky and Clementine were barking like crazy at the policemen on horseback up ahead, while Skipper, Sunshine, and Bella were alternating between exploring the confines of the picket fence wrapped in Christmas lights that held them in and rolling around playing.

They reminded me of my two, Patsy and Cline, who were cooling their heels—or rather their paws—back at home at the most exclusive and expensive doggie spa in Nashville. I felt a nudge and looked down to see that the puppy Mari called Lady had determined that my lap was where she belonged. I tried to pay no attention, but those eyes. . .

Any pet lover knows when a dog has decided *you're* the one who ought to listen to *him*. Or, in this case, to her.

I gathered up the persistent puppy and tucked her under the blanket I'd thrown over my legs. The little girl—all or part Springer Spaniel, I guessed—instantly captured my heart with her glossy liver-and-white coat with beach waves of fur I never could manage, even with all the money I spend on hair products.

"Let's get this show on the road," someone called from up ahead, signaling a response from the drum line of the Brenham High School Band.

I glanced over at Mari, who was dividing her time between calming the dogs with toys she retrieved from her backpack and repairing the damage they caused to the arrangement of star lights that had been glued randomly to the picket fence.

As the drumbeat picked up, Mari stood and pulled a thick white ribbon out of her backpack and handed it to me. "I almost forgot. You'll need to wear this sash."

I eyed the length of cloth with the words *Trina Potter Country Singing Sensation* sewed on with glow-in-the-dark trim. "Oh no, sweetheart. I won't be putting that on."

Mari laughed. "Suit yourself, but Grandma Peach made it. Apparently, it was Tyler's way of calming her down after he told her she couldn't advertise her pies or her pet clothes business on his float or have your song about her playing on the float's loudspeaker during the parade."

I gave the sash another look. "So I either wear this or explain it to Mama?"

My niece nodded. "And good luck with that second option, because I guarantee she'll notice if you don't."

I groaned as I shrugged into Mama's work of art. "Are you sure you don't want to join me up here on this bench?" I asked Mari. "You're the real star here with your dog rescues. I just write songs and try not to forget the words when I sing them. I'm sure if these dogs could talk, they'd agree."

Mari grinned. "It's probably a good thing they can't talk, Aunt Trina. Most of them weren't too happy about the bath and the medical treatment they got when they were first rescued. And as to sitting up there? No, thank you. I'll stay down here and make sure these crazy canines don't jump the fence."

"You never were one for the spotlight," I told her. "Busier than a bee in the background but never wanting to take credit for the good you do. So much like your mama."

Mari's face softened, and I wished I could take back those words. She and I didn't talk about my big sister much, but when we did, it was never planned. Nor was it easy.

And it generally ended with both of us in tears.

I miss Vanessa more than life itself. I'd have given up every one of my gold records and moved back home if it had kept her alive.

But none of that would stop what the cancer had started. And it only took one trip to Brenham to see that Mari ought to be the one to care for her mama. Not because I couldn't or wouldn't do it but rather because my niece wanted to do it.

She needed to.

So I made the difficult decision not to come around too much lest Mari think she ought to step back and let me take over. I tend to take over things—again I blame my mama for this—and I have no doubt I would have done exactly that.

In the end, it had been Mari who had stayed with her mama until she was gone. Mari who delivered the news to Mama and me that Vanessa was gone.

I sighed as I tried hard to keep my smile in place. Mama was here, so it wasn't like Mari was without family, but the girl shouldn't be walking the grief road alone.

The float jerked forward, and my little companion let out a bark. At the same time, the marching band struck up a rousing version of "Jingle Bells."

"It's all right." I scratched my new best friend behind her ear. "It's just a bunch of noise. Don't let it bother you, honey."

At that last word, that little dog stared up at me with the biggest brown eyes you've ever seen. She was giving me a look that said I'd spoken the magic word.

"Oh, I see. Your name is Honey." The pup cuddled against me, and I gave her ear another scratch. "Well, that was a good guess. I'll be sure Mari knows. Now hang on, because we're about to go for a ride."

Mari glanced up at me. "The dog you're holding is a little jittery around loud noises, so hold on tight. She was the closest one to the. . ."

Her voice trailed off. I knew instantly that Mari had said more than she'd intended. But about what?"

"Closest to what?" I demanded.

She looked away.

"Marigold Evans. What aren't you telling me?"

My niece swiveled to face her. "A few days ago, there might have been an explosion at the rescue."

"Might have been?"

Honey yipped at my outburst. I smoothed her fur and her rising tension with a sweep of my hand.

"Okay," Mari admitted, "so there was an explosion, but no one was hurt because the police came and detonated the device before it blew up next to the rescue."

"What kind of device?"

"Some kind of homemade bomb." She shook her head. "That's all I'm saying. Now smile and wave, okay? This is a Christmas parade, not an inquisition."

CHAPTER 2

"You never mentioned anything about an explosion at your rescue facility," I said to Mari, feeling as though the breath had been knocked out of me.

"It's not a big deal, Aunt Trina," my niece told me, irritation crossing her face. "Just an isolated incident. Probably someone's idea of a joke. No one was hurt." She paused to gather up a squirming pup into her arms. "I promise I'll tell you about it tomorrow."

"I see nothing funny about this." I pasted on my best pageant-girl smile. "You'll tell me tonight after this parade is over, and then I will decide whether to worry or not."

Mari made no response. She'd turned her full attention back to her furry charges. I tucked Honey closer to me and resolved to get to the bottom of this explosion thing as soon as possible.

In the meantime, I'd smile. And wave. And maybe even enjoy myself a little.

But I would know everything I could about a homemade bomb at a place where my niece visited regularly. And where precious pups like Honey called home, albeit temporarily.

In the meantime, I forced my attention back on the smiling and waving.

I've been in a parade or two during my lifetime. I mean, I did my fair share of pageants and such, and I might have won the honor of being senior class prom queen—we won't talk about how long ago that was!—Miss Cotton Gin, Bluebonnet Queen, and a few others. I have to say that this one, with all of Brenham's finest trailing down the main roads lit up like Christmas trees, was the most fun.

Poor Honey spent most of the route hidden inside the fur-trimmed red blanket that covered my lap. Mama had produced the blanket at the last minute, and I suspect it was because she didn't approve of me wearing jeans with holes in them, even if I'd bought them that way.

"Faded and holey makes no sense," she'd said when we were discussing my wardrobe that morning at the breakfast table. "Don't you want baby Jesus to see you in your best?"

I was sorely tempted to argue that baby Jesus had grown up to be the very same adult Jesus who taught His followers to judge folks by their hearts instead of their appearance.

Then I saw Mama beaming down at me from her seat in the VIP box, and my heart melted. Oh, how I love that woman, even if I will never understand her ways.

I looked over at Mari. Now her, I understand.

Just like music is my solace, hers is animals. I wanted to do more to help her reach her goal of having a permanent home for her rescue operations. I made a mental note to speak with her about this before I left.

As if she felt my attention on her, my niece glanced back at me. "Are you doing okay, Aunt Trina? We're almost to the end of the parade route."

I figured we must be since I'd lost count of how many times I'd heard the marching band play "Jingle Bells." Still, when I responded, my smile was genuine.

"I'm doing great, honey." At the mention of her name, the pup in my lap lifted her head. "Not you, Honey," I said with a chuckle. "The other one."

"I'm sorry for that comment about an inquisition, Aunt Trina," Mari said, her expression contrite. "It really wasn't a big deal. I promise."

There was plenty I could have said at that moment about what did and did not constitute a big deal, with an explosion coming in right at the top of the big-deal spectrum. However, I decided to let it go and instead offered her a conciliatory smile.

"I love you, sweetheart. Now enjoy the parade." When she continued to look in my direction, I added, "Smile and wave, Mari."

Her laughter drifted toward me along with the crowd's cheering and the chorus of "Jingle Bells." Then she added, "I love you too, Aunt Trina."

Mama and her friend Pastor Nelson met us at the end of the route. Lately her romance with the pastor seemed to have cooled a bit, but Mama refused to tell me why. The last time there was an issue between them, it got resolved quickly.

I wondered if Mama was losing interest. Unless it's for baking pies or sewing, she has the attention span of a gnat. She looked resplendent in her Christmas gear, which involved a head-to-toe dose of red and green in the form of a Christmas-themed sweater, red jeans, and a hat that matched mine. She finished off the ensemble with the reindeer antlers and a necklace of Christmas lights that blinked on and off.

After making sure that Mari and her special friend Parker didn't need my help removing the elf costumes and corralling the pups back into their kennels, I climbed down from the float to sign autographs and pose for pictures with friends and fans. That's a part of my life that I don't think I will ever get completely used to. I love standing on the stage and singing, but when I'm offstage, I am just plain Trina Potter from Brenham, Texas.

Or at least that's how I feel. My management team disagrees, but they weren't there right then. It was time to direct the cameras to Mama.

"There's the real star," I told them.

Of course Mama's expression told me she was pleased. Peach Potter never did mind a spotlight aimed in her direction.

I looked her up and down and then grinned. "What? No Christmas shoes?"

Mama frowned. "Well, I don't want to talk about it, but if I did I would tell you all about how that iron of mine ought to be replaced because it gets way hotter than it says it will. When your iron is too hot, you scorch the transfers. Nobody likes a melted dachshund in a Santa hat. Not that I want to talk about it."

"Okay, Mama." I gathered her in my arms and gave her a hug. "You're beautiful, melted dachshunds or not."

"Miss Potter! Over here!"

I turned toward the sound of my name only to have a flash go off. Temporarily blinded, I hung on to Mama until I saw only spots in front of me.

"Goodness gracious," Mama chided. "No manners at all."

"Are you Trina Potter's mother? The one she wrote the song about?"

At that question, my mother's cantankerous attitude went sweet as pie. "Why yes, I am," she said silkily. "I'm also the owner of Mama Peach's Pies and an as-yet-unnamed designer pet clothing company. And who might you be, young man?"

Next thing I knew, Mama was telling the reporter about the trauma of my birth and her subsequent difficulties in raising me to be a decent human being who loved Jesus and knew not to wear white after Labor Day or pay for clothes that weren't quality.

The glance she gave back at me clearly indicated the struggle was ongoing.

I felt a nudge and looked down to see Honey peering up at me, still in her elf costume. Of course I scooped the little rascal up at once.

I slipped away from Mama's interview with Honey in my arms. It only took a minute to find Mari and Parker in the parking lot.

"Missing someone?" I called as I closed the distance between them.

"Lady," Mari said. "You know you're not supposed to go wandering."

"I think she was looking for you," Parker said. "I've never seen her be so affectionate with any of the volunteers."

"Probably because you're all calling her by the wrong name. It's Honey."

"And you know this how?" Mari asked.

I held the squirming pup as my niece removed the elf costume. "She told me so on the float." Then I laughed. "Okay, now I'm starting to sound like Mama. Speaking of your grandmother, I've got to go see if I can interrupt my life story as told by Peach Potter. Take this sweet girl."

I handed her to Parker, and she immediately tried to wriggle free. "What am I going to do with you?" I said to the pup.

"You could adopt her," Mari said brightly. "She was a surrender. Her person is too ill to care for her."

"Oh, sweet girl," I said to Honey. "I'm so sorry, but besides the fact you'd be roommates with two ornery dogs named Patsy and Cline who would be terrible role models for you because they have never learned that the food on the counter belongs to the humans not the dogs, I think you need someone who isn't gallivanting all over the country and forcing you to ride on a tour bus all the time."

"She's small and portable," Parker offered.

His smile was so dazzling that I could only laugh. "I'll keep that in mind." Then a thought occurred. "You're Parker, right? Parker Jenson?"

"I am."

"Well, Parker," I said knowing full well that my niece was only pretending to be interested in securing the latch on Honey's kennel, "what do you know about an explosion at Mari's rescue facility?"

His face registered surprise, and his eyes darted toward Mari. "I, um, well. . ."

"I'm guessing my niece has given you specific instructions not to talk to me about it?"

"Not exactly," he said, crimson climbing into his cheeks. "Actually, it was more like 'don't let Aunt Trina know,' " he said. "But now that you know, I guess it's okay to talk about it."

"It's really not," Mari said, joining them.

"Not okay or not a big deal?" Parker asked her.

"Both," she said firmly before turning her attention to me. "The police are on it, Aunt Trina. Someone rigged up a little bomb and positioned it close to where the rescues get their outdoor exercise."

"Any of the dogs could have stumbled on it," Parker said, his voice harsh.

"But they didn't," Mari soothed. "And everything is fine now, right, Parker?"

Parker paused a beat then nodded, his eyes now on Mari. Did he see what I saw? My niece might seem calm, but the look in her eyes told another story.

"Yeah, sure. It's fine," he said.

Whether the vet tech actually believed what he was saying, I couldn't say. I would figure that out eventually.

Dr. Durham—Tyler—stepped into our circle. "Something wrong here?"

"Nothing," Mari said quickly.

I offered him a smile. "Nothing but an overprotective aunt trying to find out the details of a bomb that was found near Mari's rescue location."

Tyler's attention swiveled to Mari. "What's this? I hadn't heard anything about a bomb."

"Because it wasn't a big deal," Mari said, giving me a look that said she was not pleased with me. "Maggie Jamison is the one who found it. She called the police, and they called the bomb squad. No one was hurt."

"Thank the Lord for that," Tyler said. "What did Maggie make of it?"

"She put it down to kids messing around," Parker added. "She's pretty far off the main road. It's possible someone thought they would try out what they learned on the internet and toss a bomb into an empty field just to watch it blow up."

"Only it didn't blow up, right?" Tyler asked.

"It did not." My niece gave me a pointed look. "Apparently there was one witness to a vehicle stopped in front of the spot where the bomb was found. I'm sure the culprit will be found soon."

"So you're not worried?" Tyler asked her.

"No," Mari said.

At the same time, Parker said, "A bit. Only because someone might have been hurt," he hurried to add, his eyes on Mari. "I just keep thinking that if you or one of the dogs had come up on that thing. . ."

"Of course I'm a little worried, but that didn't happen," Mari said firmly, giving me a covert glance.

It was clear that my niece didn't want to alarm me. What wasn't clear was why.

"How about we move the party to the office?" Tyler turned to me. "You'll be joining us, won't you? And your mother, of course."

"Thank you," I told him. "We would love to."

"Great. Since the practice is new and this is our first Christmas, I'm inviting everyone who had a hand in getting us up and running. We couldn't have done it without your mother's pies."

I grinned. "Let me guess. She brought a pie down just about every day to see what was going on."

Tyler laughed. "I won't guess what her motives were, but the construction crew and I were awfully glad every time we saw her car pull up."

"I bet you don't think that now, what with Hector's dislike of all things veterinarian."

"No comment," Tyler said. "Although Kristin and Hector seem to have hit it off. So shall we continue this conversation at the party?"

CHAPTER 3

I managed to corral Mama and get her into the car for the short drive over to Lone Star Vet Clinic. On the way there, she explained that her affection for the pastor had cooled a bit.

"I'm too young to settle down again," she declared as I searched for a parking space near the vet clinic. "If it's meant to be, we'll know eventually. Plus, he's busy on Sundays and Wednesdays and working on his sermon most of the week. With all of those parishioners calling and wanting visits, he just cannot give me his full attention."

I found a space and eased the rental car into it. When I glanced over at Mama, she looked so sad.

"Mama, what is it?"

She turned to face me. "Since when did I get so self-centered?"

No way I was answering that question. "What makes you think that?" was a better response.

"I had a very nice pastor on the string, and I have basically cut him loose. Do you know how many casserole ladies are waiting in line to feed him a meal?"

Knowing she meant literally and not figuratively, I remained silent and let her continue.

"I'm just not cut out to be a pastor's wife, Trina." She shook her head. "I love Jesus with all my heart, but I just don't have it in me to help a man shepherd a flock."

Now I knew she meant that figuratively. Her love of that awful cat and Mari's dogs did not translate to a like of any other animals. And she certainly wasn't about to have farm animals living nearby.

A few minutes later, we arrived at the vet clinic. There I found the Christmas party in full swing. Dr. Kristin met me at the door with a party hat. Only then did I realize I still wore my headband and sash from the parade.

"Here," I told her. "I'll trade with you."

Kristin dutifully slipped the sash over her shoulder and tucked the headband on her head, then led me inside to cheers all around. Elvis was on the sound system, and someone was doing a decent interpretation of him as Santa over in the reception area. As I looked closer, I could see it was Dr. Durham—Tyler—beneath the white beard and dark sideburns.

"An Elvis Santa," I remarked to Kristin. "That's something I've never seen before."

Kristin shrugged. "Tyler says Elvis karaoke will be a Christmas tradition here. The practice was opened earlier in the year, so this is the first clinic Christmas party for all of us."

"I'm honored to be included, then," I told her. "And I think Santa Elvis karaoke should definitely be a tradition."

"Me too." Kristin smiled. "Also we've got Deke 'the BBQ King' King, cooking for us tonight. Have you heard of him?"

I thought a minute. "No, I don't think I have."

"He's a client, but he's also a competitive barbecue chef. Do they call them chef?" Kristin shrugged. "Anyway it'll be fun. Do you need introductions? There are a few who weren't with us this morning."

I glanced around the clinic's main space, decorated with all the requisite holiday decor, and spied someone I recognized. Before I could cross the distance to speak to him, Wyatt Chastain found me.

"No need for an introduction to this one," I told Kristin. "Wyatt Chastain was my prom date."

Kristin grinned. "Is that so?"

Wyatt nodded. "And you thought my only claim to fame was being the guy who calls out the vets at odd hours to see to bovine emergencies."

"And does legal work for the clinic." Kristin offered both a smile. "I'll let you two get reacquainted then."

I watched her walk away and then returned my attention to Wyatt. Somehow the band nerd had become the handsome man standing in front of me. "Why are you here, and how are you, Wyatt?" was all I could think of to ask.

Why hadn't I kept in touch with him? To be fair, I'd moved to Nashville and lost myself in my career while he'd gone off to college and then law school. Still, Wyatt had been the one who encouraged me to chase the path of music, and I'd thanked him by promptly forgetting all about it.

Not completely true. One look at Wyatt and all the memories came flooding back.

"I'm here because I'm on retainer for the firm. They invited everyone who helped them get the clinic up and running. As to how I am, I can't complain," he told her. "But I still do sometimes."

Although Wyatt had been a transplanted Texan for more than two decades now, his roots and his accent were firmly situated in Louisiana's Cajun country. Thus he'd never sounded like the other boys in school.

And he sounded like none of the other men now.

"I'd ask how you've been, Trina, but I admit I've read every article ever written about you. All those hit records, all those near-miss romances with musicians and movie stars," he said in his slow drawl. "You've done quite well for yourself."

"I'll admit I've done well for my record label," I corrected. "But if all you read was the news articles, then you're not getting the real story." I hurried to change the subject. "So tell me, how does a man go from playing the trombone in the Brenham High marching band to being a lawyer?"

Wyatt's smile was dazzling as he leaned forward. "One day at a time?"

I gave him a playful nudge. "Honestly, Wyatt. You are still as exasperating as you were in high school. My mother still makes the occasional reference to that boy who played that awful song on his trombone outside my bedroom window."

"Hey now, that was my big shot to get the future prom queen of Brenham High to go with me instead of all those other guys lining up to take you."

"It was a gutsy move," I said then laughed. "But how could I turn down a guy in a Hawaiian shirt and hula skirt playing the theme from *Hawaii 5-0* on a trombone while standing in front of a sign that read 'I can't take you to Hawaii, but I will take you to prom'?"

"Are we actually talking about prom now?" A peroxide blond with a painted-on smile wrapped herself around Wyatt. Her eyes opened as wide, and she smiled as broadly, as the Botox would allow. "Hello, Trina."

"Hello, um. . ." I searched my mind for just who this woman might be. Had I missed a Christmas card or wedding invitation from Mr. and Mrs. Wyatt Chastain over the years?

Another sweeping glance at the woman in the clingy red dress and matching sky-high heels, and I know I would have remembered something like that.

Someone like her.

And then it occurred to me. There was only one person on the Brenham High cheer squad who would have grown up to look like that.

"Bitsy Decker?" I said.

"It's Bitsy Bonnano now, but I might go back to Decker once the divorce is final."

"As your lawyer, I'd say keep it, Bits. You've got a following."

She turned her charm on Wyatt. "You do say the sweetest things."

I did my best not to roll my eyes. Bitsy might be about to lose a husband, but she was clearly already hunting for the next one.

Check that. She'd found him and was circling for the kill.

"So I heard about the bomb," Bitsy said.

I frowned. "Did you, now? Mari led me to believe it wasn't a big deal, so how did you hear about it?"

She blinked her eyes, fluttering those long lashes a moment. "Oh, it was a big deal, all right. The bomb squad came in to make sure there weren't any others."

"And no idea of who did it?" Wyatt asked her.

"I'm sure there are suspects." She made a pouting face. "Can you imagine? I've dated half the Brenham police force, and not a one of them would tell me a thing though."

"You're slipping, Bits," Wyatt said.

She waved away his comment. "My sales records don't say that. I'm the top producer in the farm and ranch category."

"She sells them," Wyatt supplied. "Which has nothing to do with charming policemen."

"Most of the time anyway," she said with a chuckle.

"Right. Well, congratulations, Bitsy," I told her.

"Thank you." She produced a business card from her purse and handed it to me. "In case you ever decide to come home to Brenham. If you do, I'm your girl for real estate. Anyway, you're doing all right for yourself, Trina," Bitsy said, her gaze sweeping the length of me. "Tell me the truth. Who did you write 'Snake Charmer' about?"

I'd written it about someone I'd just broken up with, but I was not about to name names. I decided to stick with the response that my publicist had come up with before the song released. "The person it's about will recognize himself. That's all I can say about that."

"Oh, it's Rory Wilson, isn't it?" She looked over at Wyatt. "He's dreamy and has way more hit records than Trina." She turned back toward me. "It was him, wasn't it?"

"I'm just going to go over there and watch karaoke for a while," I said to Bitsy and Wyatt, ignoring the question. "It looks like it's almost Mari's turn."

I made my way through the crowd until I found a spot at the edge of the makeshift stage. The song transitioned to another tune off the Elvis Christmas album. Mari took up the microphone along with the hat, beard, and sideburns and then found me in the crowd and grinned.

With Parker singing backup, my niece belted out "Blue Christmas" while her coworkers cheered. I might be the one who makes a living in the music field, but my niece can sing!

Mari's smile and the way Parker gathered her into his arms for a hug at the end of the performance warmed my heart. It had been a very long time since I'd seen her so happy.

Too long.

Wyatt tapped me on the shoulder. "How about we take a turn at this?"

I caught a glimpse of Bitsy moving through the crowd toward us. "Come on, Wyatt baby," she called. "Let's show these folks how good we are together."

"Sounds like you've got a partner for your duet."

He shook his head. "Nope. This is your song. C'mon." With that, he wrapped his hand around my wrist and gently tugged me toward the stage.

"Oh no," I told him with a laugh. "I'm just a visitor at this party. You do it without me."

"Oh come on, darlin'," he said in that unique drawl of his, "I will if you will."

"Wyatt," Bitsy said, now standing at his elbow. "Trina obviously doesn't want to. I, however, am glad to."

"No, really." I shook my head. "The spotlight is on you and Bitsy tonight."

Wyatt walked over to Travis, who was in control of the karaoke machine, and picked out a song. "Trina," he called, "this one's for you. Now come help me sing it."

The music began, and I recognized the song immediately and started laughing. Wyatt pointed in my direction as a song about coming home for Christmas blared on the sound system. Bitsy glared at me, her expression letting me know I'd better stay put.

"Come on, Aunt Trina," Mari called.

"Trina, Trina, Trina," the crowd began to chant.

Just about the time the first verse ended, I relented. "But only if Wyatt wears the wig and sideburns."

Travis paused the music to allow Wyatt to comply, then started the song over again. As we sang, I watched Bitsy disappear into the crowd.

I had forgotten how very much I missed being around people who didn't care what I did for a living. By the time I noticed Mama looking tired, I realized several hours had passed.

"Come on, Mama Peach," I said, using the name the employees of the clinic called her. "It's time to go home."

I said reluctant goodbyes to everyone, then headed Mama toward the car with Mari following close behind. Once my mother was safely loaded inside, I turned to tell Mari good night.

To my surprise, my niece hauled me into her arms and hugged me tight. "I've missed you so much, Aunt Trina," she said. "You don't even know how much."

"Oh, honey," I said, blinking to keep the tears away. "I've missed *you* so very much."

We stood there for a minute, and then Mari stepped back. "Monday is my half day. Come with me out to Maggie Jamison's property. That's where we're keeping a few of the rescues for now. I will show you what I've been up to."

I pressed a dark hair away from Mari's face—a face so like my sister's. "I would love to."

After making plans to meet up at Maggie's ranch, I gave Mari another hug and then climbed into the car for the short drive to Mama's house.

"She's hurting, Trina," Mama said before I could start the car's engine.

"I know, Mama. I wish I could fix it for her."

Mama looked over at me, her once-bright blue eyes now faded just a bit but her face still as pretty as ever. "There's no fixing it. We both know that. Time will ease the pain out of the forefront and give it a better place to live."

"A better place to live," I echoed. "I like that. And I guess all three of us need to find a place for that pain to live."

Mama reached over and patted me on the arm. "And while we're on the subject, how about you look for a better place to live too? Home is always a good place to be."

"Home?" I swiveled to face her. "You want me to move back to Brenham?"

"You did sing about it tonight." My mother raised one eyebrow, giving me her favorite I-said-what-I-said expression.

"I couldn't possibly," I said, starting the car. "I'm rooted to Nashville now, Mama. It'd be impossible to just up and move."

Mama made a snorting sound. "You're rooted to whatever you choose to be rooted to, Trina Potter, and I won't hear you say that anything is impossible. You never have before. The impossible just takes longer."

I placed my hand atop hers, and we rode the rest of the way back to Mama's house in silence.

CHAPTER 4

On Monday morning I set out extra early to give myself time to find Maggie's place. The call came from Mari just as I was about to turn on the road leading to the Jamison ranch.

"What's up, buttercup?" I asked after answering using the hands-free device in my rental car.

"I'm so sorry," Mari said, "but I'm going to be late. It's been crazy busy this morning, and we just had an emergency come in. I can't leave Parker as the only vet tech when the waiting room is full."

"Don't worry about it," I told her. "I'll see if Maggie is home, and she and I will have a visit. Then you can join us when you're done."

"I truly don't know when that will be." She sounded exasperated.

"It's fine," I soothed. "If Maggie isn't available to show me around, then you and I can come back later today or after work tomorrow. I'm not going back to Nashville until Wednesday morning, so we've got time."

Maggie and I go way back. She wasn't a Jamison back then. Since we'd last spoken, she'd been married and widowed. Still, when she met my car at the end of the long road leading to her home, she looked mostly the same.

Tired around the eyes a bit, and she'd allowed a sparkle of silver in her hair, but otherwise she was still the Maggie I remembered.

We embraced, and then Maggie led me inside. Before I knew it, we were seated across from each other at the granite-covered island in her kitchen with steaming mugs of coffee and a plate of warm-from-the-oven oatmeal cookies.

We'd covered all the basics: how long it had been since we'd seen one another, how much we both missed my sister, and our mutual admiration for my niece. Then we fell into a comfortable silence as Maggie sipped her coffee.

Maggie's kitchen was warm and sunny with a view across a generous patio to the pastures beyond. A stand of pine trees climbed toward the top of a small hill and obscured the view, but if I remembered correctly, there was a barn just on the other side.

"Just like old times," I commented as I reached for a second cookie. "All that's missing is you and my sister gabbing about boys or whatever was going on at school."

"Or complaining about our daddies trying to tell us that makeup and short skirts will attract the wrong kind of man, and our mamas getting after us to study our lessons so we can be the first of our families to go to college."

I chuckled, remembering being the tagalong little sister and listening to all their complaining. Had it really been so long ago?

Maggie slipped a cookie to the gorgeous black lab that was practically plastered to her side. "I wish they hadn't been right. What in the world were we thinking?"

"You were thinking every boy who was cute was the one until the next one came along. And back then none of us planned on actually paying to go to school when we didn't even want to go while it was free. Except band practice," I added. "Or cheerleading for you and Vanessa."

"Nessy and I lived for cheerleading back then," she said. "And boys. And short skirts and makeup. No wonder our parents were worried sick about us. But I think we turned out all right. Mostly anyway."

We laughed together. Then Maggie sobered. "We sound like a couple of old ladies. We're still young enough, Trina, aren't we?"

I wrapped my hands around the pale blue *Golden Girls* mug and thought about that a moment. "I think that depends. Mama thinks I am, and Mari probably thinks I'm not. My body varies somewhere between the two depending on the day."

"Isn't that the truth?" Maggie said. "Speaking of Mari, she sure is a sweet thing. She's the reason I've got my Midnight here."

I glanced down at the beautiful black Lab keeping watch over Maggie and likely whatever Maggie put on her plate. "Is Midnight a rescue?"

"Sure is," Maggie said. "You could say that Midnight showed up at exactly the right time not only to fix things for me but also to cement my involvement in Mari's rescue."

I smiled as I considered how often these things happen. A series of unplanned things that turn out to be much better than anyone could have planned.

"About the rescue," I said. "Would it be possible to get a tour?"

Maggie gave me a quizzical look. "I don't follow."

"Mari said that the rescue was based out here. I just figured there was a building or something set up for the animals." I shifted positions on the stool. "Isn't there?"

"I've got some crates set up in a little building behind the barn. It's watertight and wired for electricity—it used to be the foreman's office when this was a working ranch—so it's nice and comfortable. Parker got the heat working, so the rescues are toasty warm when it's cold. I guess we'll have to rig up some kind of cooling system for summer because that air conditioner never did cool well enough to suit, but we'll cross that bridge when we get to it." She paused. "So to answer your question, no, there isn't a facility. Just me, those vet techs, the vets when needed, and whoever else Mari convinces to come out and volunteer."

Not at all what she pictured. And yet quintessentially Mari.

"I see."

Midnight made a little snuffling sound, and Maggie chuckled. "I'm being told there's room in that belly for another cookie." She patted the dog's head. "But cookies are not good for any of us in large quantities, and it's just about time for your kibble."

"That is the truth."

I watched Maggie retrieve a container of food as Midnight's claws clattered on the stone floor. Once his bowl was full and the food container had been returned to the pantry, Maggie offered me a smile.

"Want to come help with the pups out in the shed?"

"I would love to."

We left Midnight, now oblivious to our presence, and stepped out into the late morning sunshine. It was warmer today, so the walk from the ranch house to the shed was pleasant.

As we reached the top of a small hill, I spied a much larger brick home off in the distance. "Mari told me you've got family living on the property too."

"Technically, I'm living on their property," she said. "I can stay there as long as I live, but when I'm gone, it'll go back to the family." She paused. "Or if I decide I've had enough of living out here and pack up and go, then it's theirs sooner."

"Have you ever considered that?"

"A timc or two," Maggie said. "But where would I go? Brenham is home. I've got my horses and plenty of room between me and them." She nodded toward her in-laws' big home. "It suits me here, at least for now. I'm not bothered by the fact I don't get invited to Sunday dinner. It works for both of us."

I decided now was the time to bring up the bomb that had landed in her pasture. "I heard you had some excitement out here recently."

Maggie paused her steps and turned to face me. "I wondered how long it would take until we got to that. Yes, there was a bomb here. Brenham's finest disposed of it. Nobody's figured out who did it or why. I'm trying not to take it personally."

"Do you think it was aimed at you?"

She shook her head. "I suppose it's possible. More than one Jamison family member would like me to head for the hills so they could move into my house. But that's low even for them." Maggie shrugged and started walking again. "I figure there is one of three explanations for it. Either it's kids building things they found on the internet, the in-laws are tired of having me on their property, or it's someone who doesn't want Mari to have a rescue here on this property."

I inhaled the pine-scented air and let out my breath slowly. "And of those, which is the most likely, in your opinion?"

"I've given that some thought, actually. There's enough money in the vaults over at the big house to do it up right if they wanted me out. Either pay me to move or pay someone to make me want to move, is my guess. They've done neither."

"A bomb does seem a little extreme," I told her.

"Agreed. And they know I'm not one to scare easily. It isn't like that thing was on my doorstep or under my pillow." She shrugged. "So I'm down to kids with too much time on their hands or somebody not liking that there's a dog rescue here."

"The kids explanation is where I land. I can't see anyone objecting to a rescue here, though it does concern me that the dogs could have been hurt."

Maggie set off walking again. I fell into step beside her on the well-worn path.

"People object to having all sorts of things near them, Trina. My neighbors aren't close by, but all it takes is someone driving down this road and seeing something they don't like—say a rescue gets loose and runs out in the road, chases one of their animals, or whatnot—and they'll have something to say about it."

"Something to say is one thing," I said. "But tossing an explosive out in a field where dogs are exercising is another altogether. It's a farm community, Maggie. Why would anyone not want dogs around?"

"You've got me," she said. "Though when we're full and they get to barking, it can be noisy. However, I doubt anyone but me can hear them."

"What about your in-laws?"

"No, that fortress is airtight, and my mother-in-law is nearly deaf. But who knows who else comes and goes from there?"

I hadn't considered that angle. Anyone who might have been at the big house could have placed that bomb in the pasture. But why? That's where I kept stumbling.

There seemed no good reason to scare anyone with such a prank. And intentionally harming innocent animals—or worse, Mari or one of the volunteers? Unthinkable.

"I very much appreciate all the help you've given my niece," I told her, pressing my runaway thoughts back into place. "I wonder if the time has come for her to move off your land and into a dedicated facility."

"That time is long past," Maggie said. "Not that I mind them here. I certainly do not, and if I owned this property, I'd carve off a piece of it and deed it over. But your niece, she's determined to do this her way." She nodded to a small wooden building surrounded by a fenced-in pasture. "We're here."

The former office was cottage-like in its appearance, with big windows on two sides and a door that had once likely been a deep shade of green but was now faded to the mossy color that was currently trendy.

"It's empty right now," Maggie said, pressing her key into the lock. "The volunteers took everyone home after the parade. After the news folks did a live feed with your mother, they were inundated with offers of homes for the pups."

"That's wonderful," I said, thinking of Honey. "I hope they'll all find their forever homes."

Maggie stepped back to let me step inside. "That's your niece's whole reason for doing this. Forever homes for all of them."

"If only she was settled in a forever home," I said under my breath as I glanced around the comfortable space.

Wooden paneling painted a pristine white covered the walls. A corkboard likely left over from the time when this served as an office was now covered with photographs of dogs. I moved closer and saw that each picture had a note on it stating the dog's name and the name of his or her new owner.

"Those are the successes," Maggie said with a grin. "I was the first—technically the second since Beau Jangles went home with Mari—and look how many there are now."

I grinned. "Mari's going to need another corkboard soon."

Maggie's phone rang, and she retrieved it from her pocket. "It's the cops," she told me as she answered.

I didn't even bother to pretend I wasn't trying to listen. Unfortunately, Maggie's side of the conversation gave few clues. Finally, she ended the call and tucked the phone back into her pocket.

"Well?" I said. "I'm guessing they called about the bomb."

Maggie nodded. "Seems as though there are two new developments. The bomb had no fingerprints on it, so the officer said that makes them think it probably wasn't kids playing around. Kids would assume it was going to blow up and wouldn't try to cover their tracks."

"That makes sense," I said.

"It does." She paused. "The other news is that they've got a witness who saw a vehicle leaving the scene."

"Yes, I heard there was a witness. Have the police been able to identify the vehicle?"

Maggie nodded slowly. "I'm afraid so."

"What do you mean?"

My sister's old friend met my gaze. "Apparently, it was a white van. The witness got the plate number and everything."

"That's great, right?" I asked with a feeling of foreboding.

"No," Maggie said. "That's not great. It's the van that was donated to the rescue organization."

CHAPTER 5

I drove all the way to Mari's apartment with a sense of foreboding. Why in the world would a van that was donated to her rescue organization be involved in something that could have harmed the very dogs she was saving? It made no sense.

Apparently, the Brenham Police Department wondered the same thing. I learned this when I knocked on Mari's apartment door and it was opened by a police officer wearing a name tag that proclaimed him to be T. Dennison.

"Where is Mari?" I demanded as I attempted to step inside. "Mari?" I called. "Mari, are you here?"

I know my niece could be messy, but there was no way what I saw was caused by her. Two officers were unzipping pillows on the sofa and peering inside them, and it sounded like someone else was either in the bedroom or the bathroom making an abundance of noise.

T. Dennison grasped me gently by the arm and led me outside, then closed the door firmly behind himself. If he hadn't been wearing a gun and a don't-you-dare look, I might have pushed right past him and gone back in.

"Who are you?" he demanded.

It had been a long time since a person hadn't recognized me. Had I not been scared out of my wits that something had happened to Mari since we spoke this morning, I might have appreciated the anonymity.

"I'm Marigold Evans's aunt, and I demand to know what's going on here."

He released me. "Trina Potter," he said slowly. "Okay, yeah. You look like her."

"Because I am her," I said testily. "Now, where is my niece, and why are police officers going over her apartment?"

"Miss Potter, I can't tell you that right now."

"I'm sorry," I snapped, "but I do not agree. You absolutely *can* tell me that right now. If my niece is in trouble, I am her aunt and should be informed, don't you think?"

A car door opened and closed in the parking lot, and he turned to watch until the owner started the engine and drove away. Then he looked back at me.

"Miss Potter, maybe you ought to go down to the police station. That's where you'll find Miss Evans."

My hackles rose. "Have you arrested my niece? Because whatever you think she did I can guarantee she did not do."

"How about I walk you to your car?" the officer said.

"How about you answer me first? Why are you tearing my niece's apartment apart while she's at the police station? If it's about the van, I can assure you that she is not a bomber."

T. Dennison frowned. "What do you know about a van?"

"I was at Maggie Jamison's place when the call came through about the van's connection to Mari's rescue. It was donated. Turn the donor's place upside down and leave Marie out of this."

"Okay," he said crisply.

"That van is used by the rescue volunteers for the purposes of the rescue. Since the rescue is currently based out of Maggie's property, then of course people would see it on that street."

"I agree," he said.

"Then why are police officers searching her apartment while she's at the station?"

"It's necessary," he said.

Necessary? This T. Dennison fellow sure was tight-lipped. "What are they looking for?" I demanded.

"The keys," he said on an exhale of breath. "Go on down to the station, and I'll be there shortly to explain everything. I will call ahead so they can tell your niece you're on your way."

"Speaking of," I said, "why hasn't Mari called me herself? Was her phone taken away?"

Officer Dennison shook his head and turned to go back to Mari's door. "Not by us" trailed behind him. A moment later, the door opened then quickly closed, and I was standing in the parking lot alone.

Although the officer told me Mari did not have a usable phone, I tried calling anyway. Sure enough, it went straight to voice mail.

When I arrived at the station, the desk officer ushered me to the door of a room off the main lobby. The sign proclaimed this to be Room 7 but gave no indication of anything else.

He turned the knob without a key, so at least Mari wasn't being held against her will. Yes, I know the officer said she wasn't in trouble, but there's just something about walking into a police station with the express purpose of seeing a family member that will make a body nervous.

The officer stepped aside and indicated that I should go in. I found a sterile-looking space not much bigger than the room Mama had given over to her cat back at her house. In the center of the room, four people sat at a round metal table littered with bottles of water and what appeared to be vending machine snacks.

"Marigold Evans," I exclaimed when I stepped inside the room. "What in the world is going on?"

Mari jumped up and offered me a hug. "I'm so glad you're here, Aunt Trina." She turned to gesture to the others. "You remember Parker and Cassidy from the Christmas party. He's a vet tech like me, and she's our office manager."

"Of course," I said, offering a smile to each of them.

Both of Mari's friends stood to greet me.

"And this is Mollie Kensington," Mari said, indicating a mousy young woman with dark hair and a fringe of bangs that hung so far into her eyes that she had to look up from under them to make eye contact with me.

Mollie stood and closed the distance between us to shake my hand. "Hello, Miss Potter. I'm a reporter for the *Banner-Press*. Mari and I met when I interviewed her about rescuing Beau Jangles."

Beau Jangles was Mari's absolutely darling Cavalier King Charles spaniel. She rescued the pup from a storm drain and ended up adopting him. Cassidy had let slip a few details—the crawl through a sewer pipe with a cheeseburger and a hungry dog with fur so matted his breed was initially indistinguishable—but I suspected there was more to the story than either young lady wished to tell.

I offered a greeting to the reporter and then returned my attention to Mari. "What is going on? I just left your apartment, where I witnessed several officers turning it upside down looking for keys to the white van that was donated to the rescue." I paused. "And while I'm asking about things, would you please tell me who would want to implicate that vehicle in the whole bomb-in-the-field thing?"

"Miss Potter?"

I turned at the gentle sound of Parker's voice. He held an unopened bottle of water out toward me. "You might want to sit down."

I let out a long breath. "Yes, all right. Thank you." I accepted the water and settled on a vacant chair between Mari and the reporter.

"So," Mari began, "it all started when Parker and I were assisting with the surgeries. As you know, we had an emergency just before I was supposed to leave to meet you. There was a car accident right out in front of our building. One of the vehicles was carrying a half dozen show dogs to an event in Austin."

"Only two needed surgery," Parker interjected, "but the rest needed triage to be sure they were okay. So Mari and I stuck around and helped with all of that."

"All the dogs are going to be fine," Mari added.

"Well, I'm glad about that, but I'm still confused as to why we're all here at the police station."

"Okay, so, after we finished up at the clinic, I was going to drive up to meet you, and Parker planned to follow in the van. We used it a few days ago for a rescue, and Parker had taken it back to his place to try to get it clean inside."

She gave me a you-don't-want-details look. I nodded.

"The plan was to leave the van at the Jamison place," Parker said. "Maggie was nice enough to let me park my vehicle in her garage while I had the van. So I was going to grab my car and head home."

"But that obviously didn't happen," I offered.

"Oh, it did. Sort of," Cassidy said. "See, Mari and I were yakking and singing to the songs on the radio—she's a very good singer—and all of a sudden we notice that Parker isn't behind us anymore. So Mari circled back around and found him walking down the road."

"The van overheated," Parker said. "I didn't know what else to do since neither of them was answering her phone."

"To be fair," Mari told her, "mine was chewed up by one of the accident victims. You'd be surprised how much damage a freaked-out Doberman can do."

"And mine was fine," Cassidy said, "except that I only thought I was charging it at my desk this morning, but instead the charger wasn't plugged into the wall. I should have noticed that the little green thingie with the lightning zapper wasn't showing up, but honestly I'm just so busy getting organized for the new year that I didn't pay any attention."

"Right." I looked over at Mari, noticing for the first time that the reporter was typing away on an iPad she had placed in front of her on the desk. "So, Mari, again. . ."

"Why are we at the police station?" Mari and I said in unison.

A knock prevented my niece from answering. Officer Dennison opened the door and stepped inside dangling a key from his index finger.

Mari jumped up and hugged the policeman, then accepted the key from him. "Thank you, Todd."

"Todd?" I asked, my gaze traveling from my niece to the officer.

"Todd Dennison," he told me. "I've known your niece and her friends for a while now. We met when she was rescuing the spaniel. I thought he'd be mine for sure, but Mari ended up keeping him."

"More like Beau Jangles decided he would keep her," Parker said.

"Oh, but your dog is adorable, Todd." Cassidy turned toward me. "Todd is great about letting us know when he sees a dog in need of rescue while he's out on patrol. One day not too long after Mari made the decision to keep Beau Jangles, Todd called and said—"

"I said there's a dog on a barn. Come and get him." Todd chuckled. "I don't think they believed me."

"But when we got there," Parker interjected, "sure enough there was this dog that had somehow climbed up on the roof of this abandoned barn out in the middle of nowhere. There's no telling how long he was out there."

"He was definitely hungry," Mari said. "The minute Parker offered him a cheeseburger, he figured out how to get down from there pretty quick."

"He's mine now, and the rest is history," Todd said. "And he still loves cheeseburgers."

"Okay," I said. "So Todd helps the rest of you rescue dogs."

"Pretty much," Parker said.

"These guys are doing a good thing for the animals," Todd said. "I just keep on the lookout for possible rescues."

"And he keeps the van running," Cassidy said. "Todd is handy at car stuff."

"Parker helps," Todd said.

"Okay, so just one more time," I said, trying to follow this rabbit trail back to the place where answers were found. "The Brenham police were looking for keys to the van at your place, Mari, and they had you waiting here."

"That's right," my niece said.

"Why?"

Todd's expression turned serious. "You already know there was a report by a supposed witness connecting the van to the bomb found on the Jamison property."

"A bogus report," Cassidy interjected.

"Right," I said.

"And we all know why the van would be on that road. It's generally parked in Maggie's garage or out in the barn," Todd continued. "We don't know whether this supposed witness knew this or not. Until proven otherwise, we have to assume that the witness did not know that, and the tip was an innocent attempt to help us solve the question of the bomb."

"Okay, but why the big search at Mari's place? I counted three cars there."

"It was a test," Parker said. "Todd figured if the witness had any kind of grudge against the rescue, then seeing all the cars at Mari's place might bring him or her out to watch."

"I find that perpetrators often turn up in the crowd at a crime scene," Todd said. "We treated Mari's apartment like a crime scene so that I could watch to see who turned up."

"What you're saying makes sense," I told them, "but why did the officers go to such lengths to pretend they were searching inside where no one can see them searching?"

"Because they really were searching." Todd gestured to the key he had placed on the table in front of my niece. "Mari lost the spare key to the van."

CHAPTER 6

"The original broke off in the lock when the forensics team tried to open the door," Parker said.

"Forensics team?" I asked. "You're all talking in riddles. Missing key, unreliable witness, forensics team? Can someone just tell me in as few words as possible how we all came to be sitting here?"

"I can," Parker said. "Todd asked us to bring in the van so their team could sweep it for anything that might have been used to make the bomb. Just to eliminate the van from being part of the investigation. Someone on the forensics team tried to use the key to lock the door."

"Bad idea," Cassidy said as Mari nodded.

"Very bad idea," Mari echoed. "I had a spare, but Beau Jangles hid it. His new trick is he hides shiny things. Anyway, Todd and his guys found the key—"

"Under the nightstand," Todd interjected.

"Clever," Mari said. "Anyway, the van will be here overnight. We were just waiting for Todd to get back so we could go claim Beau Jangles at the clinic. If you're still interested in a tour, I can take you now."

"Not necessary," I told her. "Maggie gave me the tour already. But I would like to hear more about your future plans for the rescue. How about we get your friends home and then you and I have a talk?"

A short while later, Mari and I were settled on the porch of Royer's Pie Haven in nearby Round Top. This little city came alive twice a year, in March and September, for the Antiques Weeks extravaganza, but on this quiet Monday afternoon in December, it was practically deserted—pardon the pun.

It was a warm day for late December, nothing unusual for this part of the country. The leaves were only just beginning to fall in a multicolored show that covered the ground and crunched under the feet of the few who passed by.

Over plates of pie—delicious fruity Junkberry pie for Mari and salty chocolate Texas Trash pie for me, both topped with our local delicacy, Blue Bell Homemade Vanilla ice cream—Mari discussed her dreams for making the little Second Chance Ranch rescue operation into an actual rescue with a 501(c)3 designation and a permanent location.

My niece shared her heart with such passion that she had me in tears. I was literally crying into my ice cream.

"This needs to happen, Mari," I told her, scooping up a spoonful of the ice cream and pie.

"It will," she told me. "When the time is right."

I put down my spoon and reached across the table to grasp her free hand. "Honey, let me do this for you, please."

Mari seemed to consider my words for a minute. Then she met my gaze and offered a grateful smile. "Thank you, Aunt Trina. But I need to do this on my own."

I leaned back in my chair and assessed this self-assured young woman sitting across from me. Finally, I nodded. "Yes, I can see that you do. But I need to tell you right now you come from a long line of stubborn women."

Mari matched my grin. "Rumor has it that stubbornness gets stronger with each subsequent generation."

"Touché." I took another bite of pie. "Oh, this is good."

"So good," Mari echoed.

"And we can never tell Grandma Peach that we were here."

Mari reached across to join pinky fingers with me. "Never."

"Hey," I said. "I love you, kid. Your mom would be proud of the woman you've become."

Her smile wavered only slightly. "Thank you, Aunt Trina. I hope so. Sometimes this grand plan of mine to have my own nonprofit rescue in a dedicated location seems so far away and impossible. I try not to let that get me down, but sometimes it does."

"I could always—"

"Help," she supplied. "I know, and I thank you so much for that offer and for everything you've already done. You're amazing and I love you. I hope you understand, but I need to do most of this on my own." Mari mustered a thin smile. "With the continued help of donors and volunteers, of course. But I need to do this. I told Mama I would do it that way, and I plan to keep my word."

The mention of her mother hit me in the gut. I wanted desperately to be my sister's voice to her daughter.

The words came quickly.

"You know what?" I said cheerfully. "If it is meant to be, and I believe it is, then it's going to happen, Mari. Like Grandma Peach always says, the impossible just takes a little longer."

Mari grinned. "Mama used to tell me that too."

"Well, they're right."

"Thank you, Aunt Trina," she told me. "Sitting here with you is like having my mother back for a little while."

"Oh, honey," I managed. "Thank you for telling me that."

We sat in our shared grief for Vanessa a moment. Then Mari's smile rose again. "So, tell me what it's like to share a room with Hector the devil cat."

"Oh, Mari," I said with a chuckle, "no one shares a room with Hector. Mama has me sleeping on the sofa." I paused to shake my head. "No, that's not true. I'm on the sofa by choice. She had the guest room ready for me."

"Okay, but. . ."

"But the guest room also is full to the brim with her sewing machine and all the fabric she uses for the dog clothes orders. Plus there's the boxes that are being readied for mailing, the clothes that are going to be used for her next photo shoot for Etsy, and, well, you get the picture. She tried, really. But I felt like things would go better if I stuck to the sofa. I think she was relieved when I told her that's what I'd be doing."

"I see," Mari said, joining me in laughter. "That's a big comedown from your tour bus or the hotel suites you're used to."

"I never got used to all that fancy stuff, but I don't even want to contemplate how long she's had that sofa," I told her. "And you have no idea how loud that woman is in the morning. She's up baking pies before sunrise, then off to work on her dog clothes. That sewing machine is loud.

Do not ask me how I know."

We dissolved into laughter, lightening the mood and setting the tone for the remainder of my visit. Never again did we discuss the bomb scare, the situation with the rescue, or the gaping hole in our lives that Vanessa Evans's passing had brought.

But we did laugh. We talked endlessly about good memories, good food, and that awful cat of Mama's. On Tuesday night, we all piled into Parker's home for a going-away meal.

Apparently, he had been nominated because everyone else's place was deemed unsuitable. Also, Mama had not been polled, which must have vexed her something awful.

This much I realized when we arrived at the location and began to unload the ridiculous number of pies she'd made for the occasion.

"I didn't realize we would be squeezed in like sardines," Mama said as the door opened and Mari and her friends spilled out onto the small patch of grass that passed as a lawn.

"Hush, Mama," I told her. "You need to be nice tonight. This means a lot to Mari and her friends."

She looked over at me, her face the mask of innocence. "You know I wouldn't hurt that child's feelings for anything. Of course I will be nice." She paused a beat. "But I cannot promise what I will say to you on the ride home."

I took that as a suitable truce and nodded. "Fair enough. Now let's go enjoy ourselves tonight."

"Because you'll be gone tomorrow. I know that too well, and I will miss you terribly."

Her words took me aback. Other than our one conversation about me returning to live in Brenham, Mama hadn't said a word about me flying back to Tennessee. I figured she was fine with it. After all, she had a busy social life here along with her pies and her doggie clothing design ventures.

Mari hugged me and then headed for the back of the car to retrieve a pie. Cassidy followed suit.

"We're going to need to make several trips," the clinic's office manager declared.

"I don't mind," Mari said, pausing to give Mama a peck on the cheek. "Making pies is how Grandma Peach shows she loves you. And as you can see, she loves me a lot!"

My time at Brenham ended far too soon, but there were things that needed tending back in Nashville, so off I went. I worried about Mama and Mari being without me at Christmas, but I needn't have.

The pair of them bombarded me with videos of their Christmas Eve at church, Christmas Day at Mama's place, and even a trip around the city to see the decorations the day after. One thing I noticed right off was that in all of those videos, a certain blue-eyed vet tech was close by if not in the mix.

Although I wasn't sure that Mari was aware of it, there was a romance budding. I sent a prayer skyward that if Parker was the one for my niece, it would become clear to her very soon. He seemed so perfect for her that it would be a pity if her inattention to his attempts at romance went unnoticed until he finally quit trying.

Sweet Parker didn't look like a quitter. And he loved dogs. Surely Mari would come to her senses soon.

We hadn't taken too many pictures while I was visiting. I liked it that way when it was happening, but now that I was back in Nashville, I found myself wishing for more documentation of what we'd seen and done.

One thing I wouldn't soon forget was Mama's reminder about the impossible taking longer. That stuck with me just as I hope it did with Mari.

Tennessee Williams made a career out of a story called "You Can't Go Home Again." Was he right?

Every time I decided he was, I would recall my precious Mari's face as she talked about her plans for a permanent shelter for her rescue pups. She could certainly use some help there, and not just the generous deposit I put in her bank account when I got back to Nashville. And Lord knows Mama wasn't getting any younger.

The more I thought about these things, the more I knew what I had to do. No, I couldn't consider moving back to Texas. Not when I was trying to keep my career going here in Tennessee. But I could arrange to spend more time there.

Surely that wasn't impossible, even if my team told me it was. After all, there had to be a way to keep up with my music career while living elsewhere. The only downside I could see, other than the cost of travel, was that I wouldn't be close by to attend any of the record label's impromptu meetings or fill in for a last-minute cancellation at the Opry or another local venue.

Still, I walked out of the meeting with my producer, a representative from my agency, Music Talent Today, and various representatives of Styler Records—my current record label—wondering just who worked for whom. Like Mama said, the impossible just took longer.

At the door, my agent, Olivia Burton, stopped me. "Can we talk a minute?"

At my nod, she ushered me over to a quiet corner. "I'll run this by the team," she told me. "Surely there's something we can do to accommodate you. But I need to know how much time away we're talking about."

I knew a solid number was impossible. "Olivia, do you have an aging parent?"

She sighed. "I did. And I totally understand what you were trying to accomplish back there. I didn't take the time I should have. I always thought there would be more of it." Olivia looked away then returned her attention to me. "I am willing to advocate for you, but we need to know whether your commitment is stronger to the music or your mother."

"I want both, but I will default to being with my mother every time. I'm just being honest." I paused. "Why don't you see what plan the team thinks is reasonable? Maybe we can meet again after they've had time to come to a consensus."

"And in the meantime, we continue to book you?"

I nodded, though my heart wasn't in it. What was happening to me? There was a time when I would go without sleep for three days straight if it meant I got the gig I wanted or the studio musicians I needed.

"I'll be in town for a few more weeks," I told Olivia. "After that I'll be commuting back and forth between Nashville and Texas. And just so you know, if my mother needs me again, I'll go sooner than that. However, we can always do video meetings, and I will make myself available for media or recording sessions, if necessary."

"All right," Olivia said. "I'll be praying that your mother stays healthy so you don't have to choose between caring for her and your career."

"Thank you." I reached out to hug her, and then we parted ways.

My producer, Gilbert "Sticks" Styler, caught up with me in the lobby.

"Hold up, Trina," he called. "You and I need to talk."

Sticks was handsome, if you liked the shaggy ponytailed type. He'd made his fortune and gained his nickname playing in a British boy band, and then when he got bored with the money and fame, Sticks retired to Nashville to produce other people's songs.

If Sticks had been born a generation earlier, he'd have been a hippie. As it was, he was a successful record producer with a string of hits and a few quirks and grooming habits that most folks overlooked—like dying his hair platinum blonde.

Oh, and he also owned the record label.

"There's nothing to talk about, Sticks," I said. "I got your message loud and clear. You want my mind on writing songs and making records."

He fell into step beside me, his pale hair glistening in the sunshine. "Actually, I want you happy to write songs and make records."

"Message received," I told him, smiling to the receptionist as I walked past her. "And I am happy to write songs and make records, so all is well."

Just before I reached the massive double doors that led to the parking lot, Sticks stepped in front of me. "I'm not an ogre, Trina."

"Never said you were," I told him.

He looked down at the marble floor and then back up at her. "I understand wanting to go home. I get homesick for England sometimes."

"I didn't know that."

He scrubbed at his jaws with his palms. "Yeah, well I don't mention it to the talent, now do I? I order up some fish and chips, put on an episode of *Dr. Who*, and just get on with it."

Much as I like fish and chips and television shows about time travelers, I didn't think that was the remedy for me. However, I respect Sticks and like working for him, so I just nodded.

"Why don't you bring them here? Your mother and niece, that is. I met your mum. She'd love it in Nashville. She could make little dog clothes for the stars and bake pies. And I'm sure your niece wouldn't be bored."

My temper flared, but I managed to keep my expression from slipping. "My niece is a vet tech who founded a dog rescue. She's never bored, but her organization is located in Texas, not Tennessee."

"So we will move the organization here." He shrugged and looked at me as if that was the solution to everything.

"Just like that," I said, unable to keep the sarcasm from slipping into my tone.

Letting out a long breath, he smiled. "Yes, just like that. So it's settled then?"

"Thank you," I told him. "I appreciate the advice and the suggestions, and I understand that they come from a place of concern."

It wasn't the answer to his question. I just hoped he didn't realize that. If pressed, I would elaborate that I was certain his concern was for the record label, not me or my family.

So I hurried out without a backward look. Something would change. Eventually.

Until then I settled into my old routine as winter turned to spring. Between writing sessions, recording sessions, and live performances, I stayed too busy to think about anything other than music.

Mostly.

And on those nights when I wanted to be back home, I took my producer's advice. Or rather a modified version of his advice. I ordered up Tex-Mex food, turned on an episode of my favorite Texas travel show, *The Daytripper*, and just got on with it.

Then one night I stepped off the stage after a performance at the Grand Old Opry to news that changed everything.

CHAPTER 7

My assistant thrust a phone at me the minute I stepped into my dressing room. "Someone named Wyatt Chastain is on the phone. He says it's urgent. Something about a peach."

"Mama Peach?"

"Yes, that's it."

I snatched up the phone. "Wyatt, what's happened to Mama?"

"She's going to be fine," my old friend said, his tone soothing. "But she's had a fall. She'll be in the hospital for a few days, but otherwise she's fine."

Panic rose. I'd worried about something like this happening for years. My mother was not about to slow down, even if I begged her to.

"Details, Wyatt. I need details. Where did it happen? How? All that."

He chuckled, and I almost went through the phone to tell him face-to-face that nothing at that moment was the least bit humorous. "She made me promise to let her tell the story. Apparently, she didn't think I'd tell it right. Also, she doesn't want Mari to know. No idea why. Suffice it to say, Peach is still feisty, and according to her, she'll be fine. I doubt she'll let this slow her down much."

"I'm afraid you're right. Would you tell her I'm on my way?"

"I'll let her know."

"And that I love her," I added.

"Of course."

It didn't occur to me to wonder why Wyatt of all people had made that call until I was sitting in a seat on the Styler Records jet, bracing myself for takeoff. My mind had been so focused on getting to Mama that I hadn't considered the details.

The jet roared forward, and I clutched the armrests. It was no secret that while I didn't mind flying, I was never comfortable on an airplane until I was sure it was actually going to get into the air.

Funny, I never worried about the landing.

Once the plane was airborne, I went hunting for Wyatt's email address. I couldn't make a call until we landed. Unfortunately, we wouldn't touch down until after midnight, and I didn't dare bother him at that hour.

Instead, I hunted around until I found a contact form for his law office and settled in to write out my questions. I added the part about how I'd be at the hospital first thing tomorrow and then pressed SEND.

The next morning I walked into a hospital room at Baylor Scott & White Medical Center to find my mother propped up in bed sewing brass buttons on what appeared to be a soldier costume for a small dog.

Or doll clothes. It was hard to tell and not at all unlike Mama to add a new line of clothing to her business in the middle of a crisis.

The reason for this crisis—a broken ankle due to a fall—was currently encased in plaster and suspended above the blankets with some sort of metal contraption.

Mama looked up from her work and grinned. "Trina! What a nice surprise. I didn't expect you."

"I came as soon as I heard." I walked over to give Mama a hug. "Are you hurting?"

She dismissed my question with a wave of her hand. "I'm fine. They're making a lot of fuss for nothing. I listened to your show at the Opry last night."

I sat on the chair beside the bed. "Did you like it?"

Mama patted my hand. "No, I didn't like it. I loved it. As usual, you were the best singer on the show."

"You're a little biased, don't you think?"

My mother picked up her project again. "I just tell the truth, Trina."

"Okay, Mama. Thank you," I said. "Speaking of telling the truth, why don't you want Mari to know you're in the hospital?"

Mama never looked up from her needlework. "She worries as much as you do."

"She's going to find out."

"Not unless you tell her. Now find something else to talk about, would you?"

I'd get to the bottom of this strange request to keep Mari uninformed, but obviously, interrogating Mama wasn't how it would be done. I decided to do as she asked and change the subject—for now.

"What're you making?"

My mother grinned, her countenance transformed. "It's a special order. One of my best customers is a historical reenactor. He wants to bring his Chihuahua to a convention they're having in San Antonio and thought the pup should have a costume of his own."

"Of course he should," I said as I imagined a pint-size pup wearing something like she was working on. "So how did you get your sewing things here?"

"Wyatt had his assistant go fetch them for me."

"Brilliant," I somehow managed to say without laughing. "Now, let's get back to talking about how you got here and when you'll be going home. And while you're at it, you can tell me why Wyatt was the one who called me."

Once again she dismissed my question with a sweep of her hand. "I fell. I broke instead of bounced. I ended up here but will be going home tomorrow or the next day. That's all there is to tell either by me or Wyatt Chastain."

"Mama," I said, "there has got to be more to the story than that."

"If there is, I won't be the one telling it. Now, why don't you hand me my sewing kit? I think Santa Anna needs another brass button on his uniform."

Have I mentioned that the women in my family are stubborn? After I complied with her request, Mama set her lips closed and didn't say another word until the nurse came in and shooed me out.

Wyatt hadn't answered my email, but I knew where I could find him. The hospital was out on Highway 290, and his office was downtown. The commute between them was short, so less than ten minutes later I arrived at his law office across from Faske's Jewelers on West Main Street.

While the exterior of the building was nothing to brag about, the glass door with CHASTAIN LAW written in gold letters hinted of the swanky interior. Still, an elegantly paneled foyer with gleaming marble floors and a beautiful antique brass chandelier overhead were not at all what I expected.

The minute that heavy leaded glass door closed behind me, I felt like I'd stepped into a fancy law office in Houston or Dallas. Apparently, Wyatt was doing well for himself.

A young man dressed in a conservative navy suit and red striped tie looked up from his laptop computer and frowned. A moment later, he stood. "You're Trina Potter, aren't you?"

"Yes, I am."

He stuck out his hand. "I'm so glad to meet you. I saw you in the parade at Christmas. My cousin Bubba drove your float. He also owns the hauling company and a few others." As if an afterthought, he added, "Oh, I'm Desmond."

This sharply dressed young man looked nothing like the sweet but rough Bubba who had his fingers in all sorts of business pies in Brenham, including the speedy delivery business. I elected not to tell Desmond this.

Rather, I returned the smile with one of my own. "It's very nice to meet you. I assume you work for Wyatt."

"Yes, ma'am. I'm Mr. Chastain's associate." Desmond dropped into his chair, fingers soon flying across the keyboard. Then he looked up. "I'm sorry, but I don't see that you have an appointment."

"I don't," I told him. "Is Wyatt here?"

"Not at the moment," Desmond said. "But if it's a legal matter, I can speak to you."

"Actually, it's personal," I said. "Will he be back in the office anytime soon?"

"No ma'am." He closed the laptop and looked up at me. "You're a friend of his, aren't you?"

"I am. How did you know?"

"Your birthday's on the calendar."

That was unexpected. I hadn't held a conversation with Wyatt Chastain that lasted more than ten minutes since high school, and yet he had my birthday on his calendar? I'd nodded at him across the aisle at mutual friends' weddings over the years, accepted his words of sympathy at Daddy's funeral, and danced with him twice at our five-year high school reunion. But as I got more famous, I spent less time in Brenham and even less time out in public here in my hometown.

There was no good excuse and a whole bunch of poor ones for why I'd let my friendship with Wyatt lapse. That's why I'd been happy to exchange phone numbers when we'd met again at the Christmas party, but I sure hadn't thought that reunion worthy of putting his birthday on my calendar. I realized Desmond was looking at me as if it was my turn to speak.

What was it we were talking about? Oh, birthdays.

Specifically mine on his calendar.

"I'm sure he has plenty of birthdays on his calendar," I offered.

Desmond shook his head. "Just yours and his dog's."

Again, unexpected. "Really?"

"Yes, really. Although, now that I think of it, I ought to put mine on there."

"Definitely," I said. "So if Wyatt isn't here, where can I find him? I really need to talk to him today, if possible."

"Since you two are friends, I guess it won't hurt to tell you. Mr. Chastain left a message on the voice mail early this morning that the bull got out and he needed to handle the situation." As if he interpreted my confused expression, Desmond went on. "He's got a ranch. That's the excuse he uses when he'd rather be at the ranch instead of in the office. Pretty much he's taking a work-at-home day."

"Thank you, Desmond. Just one more thing. . .the address?"

He wrote an address on a notepad and then tore off the sheet and handed it to me. "Thank you. You've been very helpful."

"Be sure to tell Mr. Chastain that. I'm still in my probation period, and I'm hoping he will hire me permanently."

I folded the note and tucked it into my purse. "You can count on me to put in a good word for you, Desmond."

He was still smiling as I turned to leave. I stepped out into the mid-morning sun, temporarily blinded.

"Trina?"

Slipping on my sunglasses, I looked around. Bitsy was climbing out of a white Cadillac SUV. She wore a hot-pink top over white jeans. Hot-pink wedge heel sandals and a hot-pink scrunchie holding up her ponytail completed the ensemble.

She closed the driver's door and headed for me, her armful of gold bracelets gleaming in the sun. "It's so good to see you," Bitsy gushed as she hugged me. "Are you back for a visit?"

"Sort of," I said, extricating myself from her strongly perfumed embrace. "I came to see Mama."

Her grin fell as she leaned forward. "Is something wrong?"

I figured I'd skirt that question rather than answer it. If word got back to Mari that I had talked about my mother's hospitalization with someone else before I spoke to her about it, she'd be hurt. And rightfully so.

"Just the usual adventures," I said lightly.

"It sounds like she needs someone to keep tabs on her. I know your niece has a full plate, what with her job at the vet clinic and then all the work she does rescuing dogs. I wonder if she's up to watching your mama as she ought to be watched. Last I heard, Mama Peach was baking pies for every charity in town plus more than one eligible widower."

"Is that so?" Bitsy's criticism hit the target. Of course, her expression was nothing but innocent.

"It would be nice to be around more," I said. "But you know how things are. Life led me out of Brenham years ago. Mama and I stay in touch though. Thank goodness for cell phones and computers."

"Sure," she said, stepping back to her SUV to grab what looked like a picnic basket out of her back seat. "I understand. But sometimes phones and computers aren't enough, and you have to lead yourself back home, you know? And when you're ready, I'm your girl. Besides, I wouldn't want you to wait too long."

"I'm sorry. Wait too long for what?"

Bitsy leaned in to close the back door with her hip and then strode toward me. "Land is always a good investment, especially in Texas, and especially now. But honestly, if I were you, I'd be more concerned about finding a safe place for my mama and maybe even for my niece and her mutts."

"They're rescues," I said, not sure whether I should take offense at her tone or not. "And my mother is just fine where she is."

Was she really? I had to guess that she was, but the thought occurred that I probably should make sure.

Bitsy's expression did not change. "I mean Mama Peach is young at heart, but for how much longer?"

Before I could respond, she continued.

"She'll need help soon enough, and buying land in anticipation of that just makes sense."

I was busy trying to connect the dots between two very different points when she went on.

"And if that land had a place on it that would serve as a home-away-from-Nashville for you, then wouldn't that be *fun*?"

Fun? I wouldn't necessarily use that word. Having Mama within reach was a good thing but also could be a not-so-good thing.

"Just think about it." Bitsy sat her picnic basket on the sidewalk at her feet and fished around in her oversized pink purse until she found a jeweled card carrier that glinted in the sun. "Call me when you're ready." She met my gaze and then thrust the card at me.

Bitsy's smiling face decorated half the card while her contact information filled the other half. "Thank you," I said. "If I decide to look around for property, I'll give you a call."

"Just not this afternoon," she told me, retrieving the picnic basket. "I'll be busy."

"Well, all right, then." I turned to walk away.

"I'm having a picnic with Wyatt," she called.

I stopped and turned around. "That sounds nice."

She grinned. "It's a surprise. Well, mostly. I did mention that I might be dropping by his office today."

There were so many things I could have said in that moment. So many ways I could have provided her with information that might show her how Wyatt felt about her dropping by his office.

However, I just couldn't. That was between her and Wyatt.

"Well, have fun," was the best I could come up with before I made my escape.

CHAPTER 8

Wyatt's ranch was at the end of a long dirt road in the middle of nowhere. The massive black iron front gate was locked tight and bore no hint of who lived here. The address on the mailbox attached to a pole along with a call button was the only clue, and it matched the one Desmond had given me.

I pulled in and parked at the gate, then pressed the call button. Beyond the fence, wind whistled through the trees and carried with it the sound of cattle in a distant pasture.

While I waited for a response, I checked my emails. There was nothing from Wyatt in response to my attempts at contacting him.

Then my phone buzzed with a new text. It was Mari sending me a photo of her latest rescue, a nut-brown dachshund and corgi mix that had been surrendered by owners who were moving out of the country.

I responded back: LOOK AT THOSE HEART-MELTING BROWN EYES.

Mari's answer was swift. I KNOW. SHE WON'T LAST LONG. I'VE ALREADY HAD SOMEONE FROM THE DOXIE RESCUE GROUP CONTACT ME.

Something outside the car groaned then creaked, and I almost dropped the phone. A moment later, the iron gates opened. I tucked my phone away and shifted into DRIVE.

A gravel road wound through the trees and then out into a clearing with pastures on both sides. To my left, I spied a herd of longhorn cattle moving toward the horizon, their horns gleaming in the June sunshine. Opposite this, a half dozen horses grazed, oblivious to my presence.

I let out a long breath. It was so peaceful here.

The road curved, and I was back in a wooded thicket with the sound of gravel crunching under my tires. I'd left my window rolled down, and now a fresh green scent of forested land filled the car. Too soon the road curved again and a house came into view in the distance.

At first glance, the massive two-story log home looked as if it had stood on that spot for a century or two. As I drew nearer, I spied a much newer log structure—a garage that easily held six vehicles, maybe more—attached to the back of the house. Two of the six modern glass and black iron doors were open, revealing a black pickup truck in one and an old beat-up car in the other.

I recognized the car instantly as the ratty old vehicle Wyatt drove in high school. Funny, I never pegged Wyatt for the sentimental type.

From somewhere off in the distance, I heard the roar of an engine. Turning, I spied an ancient pickup truck bouncing across the prairie toward me.

The paint on the thing—what was left of it—was a dull brick red that may have once been shiny when it was new. Unlike the sleek trucks they make now, this one had curved front fenders and a grill of rusted silver metal. In crackled and faded gold paint on the driver's side door were the words *Fire Chief*.

Wyatt grinned when he pulled up next to me. He was wearing a denim shirt, a straw cowboy hat, and a pair of aviator sunglasses. When he climbed out of the truck, it was no surprise that he'd completed the working cowboy look with faded jeans and a pair of brown boots flecked with mud.

"Now this is a surprise," he said, drawing out that last word into multiple syllables. "I knew you'd be in town but didn't think you'd be showing up here."

"You can thank your assistant, Desmond, for that."

He removed his shades. "Interesting that my newly hired employee would think it was fine to give a stranger my personal address. Especially on a day when I told him I was absolutely not to be interrupted unless it was a very good reason."

I wasn't fooled by his attempt to be irritated by my interruption. "Apparently, your newly hired employee recognized my name on your calendar and figured it was a very good reason." I leaned slightly forward. "Wyatt, you have my birthday on your calendar?"

His tanned face colored slightly. "It's not what you think."

I laughed. "It couldn't possibly be."

Wyatt raised one dark brow. I remembered him teaching himself how to do that using my purse mirror in homeroom.

"See, it's like this," he began and then stalled when his cell phone rang. "Hold on. I need to see who this is."

I nodded. "Yes, you should do that. It might be a very good reason."

Wyatt looked at the phone, then silenced the ring and returned his attention to me. "Where was I?" he asked as he tucked the phone back into his pocket.

"My birthday," I offered and then added, "Desmond mentioned it was on your calendar."

"Remind me to have a chat with Desmond," he muttered.

I continued to keep my gaze steady. I might have come to find out something completely unrelated to this topic, but I wasn't going any further in the conversation until this point was cleared up.

Besides, I was enjoying this.

"You're not going to let me off the hook, are you?" he said with a crooked grin.

"Nope."

Wyatt sighed. "Okay, but it's easier to show you than tell you." He nodded to the truck. "Climb in, and let's go for a ride."

I walked around to the passenger side. Wyatt loped ahead of me to open the door.

This door matched the other one with faded letters and gold paint that was cracked and peeling. "I bought it at an auction," Wyatt offered as I climbed in. "I went there for a tractor and came home with this. I would've bought the fire truck that was in the same lot, but I got outbid."

I didn't bother to ask what he would have done with a fire truck. He was a guy, and some guys liked buying things like fire trucks. Why they liked these things was a mystery I did not care to solve.

Not when there were two more that needed a solution. As we set off across the prairie back in the direction from which he'd just arrived, I decided to tackle the one we hadn't discussed yet: my mother.

He slowed to ease the truck around a stump and then hit the gas again. "So, how's Mama Peach today?"

I looked at him flabbergasted.

Wyatt gave me a sideways look. "What?"

"Actually, I was about to ask you about her."

The truck hit a dip and then bounced up. I held on to the door handle, what with seat belts apparently not being in existence when the fire chief drove this thing.

"Okay, but you first. Any idea when she'll be going home?"

"Not soon enough to suit her, but probably tomorrow or the next day." I paused. "As to how she's doing, that's a more complicated answer. Turns out her ankle is not as bad as it first appeared to be. She'll have to be in a boot but probably not a cast. That will be decided today, I think."

"Sounds promising." Wyatt made a right turn and suddenly headed the truck onto a gravel road. Up ahead was a grove of pecan trees. "You don't sound happy about all this."

His assessment surprised her. "Not true. I'm very happy things didn't turn out worse."

"But?"

"But I'm worried, Wyatt. My mother has always been a force of nature."

He chuckled. "And that's not about to change."

"No, but it needs to," I said. "It's just her and Hector in that house, and that cat's not going to be any help if something happens."

Wyatt slowed the truck to a stop in the shade of a pecan tree, then shifted into PARK. Then he turned to face her. "Actually, I would disagree."

"Okay," I said slowly. "Enlighten me."

"How do you think I came to be in the story of your mama's trip to the emergency room?"

I leaned back against the door. "If you read your emails, you would know that I've been trying to find that out since I got on the plane."

He chuckled. "I've been busy. What with the fences that needed to be mended and all the paperwork I needed to catch up on, the phone meeting with Dallas Wright's daughter, oh, and the bull—"

"Got out," I supplied. "Yes, I heard. Wyatt Chastain, get to the point!"

He held up both palms in surrender. "Okay. Hector called me. That's how I came to be the one who took your mama to the hospital."

I gave him a look that let him know exactly what I thought of his nonsense. "That's preposterous. A cat cannot dial a phone."

"This one did." He shrugged. "It was after five o'clock, and I was just about to close up for the day. I was throwing files in my briefcase to bring home to work on, and my phone rang with a video call. The caller ID said it was your mama. I answered, and there was Hector staring at me like I was the crazy one."

"You expect me to believe that my mother's cat placed a video call to you? Come on, Wyatt. Stop kidding around and just tell me what happened."

"I'm dead serious, Trina. Here. I took a screenshot." He retrieved his phone and, after a moment, thrust it toward her.

Sure enough, there was my mother's cat.

"Look in the background," he said. "That's your mama. Hector must have somehow activated the computer's camera and call function when she fell."

I enlarged the photo enough to see my mother sitting on the floor in what appeared to be a pile of fabric. Frowning, I handed the phone back to Wyatt.

"I said, 'Mrs. Potter, your cat called me. Did either of you need anything in particular, or was this a social call?' I was joking with her, because frankly I had never been called by a cat before and didn't know the protocol."

"Right."

This was serious. Mama could have been badly hurt. Why then did I have to stifle a giggle at the thought of Hector's furry face on the screen?

"So the cat starts howling like crazy. You should know I had brought Ed to work that day. He's my cattle dog, but sometimes he's my office dog. He's over at the vet clinic having a spa day today, but you'll meet him eventually if you stick around."

"Wyatt," I said, a warning tone in my voice. "Back to the story, please."

"Oh, yeah, sure. So Hector is howling, and then he's hissing because he sees Ed. Meanwhile, Ed is barking like he's about to come through the screen. I'm hollering at your mother, asking if she's okay, and she's hollering at Hector to shut up."

Wyatt paused. I resisted the urge to insist he finish the story.

"Anyway, I put Ed in the truck, and we went to see if your mama was all right. When I got there and saw she couldn't answer the door, I called her, seeing as I have her number and all."

"Did Hector answer?" I couldn't resist asking.

"Nobody did, smart aleck. So I called 911 and then waited until the ambulance arrived. After I took Ed home, I went back to check on her at the hospital. She made me promise not to tell you how she'd hurt herself, and I haven't."

"Except that in this picture it looks like she tripped over that big pile of fabric she has stored just outside her office door."

He nodded. "That's how I would tell it if I was going to tell it, which I'm not because I promised."

So my mother was hiding the fact that, just as I had warned her during my visit in December, she has too much fabric. The avalanche from her stash in the hall closet had apparently been her undoing.

Of course Mama wouldn't want to discuss the fact that I was right. It all made perfect sense now.

I leaned across the distance between us to touch his arm. "Thank you, Wyatt. You took good care of my mama. I appreciate it more than I can say."

Wyatt's phone rang again, and he gave me an apologetic look. While he was on the call, I glanced around.

The massive pecan trees here were planted orchard-style with even spaces between them, likely a hundred years ago. Bright green tassels—Daddy would have called them by their proper name of catkins—danced in the breeze among the darker emerald leaves. Judging from the amount of catkins in these trees, there would be a nice pecan haul come September.

"I'll handle it," Wyatt said.

I was trying not to eavesdrop, but the close confines of the truck made it impossible not to hear both sides of the conversation. Desmond's protests about *that woman* made me turn away so as not to reveal my smile.

Apparently, Bitsy was as persistent in her pursuit of Wyatt as she was in the sale of real estate. My guess was she'd given up on finding her man at his office and was now headed for the ranch.

She had a picnic basket and a plan.

CHAPTER 9

Wyatt tucked his phone back into his pocket. "Sorry. Office stuff," he told me.

"Something you need to handle?" I offered, knowing full well the office stuff to which he referred came dressed in white jeans and pink top.

"It'll wait." He turned to reach for the door handle. "Come with me. I want to show you something."

I climbed out before he could open the door for me. "This better answer the question of why you have my birthday on your calendar," I said in a teasing tone.

Wyatt snatched his phone out of his pocket and tossed it into his truck through the open window. His grin was spectacular. "Follow me."

Okay, that wasn't an answer to my question, but I was curious enough to do as he asked. Besides, it was a beautiful day, and I needed to hold on to that while I could because Mama's reaction to my next visit just might put a dark cloud over everything.

We walked together under the canopy of pecan trees, the bluebonnet-blue Texas sky overhead. The air was fresh here but did not have the same scent as the woods.

This was a warm scent. The smell of sunshine. Of deep, deep contentment.

After a few minutes, the flat land gave way to a hill that rose up at a relatively steep grade. When we reached the top of the hill, Wyatt halted.

"Turn around, Trina."

I did as he said and tried not to gasp. From this elevation, the orchard, the pastures, and even the forest that hid the front gate came into view. I could see Wyatt's home, his garage with all of those vehicles, and several outbuildings I hadn't noticed before.

"It's beautiful, Wyatt," I whispered.

"Sure is," came out just as softly. "I bought the place for this view. And the pecans," he added. "But mostly because there's something about standing on a hill looking down over land that I own that brings me joy. Not always happiness, because owning a ranch can be a real pain, but definitely joy."

"Joy," I said, nodding. "Yes, I can see that it would."

"Sit with me?" Wyatt didn't wait for my answer to settle onto the grass at my feet. He removed his sunglasses and folded them into his pocket.

I plopped down beside him without any hesitation. Off in the distance, I could hear a bird calling. Other than this and the swish of the leaves in the trees, there was complete quiet.

Nowhere in scripture did it say that heaven was a warm sunny day on a Texas ranch, but I felt like that just might be the case. I leaned back on my elbows and lifted my face to the sky, closing my eyes.

"It's the day I bought this place," Wyatt said, breaking the silence.

I opened my eyes and gave him a sideways look. He was also leaning back on his elbows, his eyes still closed as mine had been.

In profile, Wyatt Chastain had not changed a bit. He still looked like the goofy band nerd/buddy I went to prom with. Back then, never would I have imagined he'd have turned out like this.

"I know you're looking at me," he said without opening his eyes. "And you're thinking this dude turned out to be pretty impressive."

"Actually, I was."

Wyatt's eyes flew open, and for a second, he appeared to have lost the ability to speak. Then he grinned. "So I've answered your question."

"You have?"

He nodded. "The date on the calendar is the day I bought this place."

"Why not just put *that* on the calendar?"

A shrug of one shoulder and his eyes closed again. "It's complicated."

We sat in silence for a while, and I began to wish I'd chosen shorts or a sundress and sandals instead of the jeans, sneakers, and T-shirt I'd worn. The heat wasn't yet unbearable like it would be later in the month, but I was warming up a bit too much for my liking all the same.

And if I wasn't careful, my wardrobe gal was going to be furious with me for getting a farmer's tan. Apparently, they're hard to cover with stage makeup.

But I wasn't going to think about wardrobe, stages, or anything that had to do with the music business right now. There would be plenty of time to answer emails, follow up on phone calls, and generally throw myself back into the world I'd left behind in Nashville.

Maybe later today, but not now.

At last I sat up and hugged my knees. A flock of birds circled in the distance, and I watched their aerial dance across the skies until I finally poked Wyatt's arm.

"Don't you have things to do?"

He adjusted his cowboy hat into a position that covered his face. "I'm doing them."

I grabbed that Stetson off Wyatt's head. "Wyatt Chastain, I am not going to watch you take a nap. At least give me the keys so I can drive back to my car. I've got things to do."

He chuckled but made no move to respond. Finally, I tossed the hat back at him and stood.

"All right, Trina," Wyatt said lazily. "But don't think you can fool me into believing you weren't enjoying yourself."

I gave him a warm smile. "I haven't enjoyed myself this much in a very long time."

"Yeah?" Wyatt fitted his hat back on his head and adjusted his sunglasses. "Me too."

We walked back toward the truck at a slow pace, comfortably silent. Here and there Wyatt would stop to inspect a tree or look off into the distance. We chatted about the pecan crop he expected to have in the fall, and I told him about having figured out Mama Peach's secret ingredient for her pecan pies.

"I would never expect that she'd put turmeric and cumin in a pecan pie," Wyatt exclaimed. "She's paid me with those pies though, and I can tell you they are delicious."

The truck was in sight, but I was suddenly reluctant to have this all end. "It's so quiet out here," I remarked.

"Just like I like it." As if sensing my wish to delay, Wyatt stopped walking.

They were under the shade of the massive limbs of an ancient pecan tree. As I looked up into the canopy of green, I thought about my daddy's reminder that a pecan tree could live up to three hundred years.

"Three times our lifetime and then some."

I could still hear him say it with such awe. A man plants something in this earth that seems small and insignificant, and two generations later it's not only bearing fruit but bigger than anything the planter could imagine.

"That's the Word of God, Trina," he'd said. *"Plant it deep and care for it, and it'll outlive you and grow bigger than you ever expect it will."*

"You look pensive," Wyatt said.

I managed a weak smile. "Pecan trees make me think about my daddy."

"He did have a way with them," Wyatt said. "I doubt he told you this, but when I was looking at property, I asked him if he'd come out here with me to see if it was something worth buying. I respected his opinion. He told me I'd be crazy to let this go, and so I bought it."

"Daddy was a wise man," I said.

"I know why I've been quiet," Wyatt said, looking at me from under the brim of his hat. "But I'm wondering why you have. Can't have been thinking about your daddy all that time."

I waited a minute before responding. "In a way, I guess I was. I wonder what Daddy would think of how I've taken care of Mama. The fact she's lying in a hospital bed makes me believe he wouldn't be pleased with me."

"Hey now, Trina, that's not true. Your father couldn't brag on you enough when he was living. Every time I saw him, it was 'Trina did this' and 'Trina did that.' Didn't he ever tell you any of this?"

"All the time," I told him. "I never had a bigger fan than my daddy. But my sister was living then. Now that Daddy and Vanessa are both gone, I'm the one left to watch out for Mama, who, by the way, does not want anyone watching out for her, most of all me. You might have noticed."

"I did, actually," Wyatt said with a chuckle. "And to be fair, the cat *did* do a decent job of handling the emergency."

We shared a smile that faded quickly. "I know Mari is close by, but she's young. I won't put that responsibility on her."

When I fell silent, I fully expected Wyatt to step in with a list of things I could do to fix the situation. It has been my experience that a man faced with a statement like I'd just made would, by nature, be compelled to provide the remedy.

But he didn't.

Instead, Wyatt just nodded as he stared off into the distance. Not a dismissive nod but rather a nod that said he'd listened and understood.

Finally, he brought his attention back to me. "What're you going to do about it?"

I let out a long breath. "I have no idea."

He reached over to place his hand on my shoulder. "You'll figure it out."

"Yeah," I said. "I will. Eventually."

Wyatt let his arm fall to his side. "Come on. Let's get out of here. It's either that or we play hooky from life all day and go back to sit up on the hill."

"You'd get hungry," I told him.

"You're right," he said. "But not for a while. Desmond is handling things at the office, and I don't have to be in court until day after tomorrow."

"Wyatt."

"Okay!"

We resumed our walk down the hill toward the truck, with Wyatt taking the lead in places where the path was too narrow for us to walk side by side. He'd grown taller and broader in the shoulders over the years, and he was more serious than I remembered, but he hadn't lost his sense of humor.

And his sense of when to talk and when to be quiet. I think I liked that best about him.

It was on the drive back to my car that Wyatt finally spoke up again. "Did your niece ever find out who planted that bomb out at the Double J Ranch?"

The question startled me. So much time had passed that I'd put that incident firmly in the back of my mind.

"She didn't," I said. "If I remember correctly, the police couldn't prove whether it was kids fooling around or some kind of threat either against Mari or against Maggie Jamison."

"That's what I thought."

"There haven't been any more issues like that, have there? Because I wouldn't doubt that Mari would keep me in the dark about them like she tried to do with that bomb."

Wyatt shook his head. "Nothing that I know of. Hopefully, it was just idiot kids. Thank the Lord that I didn't have the internet telling me how to do dumber things than I was already doing as a kid."

"And on video," I added.

"Exactly." Wyatt stared straight ahead, but even from where I sat, I could see his expression had changed. "Trina, do you know whether the police did an online search to see if anyone was bragging on social media about building that bomb?"

"I don't know," I said slowly. "But that's a very good question."

"A question I wished I'd asked back when it all happened," he said. "Because I'm thinking that there would be buzz about it among the kids. Remember when we were in school? If anyone did anything, we all eventually heard about it. The parents and teachers, not so much. But the kids? Absolutely."

"Wyatt, you're a genius," I said.

"You're only telling me that because it's true," he teased.

They shared a smile. It was true.

In addition to band nerd, Wyatt Chastain had been president of the Mensa club for all four years of high school. He'd also been one of only three members who qualified for president, and the other two had no wish to run for the position.

"Seriously though," Wyatt said as he pulled the truck up next to my car and shifted gears into PARK. "I don't want to alarm you, but that whole situation still bothers me. Mari's got all these rescue dogs there, and Maggie's got a bit of animosity with her husband's family. Looking at this from a prosecuting attorney's point of view, I'd say there are avenues yet unexplored because there are plenty of suspects here."

"I don't disagree, but that's where the investigation hit a dead end. All the avenues were explored, and there was no proof of involvement from any of the Jamison family. Nor did the police find a credible threat against Mari or the rescue operation."

"Yet."

One word. Three letters. But the impact slammed her.

"You think Mari or Maggie, or both of them, are in danger?"

A question, not a statement. This time Wyatt didn't hesitate. "I think—barring some idiot bragging on social media—that the bomb was put there to threaten someone. Maybe it was Maggie. Maybe it was the dogs. Not everyone would appreciate strays being collected near them, even out in the country."

"Right."

"Or maybe it was Mari who was supposed to be scared." Wyatt paused. "Whatever the reason, it hasn't happened again, and I don't see that it had the desired effect on either of those women." He paused. "And yes, I make it my business to keep in touch with my contact at Brenham PD about this."

"Thank you," I told him. "I seem to keep saying that to you today."

He waved off the statement with a sweep of his hand. "I'm a lawyer, Trina. We love a good puzzle, and right now that unexploded pipe bomb presents a puzzle I would like very much to solve."

Wyatt's phone, which had remained on the seat between us as we bounced our way back to the ranch house, buzzed with a call. He looked down at the phone and then shook his head. "I'm sorry. I really do have to take this one.

"I can see myself out," I said.

He held up his hand as if to stall me, then answered the call with "Chastain Law Office. Would you hold, please?" Placing the caller on hold, he continued. "I've enjoyed this, Trina. Can I see you again before you leave?"

"I would like that," I said, climbing out of the truck and closing the door behind me.

"Tonight?"

I laughed. "That depends on what's going on with Mama."

"Of course. We'll connect later then."

I nodded. "Sure."

"Oh, one more thing," Wyatt called as I turned to walk away. "It doesn't take a genius to know you're happy here. Why not call Bitsy and have her show you some properties? It doesn't mean you have to live here, but at least you'd have a place to come home to that doesn't involve another potential avalanche of quilting fabric and a cat that makes video calls."

CHAPTER 10

I laughed, but the closer I got to town, the more the idea grew on me. Maybe I would just look around and see what was out there. Something with enough acreage to offer privacy and plenty of room to put in a little house for Mama if the need arose.

And definitely with a spot where Mari could have a permanent base of operations for her rescue endeavors. It was that last part that made me smile the most.

I had been donating to the rescue ever since Mari made that option available to donors and volunteers. I had to be careful not to overdo it because it made my niece uncomfortable to receive large sums of money from me. That was a lesson I learned after my first donation was returned with a very sweet note telling me that while she appreciated my generosity, this amount was out of the question.

I admired her for that. I'd loved her since the day she was born, but in that moment when Marigold Evans could have accepted my donation and had her dreams come true—most of them anyway—she had declined? That was truly when I saw my niece for who she had become: a strong, principled woman who I had no doubt could achieve anything to which she set her mind.

Thus, I would have to be careful how I approached the way I made my offer of land for her rescue. It had to be done just right.

But first things first. When I returned to the Ant Street Inn, the historic hotel on Brenham's main square, I retrieved Bitsy's card.

She picked up on the third ring with a curt recitation of her name.

"Bitsy," I said. "This is Trina Potter. I've been thinking about what you said regarding buying land, and I'm ready to see what's out there."

"That's wonderful, Trina," came out with much more enthusiasm than her greeting had. "As it turns out, I have the rest of the afternoon free. If you're ready now, I can stop by your mother's house and pick you up."

"Actually, I do have a few hours before my evening plans get started. I'm at the Ant Street Inn."

"So, what are you looking for? City or country? Ranch, property? And in Washington County, or do you want to branch out?"

"Well," I said slowly, "I definitely want at least ten acres. More would be okay, but what I'm really interested in is privacy."

"Of course. Someone famous like you wouldn't want to have the paparazzi shooting pictures at all hours of the day and night." Her tone had gone bitter.

"Well, I don't know about that. I'm just a regular person here in Brenham. But I do like my privacy, and I want it to be a place that's quiet."

"Quiet and private," Bitsy echoed, the cheery tone having returned. "I've got a few options that might suit you. I can be there in ten minutes."

Trina spent the next two hours viewing properties and listening to Bitsy extoll the virtues of each of them. Unfortunately, none interested her.

"Maybe we can try again tomorrow?" Bitsy said as she pulled her SUV to a stop in front of the inn. "I'll do a little more research and refine our search. Although I thought sure you would fall in love with the Italianate mansion on the river. That place was to die for."

"Just a bit much for me," I said. "I'm not that fancy."

Nor did I need a twenty-room home with seventeen bathrooms. What in the world would anyone who lived alone need with that many bathrooms? Then there was the price tag. While I had expected it wouldn't be an inexpensive proposition to find what I was looking for, I never thought I'd be putting that many zeros on a check.

Not that I could have even if I'd wanted to.

"Okay, just so I'm clear for our next outing, you want at least ten acres with privacy?"

I nodded.

"That's fairly general," she told me.

I shrugged. "I'm not picky, Bitsy. I just want a place I can call home with some room to spread out in case Mama ever needs to come live with me."

Bitsy's perfectly drawn brows rose. "So lots of room. Check. And for the record, I would want the same thing if my mama had to come live with me."

"It's something we have to consider, I'm afraid. They're not as young as they used to be, and neither are we."

She shuddered. "I truly cannot imagine that, Trina. I love my mother and would do anything for her, but she can be a bit, well, difficult. Having the two of us under one roof would be a nightmare. That's why my next property will have two homes on opposite ends. I'll even give her the bigger one if it'll keep her happy. Not that anything would. Still, that's what I'd do."

Having met Bitsy's mama, I didn't blame her.

My visit with Mama that evening was short. She was as sweet as she could be until I confronted her with the photo I asked Wyatt to text to me.

"Mama, you have got to do something to accident-proof your home. Things like this cannot continue to happen," I told her as she studied the picture. "You were lucky this time."

"That Hector is the smartest cat I've ever seen," she said, ignoring the rest of my statement. "Just look at him making that video call. Why, I can't even do that without having Mari on the phone walking me through the steps."

I gave her a look that told her I was not amused. She ignored me.

I retrieved the phone and turned it to face her. "What if you'd hit your head?"

"It really doesn't matter what I hit, be it my rear end or my head. Hector got 911 there in a jiffy, and all is well. By the way, I just may be going home day after tomorrow. It's ridiculous because I feel perfectly fine, but the doctors want to keep me a little longer to make sure that I don't have anything else wrong with me."

"What else could be wrong with you?" I asked as one of her nurses entered the room.

"Mrs. Potter," the nurse said in a warning tone, "are you telling tales again?" She looked at me, and I noticed her name tag proclaimed her to be Robin. "She's staying until the social worker has had time to look over her home to make sure it is safe for her to return."

"Mama!" I said far louder than I intended. "Why in the world didn't you tell me this?"

She picked up her sewing basket and began digging through it. It didn't take a genius to know that my mother had said her last on the subject.

"Can I have a word with you, Robin?" I gestured toward the door, then glanced back to catch Mama peering at us over her sewing basket. "Privately." I gave my mother a look. "Have you spoken with Mari today?"

"No," she said sheepishly.

"If you don't call her right now, I'm going to talk to her before I go to bed tonight. Understand?"

She nodded.

"I love you, Mama," I told her, and then I stepped out into the hall with the nurse. Within a few minutes, I had the name of the social worker and a plan.

After declining a dinner invitation from Wyatt, I returned to my room at the inn and settled in for the night. I had plenty to do to get ready for tomorrow.

When the phone rang, I jumped. I'd been so immersed in the research I was doing that I'd lost track of time.

"Sticks," I said to the record producer as I glanced at the clock on the mantel and saw it was half past nine. "It's good to hear from you. Is something wrong?"

"I could ask you that. I'm sending emails and texts that you're not answering. Is there a reason for that?"

"Actually, there is," I said calmly. "If you read your emails and texts from me, you would know that my mother is in the hospital, and I'm here with her in Brenham. So how can I help you?"

He named a laundry list of items I needed to handle, none of which would require a late evening phone call to discuss them. Then he paused, allowing me to respond.

"I promise I will address all of this tonight before I go to bed. Is there anything else?"

Silence fell between us, and not the comfortable quiet I'd experienced with Wyatt.

"Yeah, actually there is," Sticks said. "I took a meeting with the folks at Music Talent Today this afternoon. Olivia Burton says you're not ready to sign a new contract with us."

So the real reason for the call finally came out. I paused and considered my words carefully.

"I'm sure Olivia told you we're working on a counter."

The issue was the timeline the record company wanted for recording. I had already felt a bit reluctant to commit to such a large number of albums being recorded so closely together.

How would I find enough songs in time to make the deadlines? I sure couldn't write them that fast, and that bothered me more than anything else. Then there was the issue of caring for Mama. A grueling recording schedule coupled with live performances certainly wouldn't allow for any sort of time in Brenham.

"She did mention that you two were still discussing the terms," Sticks continued, "but since when do we use a go-between to talk? Do you want to make records with me, Trina?"

I took in a deep breath and then let it out slowly. "Sticks, you're the best in the business. Who wouldn't want to make records with you?"

"I'm glad to hear it, because I just emailed a copy of the new contract to you. Sign it and send it back, and we won't have to talk about this again for a while."

"I can't do that," I told him. "You know that."

"Yeah, I know, but I had to try." He paused. "What's so great about Brenham anyway? It's not like you want to move there permanently or something, is it?"

When I didn't answer immediately, he groaned. I, on the other hand, marveled at the fact that I'd just admitted to myself, albeit indirectly, that there was something great about Brenham that just might make me want to move there permanently.

"Maybe you ought to check it out," I told him. "Brenham is pretty great."

"Sure," he said, exaggerating his British accent, "I'd make a brilliant Texan. I certainly didn't the last time I was there."

"You never know. You just might. Anyway, I need to go, Sticks," I said firmly. "Thanks for calling."

I ended the call and was about to place the phone on the table when it rang again. This time it was Mari. I answered immediately. After a few minutes of cheerful chatter about the rescue, I asked her if she'd spoken to her grandmother lately. When she hadn't, I filled her in.

"Aunt Trina, we have to do something," Mari said. "I've been so busy with work and the rescue that I haven't spent much time with her."

"I've got some ideas, but I'm not ready to talk about them just yet. I need to do more research." I paused. "Speaking of research, I did some looking online this evening."

"Looking for what?" Mari asked over the sound of barking. "Sorry, Aunt Trina. I just got to the Double J, and I'm feeding the rescues. They're a little worked up."

"It's fine, honey." I told her about the conversation I'd had with Wyatt about social media.

"Oh wow," Mari said. "I didn't even think about that." She paused. "Can I call you back in a sec?"

"Sure, honey."

A few minutes later, the phone rang again. "Aunt Trina, how would you like to go with Parker and me on a rescue? I usually take my friend Cassidy, but she's busy tonight and it's kind of late to call Maggie Jamison."

"Are you kidding? I would love to."

CHAPTER 11

Twenty minutes later, I stepped out onto the sidewalk in front of the Ant Street Inn. The downtown square was deserted this time of night except for the white van waiting at the curb, lights off and engine idling.

The door opened, and I climbed inside to find another guest on tonight's rescue: Wyatt Chastain. He offered a grin. "Since my hopes for dinner plans fell through, I was over at the diner with Parker here when the call came in from Mari."

"I didn't know you and Parker were friends," Mari said.

"New friends," Wyatt said as Parker nodded. "We were both eating alone, and I recognized him from the vet's office. I'd just picked up Ed that afternoon."

"Ed is his cattle dog," Parker supplied. "He's a sweetheart."

"Don't say that," Wyatt exclaimed. "I don't want word getting out that my guard dog isn't vicious."

I laughed. "Hey, this afternoon you told me your dog was at the spa. That doesn't sound vicious to me."

"Even bad dogs need to look good," Wyatt responded. "That's my motto, you know."

I rolled my eyes.

Parker grinned. "Anyway, we got to talking about the rescue, and that led us to the topic of the pipe bomb."

"Oh?" Mari said.

"Nothing on social media for six months almost certainly means this wasn't the work of idiot kids," Parker said. "At least that's my take. Wyatt's too."

"Which means you're dealing with idiot adults," Wyatt said. "The kind of people who think it is okay to threaten either a dog rescue or a widow living alone."

"Nothing else has happened for six months," Mari offered. "Can't that mean that it was just a fluke?"

"I would never call a bomb a fluke," I said. "I read the news articles. That was a live bomb. The bomb squad had to detonate it. That's the real thing, sweetheart."

"I don't know why it hasn't happened again, but I am very glad it hasn't," Parker said. "But as long as the person who built that thing is still out there, I will continue to worry about the safety of you and the dogs." He paused to glance in her direction. "Let's be honest. I'll still worry even after he's caught."

"You never told me that," Mari scolded.

Parker shrugged. "No sense in you worrying too. Besides, it's kind of been my job from the beginning anyway."

Mari reached over to pat the vet tech on his shoulder. "Parker to the rescue. I really appreciate it that you worry. I mean, I'm glad we're a team. I should probably worry more."

"It would keep you from diving into nasty drainage pipes or racing down a busy freeway to catch a rescue dog," Parker chided.

"I agree with Parker," I said.

"Of course you do," Mari said. "You're my aunt."

I would have said that her mother might have agreed as well, but now was not the time. Not with two men in the van who didn't know my sister or share my and Mari's grief.

However, I would be sure to use that reasoning the next time my niece did something risky. And unfortunately, I knew it was just a matter of time before it happened again.

"Hey," I said, "am I imagining it, or do I smell cheeseburgers?"

"Just one cheeseburger," Parker said, "and it's in a bag in the back with our supplies."

"That's so Parker won't eat it on the way," Mari teased. "The cheeseburger is statistically proven to catch more dogs than any other bait we've used."

"And she's not kidding about the reason it's in the back of the van," Parker added. "I'm usually starving by the time we finish a rescue."

Parker left the freeway and made several turns. Although we hadn't driven far from downtown Brenham, we were now on a dark stretch of road. With only the sliver of a moon, there wasn't much light to help with the search.

I sat next to Wyatt and listened as Mari and Parker discussed their strategy for snatching up their latest rescue, which had allegedly been seen on the second level of an abandoned oil facility. Mari was insisting she do the climbing should it be needed, and Parker was voicing a compelling argument against it.

I almost interjected with a statement about safety, but I elected not to. If I was too much of a worrywart, she would never ask me to come along on a rescue again. And as much as I wanted my niece out of harm's way, I did admire her tenacity when it came to saving lost or abandoned pups.

Wyatt leaned close. "I heard you went out looking at property this afternoon."

I wasn't ready to share this with Mari or Mama just yet. I had barely admitted this to myself.

"I thought I would look, but I didn't find anything," I whispered against his ear.

"It's always better to wait for the right one." His eyes lingered on me a moment.

"Look!" Mari sat forward in her seat and gestured to a blur crossing the road just within view of the illumination from our headlights. "I think that's him."

"Hang on, everyone." Parker made a sharp right turn onto a gravel road that split an overgrown field.

The road was more holes than gravel, sending me rocking from side to side as Parker tried to keep the dog in view of the headlights.

"Do you know where you're headed?" Wyatt asked, his attention on his smart watch.

"Down a gravel road in the dark?" was Parker's response.

"You're going to need to hang a right just as soon as you can find a place that's safe," Wyatt continued, his tone urgent.

"I'll lose the dog if I do," he insisted.

"Parker," Wyatt snapped, "right turn. . .now!"

Parker jerked the wheel to the right just in time to avoid a black iron fence. Mari let out a scream while I held on tight to the armrests, eyes closed and prayers going up.

The van shuddered to a stop, and Parker turned around to face Wyatt. "How did you do that? There's no way you could see that black iron fence."

Wyatt held up his watch. "I wrote up a mineral lease out here for the Wrights—that's Dallas and his daughter, Anna—a couple of weeks ago, so I had the location mapped out on the app. I pulled it up thinking I could help guide you to the outbuilding where the animal is most likely living. That's when I remembered I had to get past the fence last time I was here."

Mari pitched herself forward to envelop Parker in a hug. "Parker to the rescue again." She glanced back at me, then at Wyatt. "And you too, Mr. Chastain."

"Wyatt will do just fine," he told her as he unbuckled his seat belt. "Now, what say we go see if we can find this dog on foot?"

"I think that's wise," Parker said, and Mari nodded her agreement.

I looked down at my pristine white sneakers and stifled a groan. Then I thought about the near miss with the fence and decided a pair of ruined shoes could be easily replaced.

"Okay, everyone," Mari said. "Everything is in the back of the van. Let's go."

After my niece handed out supplies—flashlights for everyone, a pair of rubber boots for me, a portable dog crate, and a few other things—we set off in the direction we'd seen the animal disappear.

Wyatt took the lead, using his mapping app to lead the group through the thicket to a clearing up ahead. At least he said it was a clearing. It was too dark to tell, and Mari had forbidden more than one of us—Wyatt in this case—to use flashlights unless absolutely necessary.

No talking. No flashlights.

There were lots of rules in dog rescuing. I truly wasn't sure I could embrace the adventure the way Mari did.

After hiking single file around the clearing and back into the weeds for a few more minutes, we all paused when our leader stopped. The night was warm with only the slightest breeze bringing with it the scent of someone grilling.

"Is there a burger place around here?" I asked, only to be shushed by the others. "Okay," I said softly, "but I absolutely smell burgers. And not the burger that Parker carries for bait."

"You smell barbecue," Wyatt told me. "Just the other side of the fence is Deke King's place. Surely you've heard of Brenham's famous BBQ King? He moved here a few years ago."

"The name rings a bell," I told him. "Does he grill burgers?"

"Brisket mostly," Wyatt told me. "I think he's done well with his ribs, but the real prize is his links. His recipe is a secret, and he wins every time he enters them in a competition."

"So he's good, then?"

"Good?" He paused to shake his head. "Trina, I've been known to be paid for my legal work with Deke's jalapeño cheese and beef links. See, he makes them with some kind of seasoning that—"

"Quiet," Marigold urged. "Rescue dogs can be skittish. If he hears you two talking, he's going to run again."

I nodded, properly chastised. Wyatt leaned close enough for me to see his grin even in the low light. Then he stepped back into the lead, motioning for us to follow him.

After a few more minutes, with the scent of grilled meats fading, we came upon a small building. It might have been a shed or an outbuilding. Maybe it was even a dwelling of some kind because there appeared to be windows, a door, and quite possibly a chimney.

It was hard to know without using my flashlight to explore.

Something rustled. A limb cracked.

Or at least it sounded like a limb. I clutched Mari's free arm. "Did you hear that?" I whispered. "You need to shine that light on the building and see what's in there."

"*Shhh*," Wyatt warned.

Parker came up beside Mari. She handed him the flashlight, and I saw a look pass between them. Without a word, Mari moved to a position behind Parker and pulled me with her. Wyatt matched Parker shoulder to shoulder as the four of us walked in a square.

The idea of a marching square occurred, and I stifled a giggle. Two by two we moved toward the now-silent building. As we got closer, I could clearly see that this was absolutely some kind of dwelling.

The screen door was propped open by an ancient, rusted bicycle. The door behind it was closed, perhaps permanently since the wood looked faded and warped.

Using the flashlight, Parker scanned the perimeter of the little cabin. Then he raised the light to shine through first one window and then the other.

Another crack split the silence and then the unmistakable sound of a click.

"What was that?" I whispered to Wyatt, who was standing in front of me blocking my view.

"*Shhh*," my three companions said in unison.

Parker swung the beam of the flashlight toward the door. The light illuminated the warped wood just as it flew open to reveal a man holding a flashlight in one hand and a pistol in the other.

Then he fired.

CHAPTER 12

Everyone scattered. Except Wyatt, that is. I didn't realize this until I found myself crouching behind a tree with Mari next to me.

Parker had doused the flashlight when he hit the ground at our feet. Wyatt, however, hadn't moved an inch, and neither had the shooter.

Before the light went out, I'd seen that the man holding the smoking gun was tall and lean with thick white hair and a neatly trimmed beard and mustache. He was dressed in jeans, boots, and a pearl snap shirt that made him look as if he was a cowboy headed for town rather than a man terrifying innocent people.

People who might be trespassing on his land, I reminded myself as I held Mari close. So maybe we weren't looking so innocent after all.

"Dallas," Wyatt said in that slow drawl of his as he reached out his hand toward the stranger. "There was no need for that. Now, give me the gun."

"Aw, Wyatt," the man said, shaking his head. "Why didn't you tell me it was you?"

"You didn't give me time. Now hand over the gun, and stop frightening my friends."

He leaned forward to look around. "You got friends out there?"

"I do, but your antics had them running for cover." Wyatt turned toward us. "It's safe. You can come out. Dallas won't hurt you, will you, Dallas?"

An arc of light swept over us, but I made no move to join Wyatt. Not while that man still held his gun. Apparently, Mari agreed because she still clutched my arm. Parker, however, climbed to his feet, handed Mari the flashlight, and walked toward Wyatt.

"Dallas, this is Parker Jenson," Wyatt said. "Parker, this is Dallas Wright. He owns this place."

Parker reached out to shake Dallas Wright's hand. "We must have given you a fright, sir. I apologize. It wasn't intentional."

"He and his friend Mari work over at the Lone Star Vet Clinic. They got a tip that there's a stray dog out here in need of rescuing. See, Mari runs a dog rescue and Parker helps her with it."

Wyatt turned the flashlight toward us. I nudged Mari, and together we stepped out of our hiding place and moved toward the men.

"That'd be Mari now. Marigold Evans is her name, and that's her Aunt Trina."

"I know Trina Potter," Dallas said. "I listen to your records. Your daddy was an acquaintance of mine back in our rodeo days. Good man and a decent bronc rider, he was."

"Pleased to meet you, sir," I told him. "And yes, he sure was."

Mari exchanged greetings with the older man, then moved to stand beside Parker. I didn't miss the fact that the blue-eyed vet tech edged closer and put a protective hand on my niece's back.

Dallas leaned against the doorframe and scratched his forehead with the barrel of the pistol. He must have then realized he still held the thing, because he handed it over to Wyatt.

"It's just an old starter pistol," Dallas said. "Nothing but a glorified cap gun. I keep it around in case I need to scare anyone off."

"And it almost worked," Wyatt said as he inspected the pistol, then handed it back to Dallas. "Keep it, but don't point it at anyone unless you want to get yourself shot."

"I will," he said, reaching inside the cabin to put away the gun. "I guess it's for the best that my daughter saw fit to snatch up all my guns and run off with them. I'm trying to figure out where she's taken them, but that's a whole other story."

"As your lawyer, I'd advise you to stick with the starter pistol and to always dial 911 if you feel threatened. Give me a call at the office tomorrow, and we can talk about what we're going to do about Anna and those missing guns." Wyatt paused. "Now, about that dog."

"Yeah, that'd be Old Blue," he said. "I've been feeding him, but he's a skittish thing, all yellow colored and matted. Probably because he gets the rest of his nutrition off of Deke King's grill. Deke's aim is as bad as his eyesight at night, and he always wears gloves when he cooks or chops wood, which is probably why the pup is still living. Well, that and the shelter I've provided for him."

"So he's your dog?"

"I don't think he's decided that yet," Dallas said. "But I'd take him if I could catch him. He will need a good grooming and a checkup. He looks to have been living rough for a while."

"Would you mind showing us where you've been sheltering him?" Parker asked. "We've brought the supplies we use to capture rescues. We may be able to catch him."

It took all five of us, but after a good half hour of trying, Old Blue was finally in the crate ready for transport to the vet clinic. I was glad for the boots because otherwise my sneakers would have been as dirty as my jeans and T-shirt.

I walked back to the van with Wyatt in companionable silence, leaving Mari and Parker to visit with Dallas before they took Old Blue away. I reflected on my niece and Parker, how well they worked together and the consideration they showed to the sweet, scared pup as they somehow managed to capture him.

"Well, this was fun," Wyatt said when we reached the van. "Do you go out on rescues often?"

"My first," I told him.

"Well, obviously mine too." He rested his booted foot on the van's bumper and swiped at the dirt on his jeans. "I thought I was pretty good at keeping up with the kids, but I guess I need to start running again. I'm exhausted."

"You and Parker did the hard work of chasing Old Blue down. All I had to do was talk nice to him while Mari held the crate door open."

"If I wasn't so tired, I'd say something witty about how I'd step into a cage too if you'd talk sweet to me." He grinned. "But that would be weird."

"Very," I said, laughing. "Not that you've ever worried about being normal, at least not back when I knew you in high school."

Wyatt gave me a sideways look. "I like to think that being weird is what got me the cutest date at the prom."

Laughter drifting toward us meant Mari and Parker were returning.

Rather than respond to Wyatt, I just shook my head. I've never been comfortable receiving compliments about my appearance.

My music? Sure.

But my looks? Not so much.

As soon as they got close enough for me to see them, I noticed they hadn't brought the dog with them. "Where's Old Blue?"

"Mr. Wright asked if Old Blue could stay with him tonight. He's going to bring him to the clinic tomorrow to get cleaned up and checked out." She paused. "He's not chipped, so I guess we'll see what happens once all of those things are done."

"How could you tell he wasn't chipped?" Wyatt asked.

Parker retrieved his phone and held it out to show Wyatt. "I've got an app that can check for chips. It won't read them, but it can show whether there is one, and unfortunately in this case there wasn't."

"Hey, maybe that's good news for Dallas," I said. "He seemed interested in keeping him."

"He did," Mari said slowly, "but I'm not sure that his tiny cabin in the woods is going to be big enough for the two of them."

"Mari," Parker said. "Just say it. You're worried that Mr. Wright won't be able to feed the dog adequately. I mean, it is a small place, but dogs don't take up much room."

"They do have to be fed and cared for properly," Mari said. "That's one thing I promised myself when I was planning this rescue. I wouldn't let a dog leave the rescue unless I was certain about the place where it would be living."

"You won't have to worry about Dallas being able to feed that dog," Wyatt said. "When I said he owns this place, I didn't just mean that cabin. I meant he owns all of this tract of land and a few more besides. At one time, the Wrights were the biggest landowners on this side of Washington County."

"Whoa," Parker said under his breath.

"Exactly," Mari agreed. "But if Mr. Wright owns all sorts of property, why is he in that tiny cabin?"

"You've never met his daughter, have you?" Wyatt asked with a chuckle. "Anna Wright is, well, she's something. I'll just say that. Nice lady and smart as she can be. Dallas isn't the chatty type, so he's told me he likes to go out in the woods and be quiet when Anna is in town. I guess that's what he meant by it, although I always assumed he was just taking long walks." He turned to me. "Did you know Anna? She was our age, but she didn't graduate from Brenham High."

"I've never heard of her," I said. "Did she grow up in Brenham?"

"I can't reveal the particulars because it is covered under attorney-client privilege, but I can say that after Dallas's wife died, Anna spent most of her life with her mama's people back east. Connecticut, I think. Or maybe it was New Hampshire.

"Anyway, Dallas figured she'd be better cared for there. To hear Dallas tell it, his grief prevented him from being the daddy he thought Anna needed."

"That's so sad," Mari said. "Is that why he's living in the cabin?"

"Is he? My guess is that's a place he goes to think and be quiet. I'd be surprised if he was actually living there," Wyatt said. "He has a nice home on the opposite side of the property."

"No," Parker said. "He told us the cabin is where he lives. I didn't know all of this so I didn't ask him why. Just figured it was all he could manage financially."

"Interesting," Wyatt said. "I'll have to check into this. But I'll leave that for another time. Just rest assured that Old Blue is in good hands and will likely be fed well, even if Dallas keeps him from snatching food off the BBQ King's grill."

We all piled into the van and buckled our seat belts. Parker started the engine, and we drove back toward downtown, chattering about the events of the evening.

"Is it always this way?" I asked Mari.

She swiveled in her seat to face me. "What do you mean?"

"It was just so, well, rewarding," I told her. "I mean, we did a good thing for that poor pup. Because of us—well, you guys, because I didn't do anything—Ole Blue will have a happy life."

"Every rescue is different," Mari said. "But yes, I almost always feel that way afterward. We don't usually know what's going to happen to the dogs we rescue, but I feel good that at least I've removed a dog from a dangerous situation."

I reached up to pat Mari on her shoulder. "You were made for this, sweetheart."

"I agree," Parker said.

"Thank you, but I'm just one of many volunteers," Mari protested.

"Not true," I pressed. "You're the reason this rescue exists. Do not diminish that, Marigold Evans."

"Yes ma'am," she said with a smile.

Just before it was time to take the turn for the downtown square, Wyatt spoke up. "Hey, how about cheeseburgers? I'm buying!"

"Wyatt," I exclaimed, "we are covered in mud!"

"No one at the Brenham Burger is going to care," he said.

"I will," I protested.

"Oh come on, Aunt Trina," Mari said. "Loosen up. A little mud never hurt anyone."

"As long as your hands are clean," Parker said. "No one should eat a burger with muddy hands."

Even with clean hands, I had no plans to eat a burger or anything else tonight. "If my stage wardrobe has to be let out, I'll be in big trouble," I told them. "But I can sit and drink a glass of tea while you all enjoy yourselves."

Later, while the guys were ordering the burgers, I sat with Mari and told her about her grandmother's broken ankle. We made plans for her to go with me to the hospital in the morning before she had to be at work.

Later, when we said good night, I told Mari again how proud I was of her. As I walked back upstairs to my room, I knew what I needed to do to help my niece continue her rescue work.

One email and a phone call later, I was all set.

CHAPTER 13

The next morning at half past eight, Mari and I walked into Mama's hospital room to find her dressed and ready to go. The balloon bouquet I'd brought her from the gift shop was tied to the handle of her overnight bag, and a dozen yellow roses sat in a vase on the table beside her.

"Look what the cat drug in," she said, her tone indignant.

Look what the cat had to save with a computer, I wanted to say. Instead, I pasted on my best smile and said, "Good morning, Mama. I've brought Mari with me."

Her expression changed the instant my mother registered the fact that her favorite grandchild had come to visit. "Oh, sweet Mari, come and sit beside me. I've missed you so much."

Again I bit my tongue and didn't mention that she'd sworn me to secrecy over her hospitalization. I'm sure I'd hear that speech once I got her home and Mari went off to work.

"It looks like you're going home, Mama," I said when there was a lull in the conversation. "Did you decide that, or is your doctor releasing you?"

Mama's expression turned innocent. "A little of both, I suppose."

"I see." I gave Mari a look, then returned my attention to Mama. "I'll just let you and Mari visit while I go see about the paperwork."

I left my mother and went in search of a nurse. I returned to find that Mama had welcomed another guest. A handsome older gentleman leaned against the window, smiling down at Mama as she gushed over the lovely flowers.

It didn't take me long to figure out this man had sent them. Based on what I'd learned from the nurses, I also knew his name.

"Good morning, Dr. Bishop," I said sweetly. "I understand you're responsible for my mother's release today."

He crossed the room to shake my hand. "Guilty as charged," he said. "I couldn't let this lovely lady languish in a hospital bed when she could do just as well recuperating at home."

"Right," I said. "And how exactly did you get involved in my mother's case?"

"Oh, we go way back," Mama said. "Dr. Bishop—"

"Elvin," he said gently.

She matched the old man's smile. "Daddy, rest his soul, always trusted Elvin for all the doctoring that was needed, but I didn't get to know him until much later."

"So you were my father's doctor?"

"I was the only one he would trust," he said. "Your daddy had high standards when it came to medical care, and I must have lived up to them, because he continued to call on me to do the work as long as he was living."

"And after he passed on, well," Mama said, "I didn't have any need for Elvin until Hector came along."

"Hector?" Mari's attention swung from her grandmother to Dr. Bishop. "What does Hector have to do with anything?"

"Well, young lady," he said smoothly, "you could say that Hector brought us together."

"Mari, Dr. Bishop is a veterinarian," Mama told her.

"A retired veterinarian for the past twenty odd years," he corrected. "And I understand you are a vet tech with a penchant for rescuing dogs."

As the conversation turned toward Mari and her rescue, I watched the three of them. Mama was honest in saying that her decision to leave had been based in part on her decision and in part on a doctor's advice. However, she'd left out the part about the doctor being a veterinarian.

"Mama," I interjected as the conversation continued around me, "are you sure that going back home is a good idea? I haven't had a chance to clean up the mess you made when the fabric avalanche happened. Maybe you need to stay another night and let me get that handled first."

"No need," Dr. Bishop said. "I had my associate go over and take care of all that yesterday."

"Your associate?" I asked. "Is he a vet too?"

Dr. Bishop gave me a look that told me he was trying his best to be patient with me. "No, Blake Perry does odd jobs for me when he's not on duty as a security guard. I took pictures of the cleaned-up hallway for Peach, but I'd be happy to show them to you."

"That won't be necessary." I turned my attention to my mother. "Do you have any prescriptions to be picked up?"

"Blake is already on his way to do that," Dr. Bishop said.

Mama fluttered her eyes at the old veterinarian, and I guessed she was giving it her best attempt at flirting. Otherwise, she had something in her eyes and needed assistance. I decided to wait to see which it was.

"Elvin, you have absolutely thought of everything. Once I get the go-ahead to start making pies again, I am going to make your favorite."

"Peach," they said in unison.

It took all I had not to bust out laughing when Mari gave me a stricken look. There was definitely a can-you-believe-that conversation in our future. But for now, I needed to take the situation in hand.

"What about physical therapy, Mama?" I said. "I'm sure your orthopedist is going to insist you go."

"Already scheduled and on my calendar," Dr. Bishop said. "I've got all the time in the world nowadays, so I can make sure she gets there." He paused. "In case you're needing to get back to Nashville soon."

Was he suggesting that I leave?

"Well, that's nice," I replied, keeping my attention focused on Mama. "But I would like to hear from my mother that she will actually be listening to her doctor and going to therapy."

"I assure you—"

"Dr. Bishop," I said evenly, "I need to hear this from my mother."

"There is no need to be rude, Trina," Mama said. "Yes, I will be a good patient, and I'll go to therapy for as long as I am supposed to. Are you happy now?"

"For now. That may change if I find out you're not keeping your end of the bargain." I paused. "Want me to come by later with some lunch?"

"Actually—" Dr. Bishop began.

"Let me guess, Blake is cooking for you," I said far too sarcastically than I should have.

My statement only served to cause Mama to reach over and grasp the veterinarian's hand. "Elvin is cooking, Trina, but he did send Blake out with a grocery list. He's picking everything up for lunch after he goes to the pharmacy. Now, if you're finished giving Elvin the third degree, I will let him take me home."

"Now, Peach," Dr. Bishop said, "don't be that way. Trina is your daughter, and she's concerned about you. I would be asking the same questions if I were in her shoes. And she did come all the way from Nashville to take care of you even though you knew I was going to be doing that."

Now that was news. When I left Nashville in a hurry, it was because I thought my mother needed me. She didn't breathe a word about already having help.

"You're a good and thoughtful daughter to drop everything in Nashville and come all this way for me, Trina," Mama said.

"You're my mother. Of course I would do that," I said.

"You know what," Dr. Bishop said to Mama. "How about I let Trina take you home? I can come by later and visit. Maybe bring lunch?"

Mama was about to answer when I spoke up. "That isn't necessary, Dr. Bishop. Thank you for caring so well for my mama." I gave Mama a kiss on the cheek, then regarded them both with a smile. "You two behave yourselves. I'll stop by later to see you, Mama."

"Can we set another place for lunch?" the vet asked.

"No, don't do that. I'm not sure when I'll get there. Now that my morning is free, I have some errands to run."

Mari said her goodbyes and followed me out. We didn't speak until we reached the parking lot.

"Oh my gosh, Aunt Trina," Mari said, clutching my arm. "What was *that*?"

I merely shook my head. "I don't know, but your grandmother seems happy."

"I think so too. And Dr. Bishop is nice. He's come into the clinic a few times, and the vets really like him." She paused. "But I liked Pastor Nelson too."

"I liked him too. Who knows whether he's temporarily out of favor or they're just taking a break, as you kids say. With Mama Peach, you never know," I said. "But she's told me she's not about to settle down just yet, so you don't have to worry about her falling for this veterinarian."

Mari shook her head. "What makes you say that? I would very much like her to fall in love with someone. Why not Dr. Bishop?"

Why not indeed?

"He seems like he cares for her," I said. "But time will tell, I guess. Like I said, you never know with Mama Peach."

I walked with Mari to her car, then crossed the parking lot to climb into mine. With someone else taking on the responsibility of seeing to Mama this morning, I had more free time than I expected. I checked my emails and found the one I'd hoped would be there.

Then I called Bitsy.

She picked up on the first ring, delighted that our short trip to see a few more properties could be a longer one. "Give me an hour to make arrangements, and I'll pick you up at your hotel."

I drove back to my hotel and parked the rental car, then walked down the street toward Wyatt's office. When I stepped inside, Desmond was on the phone. He nodded toward a closed door to his right and motioned for me to go in.

I knocked twice then opened the door to find Wyatt seated behind a massive desk. At least I assumed that was Wyatt as his entire form was obscured by file folders, stacks of paper, and legal books.

He rose. "Welcome to the inner sanctum." Then he glanced at his watch. "Is my watch wrong?"

"Your watch is fine," I told him. "Mama got a better offer, so here I am."

He lifted one dark brow. "Still going to look at property today?"

"Bitsy is coming for me in an hour," I told him, unable to take my eyes off the disarray on the desk.

"So you thought you'd come and bug me until she gets here?"

I shrugged. "That did occur to me. Then I saw this mess, and now I have a different plan for how to spend the next hour."

"Seriously?" He shook his head. "You'd help me with this?"

"Of course," I told him, "although isn't that what you hired Desmond for?"

"It is," he said, "but I don't want to scare him off. I've been without help for a while."

"It shows," I told him with a chuckle. "Now let's get started, but set a timer on that watch. I don't want to be late to meet my Realtor."

"Your Realtor," Wyatt echoed. "I like the sound of that. Do you think you'll be moving back here full-time?"

I reached for a stack of books and turned toward the bookcase with them. "That's more of a dream than a reality. Too many commitments and contracts bind me to Nashville right now."

"You know," he said in a conspiratorial tone, "I am pretty good with contracts. If you were looking for loopholes, that is."

I shoved the books into place on the shelf, then turned around to face Wyatt. "I appreciate that, but when I give my word, I keep my commitment."

"Duly noted," he said. "But the offer stands."

I returned to the desk for another stack of books. "Thank you, Wyatt."

We set to work on the mess, with Wyatt sorting files and me separating invoices from other types of paperwork.

"So," Wyatt said after a while, "I had a chat with an ATF buddy of mine."

I looked up from my reading. "Oh?"

"Called in a favor, actually," he said. "I can't promise anything, but he said he'd try to get his hands on the remains of that pipe bomb and see what he can find out about it."

I frowned. "Wyatt, the bomb squad blew the thing up. How could he possibly learn anything about it?"

"Got me," Wyatt said, "but he thought there was a small chance."

Placing the stack of papers on the desk, I sat back in the chair. "You've done a lot of thinking about that pipe bomb."

His hands stilled, and then he closed the file he'd been looking through. A moment later, he met my gaze. "I have. It bothers me a lot."

"Why? No one was hurt. Yes, it's a mystery, but nothing else has happened."

"Nothing that we know about," he said. "You were out there with Mari and Parker last night. If Dallas had been holding something other than a starter pistol, they could have been seriously hurt."

"Yes, agreed," I said. "But I don't see the connection."

Wyatt settled the stack of files on the desk in front of him. "Have you talked to Mari about whether they've had any other near misses on their rescues?"

"The topic has never come up," I admitted. "Why?"

He shifted positions in his chair. "Parker and I were in the middle of having that very conversation when we got the call about the rescue last night. That's what made me think to call my friend at ATF this morning."

"So there have been other bombs?"

"No other bombs," he said. "But other times when they were in danger."

I gave that statement some thought. "Actually, wouldn't they be in danger every time they go out chasing a dog who knows where?"

"Yes."

I sensed there was more. "But?"

"I'd rather you talk to Mari about this," he said.

I pressed my palms on the desk, irritation rising. "Since Mari isn't here and you are, just tell me what you know, Wyatt."

"Okay," came out on an exhale of breath. "But understand that I got this straight from Parker. If there are any deviations from how Mari wants to tell this story, tell her to take that up with her partner."

"Spill it, Chastain," I said.

"You know that usually they go out with a third person, Cassidy. She also works at Lone Star Vet Clinic."

"Yes, I met her while I was here for the parade," I told him.

"According to Parker, Cassidy has not been going out with them as much, and she always seems to have an excuse when it's at night. She won't tell him why, but he thinks she's afraid."

"I did notice she wasn't there last night," I said. "That was six months ago. She's felt like this that long?"

"I guess so," he said. "I told my ATF buddy, but he said he'd have to believe it was her imagination that made her afraid until there was proof otherwise."

I retrieved my phone and called the clinic, then asked for Cassidy. "I had to leave a message," I told Wyatt. "But that is weird. Now about that ATF agent—I want to speak to him."

"I'll see if I can arrange it," Wyatt said. "If he's willing, I'll have him call you."

"Thank you," I told him.

Something buzzed, and Wyatt jumped. "Oh, my watch. It gets me every time."

I stood and surveyed the desk, then smiled at Wyatt. "It looks less like a hurricane hit it and more like it was just a tropical storm."

Wyatt rose, shaking his head. "Okay, so organization isn't my strong suit."

"If I were you, I'd make sure it's Desmond's strong suit, because someone needs to manage your messes," I said. "Now, I've got to go. Are you coming with me?"

"You and Bitsy on a real estate shopping trip?" he said. "I'd rather be hung upside down outdoors in my short shorts during mosquito season."

"You're so weird, Wyatt."

"Again, I'm the same weird Wyatt you went to prom with." He offered a dazzling smile. "So is that my problem or yours?"

I laughed as I opened the office door. "Bye, Wyatt."

CHAPTER 14

As I walked down the street to the Ant Street Inn, I wondered just how that fun, nerdy guy had turned into a handsome lawyer who could still make me laugh like no one else. Somehow Wyatt had gone from Hawaiian shirts to tailored suits while I was away.

Not just tailored suits, I mused as I recalled his cowboy look from yesterday. That's a look I could get used to.

I spied Bitsy waving at me from her vehicle parked in front of the inn and returned the gesture. "Ready to go find some property to buy?" she asked as I climbed in.

"I'm ready to look," I said.

"That's a start," she told me. "Now, keep an open mind, because I've got some properties to show you that you might not have considered."

"No more mansions on the river, please," I said. "That's just not my style."

"Oh, absolutely not. I promise." A few minutes later she pulled into a parking space in front of the corporate hangar at the Brenham airport. "Surprise!"

"Surprise?" I asked as she opened the door and got out.

"I told you to keep an open mind." Bitsy nodded to a helicopter nearby. "This is how we're looking at property today. From the air!"

For a full minute, maybe longer, I could only stare. First at her and then at the helicopter she'd hired for the occasion. It wasn't that I was afraid of flying.

I'd never have had a music career if I had trouble being airborne, no matter how small the plane or chopper. But why take a helicopter when we could easily drive to whatever location she wanted to show me?

This question was answered by the directions she gave to the pilot. "Fredericksburg?" I asked. "That's not even close to Brenham."

"Just a few hours by car, and if you get one of these, it's much faster than that," she'd said with a wave of her hand. "And you'll get such a good return on your investment. You might even want to put in a winery. Or, better yet, buy one. I bet I have at least one that's available for showing today."

"No," I said. "Absolutely not. Take me back. I don't want to look at properties that far away."

"Of course you do," Bitsy said. "You just don't know it yet."

And that was the end of the conversation. Apparently, Bitsy's headphones had some sort of glitch—not that I believed that for a minute—and she was unable to hear a word I said. Three hours later, the chopper landed back in Brenham, and I was done.

Bitsy kept up her cheerful banter, noting the benefits of every property we'd flown over and the three she'd insisted we land and see from the ground. She even mentioned how wonderful it would be for me to be away from Brenham and in a more private setting.

"Is that what you think I want?" I asked.

"Why wouldn't you?" she responded, eyes wide. "You're a famous singer who could never have anonymity in her hometown. Wouldn't you rather live in the middle of nowhere?"

"Nobody bothers me in Brenham," I said. "And that's where my family is. Why would I want to be so far away from my mother and niece?"

"It just seems like such a good idea," Bitsy said, her smile never wavering. "And sometimes the Realtor knows better than the buyer what she ought to be purchasing."

I shook my head and turned toward Bitsy's SUV, not caring if she was following or not. Better to stand in the parking lot until my irritation settled than to continue this conversation.

We rode back to the Ant Street Inn in silence. Just before we reached the downtown square, Bitsy pulled over and shifted her SUV into PARK. She stared out the windshield, exhaled audibly, and then swiveled to face me.

"Okay, Trina, what gives? I'm doing my best to find a place for you, and you don't seem to appreciate my efforts."

"Not true," I protested. "I can see that you've gone to a lot of trouble, and I appreciate that, but you haven't shown me any properties that are remotely similar to what I requested." At her surprised expression, I continued. "I only want a few things: at least ten acres, not located on a busy road, and with some kind of home on it that can be fixed up if it's not already move-in ready."

"Every property I've shown you is exactly like that if not better."

"But none of them are in Brenham or even in Washington County except the home on the river, and I'm not sure if that one hasn't been flooded a few times."

"It has," she admitted, "but since you were willing to do some remodeling, I thought it might work for you."

Remodeling a home of that size would be astronomically expensive should floodwaters enter the building. Bitsy knew this. What game was she playing?

"Bitsy," I said slowly, "do you have a problem with me buying a property in Brenham?"

"Don't be ridiculous," she said, but not with the amount of energy I might have put into convincing someone they were wrong.

Without another word, she shifted the SUV into Drive and pulled back onto the road. A few minutes later, she stopped in front of the Ant Street Inn long enough for me to climb out. If I hadn't snatched up my purse quickly, she might have driven off with it still on the seat. As it was, I barely got the door shut before her tires peeled away.

I stood on the curb, watching her taillights get smaller, then tucked my purse over my shoulder and turned to go inside the inn. Something stopped me just before my fingertips touched the ornate silver doorknob.

Instead, I crossed the street and turned left toward the Washington County Courthouse and the white gazebo that had been erected on the grounds back in 1976 to celebrate the Bicentennial of the United States. Next to the gazebo was a plaque from the historical society commemorating Brenham Maifest.

I paused to run my fingers over the raised letters of the plaque. Why did it seem like it was only yesterday when I'd stood right here in this spot and posed for photographs in my Maifest Queen regalia?

Bitsy had come in second that year but won the next. By then I was already gone from Brenham and headed to Nashville intent on becoming a star.

Despite the fact that I did fit the definition, I had never settled comfortably into the role of a star. I was just me. Just Trina Potter, a product of my small-town raising.

I glanced around this side of the square, enjoying for a moment the folks going about their business and the cars passing by. Just a normal day in a normal small town.

And yet it felt so very special.

Then it occurred to me. I really could have this every day if I wanted. Yes, I did agree to fulfill contracts, and I would. But someday all of that would be behind me and I could come home, couldn't I?

I returned to the inn and called Mama. She sounded like her old self, reminding me that when I came to visit her that evening I might need to pick up some Blue Bell for the pie she was teaching Dr. Bishop to make.

"Mama," I fussed, "you're supposed to be getting your rest, and you're definitely not supposed to be standing in the kitchen."

"I've been doing nothing but resting since I got home from the hospital this morning. I promise. But Elvin and I got to talking about pies, and the next thing you know, we were in the kitchen with my ankle propped up on a chair and Elvin gathering the ingredients for piecrusts."

"How's he doing with the piecrusts?" I asked.

"Well, he's doing a passable job of listening to me," Mama said. "And if he practices, he just might learn how to crimp the crusts like a professional."

"I am a long way from that," I heard the veterinarian say in the background.

"He is," Mama said, "but he's trying."

"All right, Mama," I told her. "You two behave, and I'll stop by later to check on you. Maybe bring you some dinner with that Blue Bell?"

"No need," Mama said. "The casserole ladies have mustered up and are bringing meals. I got the first installment this morning. I am not exactly thrilled that Berta Goss made that chicken and spaghetti concoction that she always brings to the church potlucks, but apparently it's Elvin's favorite, so it's going home with him."

"That will leave you without anything for supper," I pointed out.

"Nope," she told me. "Mari is bringing over pizza after work. Join us, and we'll have our own little family pizza party."

"Which I will not be attending," Dr. Bishop said.

"I've told him it's girls only tonight," Mama explained. "He took the news pretty well, but I think it's because he's getting to go home with the chicken and spaghetti."

Mama and I chatted a little longer, and then I said my goodbyes along with another promise not to forget the Blue Bell. Of course, when I got there at the appointed time that evening, I'd completely forgotten the ice cream. A quick call to Mari saved the day and the pizza party, and we all went to bed that night full and happy.

The next morning, I awakened to my phone ringing. It was Wyatt.

"Good morning, sunshine," he said in a much-too-cheery tone for the time of day it was.

"Good morning, Wyatt," I managed as I untangled the blankets.

"Did I wake you up?"

"Actually, you did," I admitted, not a bit ashamed that I was able to sleep late on a day when most folks had already gone to work.

"Well, get dressed. We've got somewhere to be in an hour."

"You're going to have to explain yourself," I said. "Else I'm staying right where I am for a while longer."

"Bitsy told me your shopping trip yesterday was a bust," he said.

"Did she also tell you that she was showing me properties in Fredericksburg by helicopter?"

Wyatt chuckled. "I'm not surprised."

I swiped my hair from my face and glanced over at the clock. "Why?"

"Well," he said slowly, "apparently she sees you as a rival for my affection. She figured if you bought land in another county, then you wouldn't be hanging around here catching my attention and possibly breaking my heart."

I let that sink in a minute. "That is the most ridiculous thing I have ever heard."

"I am wounded," Wyatt said.

"You are not." I threw back the covers. "Tell me why you want me to meet you in an hour, and I might consider it."

CHAPTER 15

One hour later, I climbed into Wyatt's pickup truck and secured my seat belt. "Good morning, sunshine," Wyatt said as he handed me a paper sack.

"You said that already." I glanced down at the bag, then back over at him. "What is this?"

He grinned. "Since it's obvious you aren't a morning person, I brought breakfast."

I might have argued the point that I'm not a morning person because my job often requires that I'm on stage until late into the evening. However, the delicious scent emanating from the bag had my attention.

I opened the bag and spied a half dozen foil-wrapped parcels. My stomach growled. The scent was heavenly.

"Breakfast tacos from Smarty's," Wyatt said. "I didn't know which kind you prefer, so I bought one of each." He nodded to the cup holder. "Same with coffee. One is black, and the other is the froufrou latte kind with enough additions to make it not taste like coffee. I had to stop the barista before she added sprinkles. They probably would have put edible glitter on it if I'd have asked for it."

"You thought of everything." I grabbed the one he'd deemed froufrou and took a sip. "Thank you, Wyatt. This is amazing, even without the sprinkles and edible glitter."

He gave me a sideways glance. "Mark my words, Trina Potter. That comment just earned you a froufrou latte with the works, including sprinkles and edible glitter."

I grinned. "I will gladly accept such a magnificent concoction. Right now, however, I am gratefully digging in. Want one?"

"You're welcome. And no, thank you. I've already had mine," he said. "So enjoy."

I reached in and grabbed a foil-wrapped taco and then set the bag aside. Breakfast tacos at Smarty's always involved the best scrambled eggs on the entire planet wrapped in a warm corn tortilla. To this already heavenly concoction, other items were always added.

The one I chose was a mouthwatering combination of egg, jalapeno sausage, and pancake syrup that was labeled Smarty's Sweet Oink and Cluck. I was just finishing off the last bite of the legendary sweet and spicy taco when Wyatt signaled to turn off the main road.

"Hey, I know this place," I said. "This is where Mari and Parker took us to rescue Old Blue. You didn't tell me you were taking me to look at Dallas Wright's property."

"I thought I did." Wyatt shrugged. "Anyway, Dallas would prefer that no one knows he's interested in selling, in part because he's a private man and doesn't want the details of his home and property listed on a Realtor's site. He's also not too fond of strangers on his land."

"That I did notice," I said.

"There's more to it than that, but Dallas would be the one to talk about those details."

I took a sip of coffee, then placed the cup back in the holder. "You're sure he's okay with us being here?"

"Trina," Wyatt said gently, "we are meeting Dallas. He set the time and place. So yes, he's okay with it. And for the record, you're the only one he's considering selling to."

"Really? Why me?"

"I don't know." He made a turn down a rutted dirt road, and I grabbed the door handle to hang on. "But I do know it's the truth because I made him a good offer and he turned it down."

"I'm sorry," I told him.

"Nope. Don't be." He shrugged. "Wasn't meant to be."

He pulled to a stop in front of a two-story white farmhouse with a wide front porch that looked out over an expanse of lush green lawn. With the woods all around, this home felt hidden and secluded even though it was just a short drive from downtown.

Rocking chairs lined one side of the porch while a wicker table and four side chairs filled the other. The front door was painted a soft sage green, just a few shades lighter than the ferns that hung from the porch eaves and swayed in the summer breeze.

"The only thing that's missing is a pitcher of sweet tea and some free time to sit in one of those rocking chairs," I said as I climbed down from the truck. "I don't know what I expected, but this is not it."

"It's an old home that's been well maintained," Wyatt said. "And of course you know it comes with a cabin."

"Speaking of that cabin, if Dallas lives out there, then who lives here?"

"I've told you about his daughter, Anna. She visits frequently, so I'd guess she does." He walked past me to climb the wide steps that led to the front door. "Or maybe Dallas does, and he just isn't claiming to."

"It's a little of both," came from behind us.

I turned around to see Dallas Wright walking up the path. He was much younger looking in the daylight, with a spring in his step and a smile on his face. He wore faded denim jeans and a pearl snap shirt with cowboy boots.

He exchanged greetings with us and then shook hands with Wyatt. "Come sit on the porch a minute. I'll bring us some iced tea. It's already warm out this morning."

We did as he asked and were rewarded with sweet tea in tall glasses. I settled on a rocker with Wyatt to my right and Dallas on the other side of him. For a moment, I sat and enjoyed the quiet.

"I'll get to the point," Dallas said, breaking the silence. "Wyatt, you're a good man, and I appreciate that you went to all the trouble of drafting those documents. You'll be paid, but I won't be signing."

Wyatt shook his head. "Dallas, you know I don't care about that."

"Doesn't matter," he said, his expression solemn. "I pay my debts."

"Well, technically it was Anna who asked me to draw it up," Wyatt protested. "So I'll send the bill to her."

Dallas thought a minute and nodded. "That'll do." Then he leaned forward to look at me. "Miss Potter, Wyatt tells me you're looking for a piece of land close to Brenham."

"Yes, sir, I am," I told him.

"And I understand you intend to have that dog rescue lady build a place for her rescues on the property."

"The rescue lady is my niece, Mari Evans, and yes, I'm looking for a property that will accommodate a base for her rescue operations. If there isn't already a building in place, I'll let her design one." I paused. "You might wonder why I want a bunch of strays on my land, but I believe in what Mari and Parker and the others are doing. You've seen it for yourself."

"I have indeed." He grinned. "And while we're on the subject, looks like Old Blue will be coming home to stay with me in a few days. Everything checked out fine with the health, and the groomer is doing her magic on the matted fur today."

"That's great news," I said.

"Just one surprise in the report, but I don't mind."

"What's that?" Wyatt asked.

"Seems as though Old Blue's a she, not a he. Might have to come up with a different name for her. I'll wait and let her tell me." He glanced up sharply. "Don't take that to mean I believe dogs talk. I just mean that a dog's name has to suit him or, in this case, her."

"Exactly right," Wyatt said. "I called Ed by a half dozen names before he finally answered to the right one. Or rather, before *I* finally figured out what the right one was."

We shared a laugh. "My two are black-and-white English Springer Spaniels named Patsy and Cline. They came to me named and were a gift from the owner of my record label. But their names fit them, and they come when I call most of the time, so it works. Except when I've got food on the counter. If I don't watch them like a hawk, they'll grab whatever is cooking and be gone in a split second."

"Patsy Cline," Dallas echoed. "That woman could sing." He looked at me. "But so can you." He shook his head. "I said I'd get to the point, and here I am socializing. Look, I have a need to sell this place, and fast. Are you interested in buying, Miss Potter?"

I wanted to ask what the hurry was, but I did not. Instead, I offered the old man a smile.

"Call me Trina, and I sure am. I'd need to see it all and hear your price before I commit to it though."

"No time like the present," Wyatt said. "Dallas, how about you show the lady around?"

I took the grand tour—first indoors and then outdoors—with Dallas providing a history of the home along the way. By the time we'd come full circle and returned to the rocking chairs, I was sold.

He named his price. I countered, then added, "And that would be a cash sale. I can close as soon as the papers are drawn up."

Then Wyatt intervened. "Dallas," he said in a warning tone, "tell her the rest before you two finalize this deal."

The old man frowned. Then he nodded. "All right. I own this place free and clear. It's mine, understand?"

"I do," I told him.

"I inherited the land from my daddy, who got it from his, and on back it goes, just like I told you when we were walking the property." He paused. "Wyatt here will tell you that while I might be eighty-nine years old, I've got full control of my faculties."

"Sharp as a tack, this one," Wyatt confirmed. "And don't let him convince you to play checkers, because you'll lose every time."

Dallas chuckled. "Well, anyway, my daughter is the light of my life. I love Anna more than anything in this world. Her mama died when she was little, so she grew up indepedent and mostly elsewhere. Oh, she visited and kept in touch, but never once did she tell me what to do. Recently, that has changed." He gave Wyatt an imploring look. "Tell her, Wyatt."

"What Dallas is saying is that he and Anna don't see eye to eye. She'd like to see Dallas move in with her in Austin."

"Fat chance," he said. "Too many people and cars for my liking."

"Be that as it may," Wyatt continued, "Anna has concerns about her father living alone in the big house."

"Which is why I spend my time out in the cabin now. To tell the truth, that big house holds too many memories for me. I sit there alone at night and it's just so blasted quiet now." He shrugged. "That cabin isn't quiet. There's sounds of the outdoors all around. I have a fireplace crackling in winter and a cool breeze off the trees in summer, although I admit I've hauled a window unit air conditioner in there on hot evenings more than once."

"Where do you plug it in?" Wyatt asked.

"I had power run to the place when I reassembled the logs out there. I may like the wilderness, but this is Texas. I'm not completely crazy." He chuckled. "Do not let my daughter hear that, or she'll take it the wrong way."

"Want me to tell the rest?" Wyatt said gently. "Or are you going to?"

"Okay," Dallas said, meeting my gaze. "I like you, and I'm willing to accept your offer, but with one catch."

"What's that?" I asked, my heart pounding because I'd already begun to think of this place as mine. Surely it would be something I wouldn't mind.

"I come with the deal," Dallas said.

"What he means," Wyatt supplied, "is that he would like to sell this property to you but retain a life estate on the one-half acre where his cabin now stands. Once Dallas has passed on, that portion of the land will go to you as your property. Until then, you cannot evict him."

"And Old Blue comes with the deal," Dallas added. "I can hire movers to come out next week and store the furniture until Anna can go through it. What she and I don't want you can have. How's that?"

"Sold," I said, offering my hand to shake on it.

Now all I had to do was explain my new purchase and my intent to spend as much time here as possible to Sticks and my agent. But not today.

CHAPTER 16

After making a few more arrangements, including securing permission to show the place to Mari and her friends this evening, we said goodbye to Dallas. Then Wyatt and I climbed back into his truck, the scent of breakfast tacos now permeating the interior.

I waved to the old man on the porch, his hand raised and a smile on his face. I knew I'd made the right decision. I hoped he believed he had too.

"Congratulations, Trina," Wyatt said as he jabbed the key into the ignition, then started the truck. "You just bought yourself a fine piece of land. Or will have once I get all the papers drawn up."

"Thank you," I told him. "This happened because of you, and I'm grateful."

"Actually," he said slowly as he backed the truck out of the parking spot and headed for the main road, "it happened because Dallas was impressed with your niece. The way he told it to me, he got a dog he'd been trying to win over, and that's all he needs besides that little cabin. The rest of it is something he is happy to part with."

"Happy?" I shook my head. "It seems like it would be difficult to give up something that has been in his family all these years."

Wyatt shrugged away the statement, but I felt like he knew more than he was saying.

Once Wyatt dropped me off at the hotel, my first call was to Mama. She answered on the first ring and was so busy chattering that she never thought to ask why I called.

Once she'd run out of topics to discuss, I said my goodbyes and hung up without telling her the news and then checked the time. Mari would be working, so I texted her instead of calling. *Busy tonight? If not, I'd like to take you and Parker to dinner. Cassidy too, if she's free.*

Her response came a half hour later. *Just Parker and me. What time and where?*

We made arrangements to meet after the clinic closed. I had just said goodbye when my phone rang with a number I didn't recognize. Normally, I would have let the call go to voice mail, but considering the events of this morning, I thought it might be related to the purchase of the Wright property.

"Miss Potter?" a sweet female voice asked. "My name is Cassidy, and I'm returning your call. I'm sorry it has taken me so long to get back to you. When Mari asked me about tonight, I realized I hadn't responded."

"Cassidy. From the vet clinic. Thank you for calling me back."

"Yes, that's the one," she said. "How can I help you?"

I considered my words before I said them. "I went with Mari and Parker on a rescue the other night. She mentioned that you weren't able to join them."

"Yes ma'am," she said. "I was busy that night. Had some things to do. You know, like my closet was in dire condition, and I really needed to. . ." She paused. "Sorry, I'm talking too much. I do that sometimes. Was that all you needed to know?"

"Not exactly," I said. "I understand that you have been on rescues in the past. With Mari, I mean."

"Lots," she said. "We've had some crazy adventures. Like there was that time we almost got arrested and Mari's car was stolen, and the officer ended up adopting another rescue. Not the one we saved that night. That was Beau Jangles. You've probably met him."

Mari had told me the story of how she'd come to own the sweet Cavalier King Charles spaniel, though she'd left out the part about the stolen car and near arrest. I think I'd have remembered if she'd mentioned it.

"Yes, he's darling." I paused. "So, Parker mentioned you've been skipping the rescues lately. I was just wondering if there was a reason."

"Like I said, I've been busy. You know. Doing stuff."

I didn't buy Cassidy's excuse for a minute, but I wasn't about to tell her that. Instead, I tried another angle. "So when you're out on rescues, do things ever get scary? Have you ever felt threatened or in danger?"

Another long silence. "Hey, sorry, I've got to go," Cassidy finally said. "The, um, well, I've got stuff to do."

"Sure, but I just have one more question," I told her. "Is there a reason I should be concerned about Mari going out on rescues? By that I mean, has something happened? Are there threats of some kind?"

"What? No," she said quickly. "Nothing like that. I mean, when it's dark or when there's things you don't expect that happen, then yeah, that's not fun."

"Like what? Specifically," I added. "Another pipe bomb or something like that? Does it bother you that the person who planted that bomb hasn't been found? I guess I'm just wondering if that person might want to cause more harm to others, specifically my niece and her team."

I cringed as soon as the words were out. If she hadn't truly been afraid before, she might be now.

"Yeah, um, I really have to go. I'm so sorry." She paused. "And really, everything is fine. I promise."

"Cassidy," I said slowly, "I would really like you to join us tonight. I can't go into detail, but I've got something special for Mari, and since you're best friends, it would be great if you were there too."

Silence.

"I promise not to bring up anything about what we've just talked about," I added.

"Well," she said slowly, "I can probably do the things I was going to do tonight on another night. If it's something you think Mari would want me to be there to witness."

"Oh, I definitely know it is," I said.

"Okay, then," Cassidy said on an exhale of breath. "I'll be there."

I hung up, not certain whether I'd learned anything from that call. If Cassidy was afraid, though, should Mari be going out? Even after spending the afternoon with Mama, I was still pondering that question when I drove into the clinic parking lot that evening to meet them.

A few minutes later, Mari escaped the clinic with a spring in her step and Parker following her. She practically fell into my car, such was her enthusiasm with whatever she was about to share. Cassidy stepped out of the door and waved and then proceeded to lock the clinic.

"It was so awesome, Aunt Trina. Parker and I scrubbed in on a surgery with Tyler, and we helped save the life of a mama and her puppies, then right after that we had another one come in, and I got to help Kristin with a procedure."

Mari went on, using technical terms that went right over my head, while Parker and Cassidy climbed into the back seat and buckled their seat belts. When my niece paused to catch her breath, I greeted her companions.

I began driving while Mari continued her story. When the story had not yet finished by the time we turned on to the main road leading to the Wright property, it occurred to me that she might have inherited this talent for conversation from her grandmother.

It was Parker who first noticed we were driving in a direction that would take us away from local restaurants. I saw his expression in the rearview mirror when I made the first turn and then the second one. Cassidy had been looking at her phone since we left the clinic and appeared to be clueless as to the obvious change of plans.

Finally, Parker spoke up. "Excuse me a sec, Trina. But aren't the restaurants the other way?"

I smiled at him in the mirror and nodded. "Yes. I hope you don't mind, but I'm taking you on a quick detour before we eat. Unless you're starving. Then we can do it after."

"Parker is always starving," Mari and Cassidy said in unison.

"Hey now," Parker exclaimed. "I feel personally attacked." His laughter belied his words, and soon the three of them were trading stories about the blue-eyed vet tech's endless appetite.

"Aunt Trina," Mari finally said as I made the last turn. "Where are you taking us?"

"You don't recognize this place?" I asked innocently.

"I do," Parker said. "This is where we picked up Old Blue from that man in the cabin."

I met his gaze in the mirror. "That's right."

"Well, that's unexpected," Mari said. "Old Blue isn't going home until tomorrow, so we can't be here to visit her. She is a her, not a him, by the way."

"Yes, I heard that," I said as I bypassed the path leading to the cabin and continued driving down the road toward the main house.

My trio of companions remained silent until I parked the car in front of the Wright home and turned off the engine. Then they all began speaking at once. I climbed out of the car and waited for them to do the same.

"Okay, Aunt Trina. I'm officially confused. What are we doing here?"

"Well," I said slowly, dragging out each syllable until I could stall no longer, "today I bought the place."

"This place?" Parker said. "You bought the Wright place?"

"Almost all of it," I said. "Mr. Wright is keeping a plot of land around the cabin, and he will continue to live there. But the rest of it is mine."

I paused to allow the combination of chattering, cheering, and hugging to stop. Then I continued. "It'll be a few weeks before the paperwork is completed and the Wrights' furniture can be moved out, so there are no immediate plans to move my things in." I paused, savoring the next piece of news. "However," I said slowly, "there is nothing stopping the Second Chance Ranch Dog Rescue from moving in immediately."

"What?" Cassidy and Mari cried.

"You're joking," Parker managed.

"I'm serious," I said as Mari launched herself into my arms. "And don't celebrate too much yet, because I am respecting your request that you do this yourself."

Her smile slipped a bit. "Okay."

"Wyatt is drawing up a lease. The rescue will occupy the property in a rent-to-own capacity. Basically, you get with Wyatt to let him know what the rescue can afford to pay, and he will write that in as the monthly lease amount. Someday when I'm gone, that part of the property will all be yours anyway, but since you're stubborn and want to do this on your own, I'm not just giving your inheritance to you now."

Mari glanced over at Parker, who nodded. Then she returned her attention to me.

"Yes," she said. "That sounds perfect. Thank you, Aunt Trina!"

"You're welcome, sweetheart. So, do you want to walk the property to see if you can decide on a place for the rescue now, or do you want to go to dinner and come back another day?"

There were two responses in favor of walking it now. Parker, however, remained quiet.

"Okay, Parker," I said. "There's a bag in the car with SkinnyPop and a can of mixed nuts. It's not much, but it should hold you over until we actually have our dinner."

An hour later, the four of them were seated at a table at the Dairy Bar. Parker had the remains of a triple meat cheeseburger with the works in front of him and was working his way through a large order of fries. I opted for my favorite, a chili pie, hold the onions, while the girls had more reasonable single-patty cheeseburgers and were sharing a medium order of fries.

After much debate and walking back and forth between the sites, the trio had agreed upon a piece of land that already had a decent-sized outbuilding on it. With the addition of fans and a few more windows on the sides for cross-ventilation, the structure would make a fine rescue facility.

I interrupted a conversation between my companions on the best way to pay for the renovations. "I'm the landlord," I said. "So I am the one who will pay for those changes. And the first one who complains pays for the meal next time."

They all laughed, and no one complained.

Then Mari leaned toward me and whispered, "Are you sure about all of this, Aunt Trina? It's a lot."

"I have never been surer about anything in my life," I told her. "Besides, between you guys on one end of the property and Dallas on the other end, I feel like the house will be safe when I'm not here, which will be most of the time."

"That's so sad—that you're not going to be here to enjoy all of this."

"Who says I'm not ever going to be here?" I asked. "I plan to work hard to try not to work so hard, if that makes sense. I've got a meeting planned for next week to see if my team and I can't reach some sort of arrangement about that."

"Oh, I hope so," Cassidy interjected. "You're just so awesome."

"She is, isn't she?" Mari said as Parker nodded, his mouth currently filled with fries.

"I hope my agent and producer agree with you when I tell them the news," I said. "But I'm not worrying about that until I get back to Nashville."

The rest of the evening passed in a blur of excitement, project planning, and conversation. I spent the next day with Mama, during which she alternated between fussing at me for buying the property without telling her first and crowing because her nemesis Donna Sue Specklemeyer had always wanted to live there.

That led to the perfect opening for me. "You know, Mama, you could always move into the house and take care of things there. I would love it if you'd consider it."

Mama looked as if she might be thinking it over. Then she shook her head. "You'll not get me out of my home so easily, Trina Potter. It's a slippery slope from freedom to the nursing home if I move in with you."

"Don't be silly," I told her. "The house would be yours to run as you'd like. I'd just be popping in from time to time and staying in a room that's my own instead of crowding in at your house or bunking at the Ant Street Inn. And for the record, as long as I am living, you will not be put in a nursing home, okay?"

"I could decorate like I want?" Mama said, obviously testing me.

I tried not to grit my teeth as I said, "Yes."

She almost smiled as she added, "And I can set up a bigger and better cat-io for Hector?"

"There is a nice sunroom on one side of the house that faces the woods. I bet Hector would love it there."

Somehow I managed to continue to discuss the benefits of a cat's sunroom with a straight face. Goodness but my mother was nuts about the ornery feline. And if Mama loved Hector and I wanted Mama where I knew she'd be safe, then I needed to at least try to like Hector.

It was the next best thing to bringing her with me to live in Nashville, something she had absolutely refused to do since the first time I mentioned it.

"Besides, Mama," I said slyly, "you can have a sewing room with lots of storage for your fabric and patterns. And maybe even room for that fancy quilting machine you've been looking at. Oh, and did I mention there's a whole other kitchen separate from the main one that's just for caterers to use? That means there are several ovens. Industrial ovens, Mama."

She acted like she wasn't impressed. I wasn't convinced, especially when she managed to slip in a question here and there about the subject.

Oh, she was definitely seeing her pie baking go to a new level if she moved out there. But would industrial ovens and a fancy space for Hector be enough?

By the time we said our goodbyes that evening, Mama had promised to make a trip out to the house with Mari the following weekend so she could see what she thought about the place. I held out little hope that the few incentives I'd offered would get her to move out there anytime soon, but at least I had begun inching her toward that goal.

CHAPTER 17

It was hard to leave my mother and go back to Nashville. Though Mama Peach was already getting around like a champ on her crutches and was holding court among the many friends and admirers who insisted on visiting her, I still worried. Dr. Bishop was spending a lot of time with her as well, and I worried about that too.

The last time I tried to discuss a move back to Texas, Sticks wasn't happy with me. Neither was my agent, but at least she'd understood and said we'd brainstorm how I could stay in the game from such a long distance away.

But was it that far really?

Just this morning, Olivia had messaged me that she was encouraged with the feedback from Styler Records in regard to our counteroffer to their new contract. And if she was encouraged, then I was definitely encouraged.

I made a quick stop by the vet clinic to say goodbye to Mari. I found her in the outdoor area out back watching Old Blue run around like a puppy. Who knew that under all that matted fur there was a beautiful dog?

"Any idea what her breed is?" I asked Mari after we exchanged a hug.

"Mr. Wright had us do a DNA swab, so I guess we'll find out eventually. I'd guess she's got some sort of terrier in her. Maybe a spaniel too?"

"Whatever it is, she wears it well," I said as I watched the dog romp.

"She'll look even better next time you see her. We've got Mr. Wright set up with pet food delivery so he can have the right foods to fatten her up and keep her healthy." Mari crouched down, and the dog came running. "After all, she's going to be our neighbor, aren't you, beautiful?"

The dog licked Mari's face and then apparently noticed for the first time that I was there. After a few tentative sniffs, she barked.

"That means she wants you to throw the toy." I did, and she immediately trotted back to deposit her prize at my feet. "And this is why I think she's got retriever in her."

My phone rang, and I silenced it. After a few more minutes, I hugged my niece and extracted a promise for her to send lots of pictures of the new facility along with repair bills and to take care of Mama in my absence.

"All of that I will do," Mari said, laughing. "Just go. Catch your plane."

I nodded and left before the tears threatened. It was a private jet that wasn't going anywhere until I was aboard, but I couldn't stay another minute without being tempted to call and cancel everything that was planned for the coming week.

Then I imagined how badly that conversation would go and hurried through the lobby and out onto the sidewalk without stopping to say goodbye to Cassidy or Parker.

I was about to climb into my rental when I heard a familiar voice calling my name. Turning toward the sound, I spied Bitsy heading toward me as fast as her stilettos would allow. Today's version of pink was a neon fuchsia sundress with a purse large enough to hold Old Blue. Matching feather earrings that hung to her shoulders completed the ensemble.

"I was just leaving," I called, hoping to ward her off.

"Whatever." She stuttered to a stop on the curb beside me. "I know you have time to talk to me. I was just out at the airport settling a helicopter bill and saw the jet with the record label on the side of it. The only thing that was missing was the red carpet, but I guess they don't roll that out until you arrive."

Oh brother. I knew she wouldn't be happy that I'd bought a property she hadn't shown me, but this was over the top. Even for Bitsy.

She looked as if she expected an answer. I refused to give her the satisfaction. Anything I said wouldn't be nice anyway, so I did as my mother always warned and said nothing at all.

"I heard you bought a house," she finally said, her tone icy. "I ought to charge you for all the wasted time and fees I paid trying to show you the perfect property."

"Go ahead," I told her. "Imagine though. While you were taking me all over Central Texas, everything I wanted was right here in town, and you didn't know it was for sale. I don't suppose you'd want that to get out, would you?"

That wasn't nice. I would be repenting in my prayers tonight, but I wasn't ready to take it back. Not when I was so mad that my hands were shaking.

"Why do you even have to come back here, Trina?" she snapped. "You left. There's nothing here for you."

"Except my mother and niece," I corrected. "Well, and there's also my home now that I've bought one."

Okay, that was a low blow, but I was not pleased at the confrontation or her behavior. Bitsy was way out of line. Mama always said that anger was a secondary emotion that was always caused by something else.

Maybe that sale meant a lot to her. Or she might be hurting financially. She did mention that she was in the middle of a divorce, didn't she? Or that she'd just finished one? I couldn't remember.

But one look at her and the car she drove up in caused me to decide that she was probably not desperate for the sale.

"Look, Bitsy. I didn't go looking for that property. It found me, so to speak. I met Dallas when I went out on a dog rescue with Mari a few days ago. Dallas found out I wanted to buy land, and the rest is history."

"And just how did he find out?"

No way was I dragging Wyatt into this discussion. "You'd have to ask Dallas," I said. "Now if that's all, I'm going to go."

"Why don't you take your mother and niece with you, then? I'm sure you've got a grand home where they could live and bake pies and save dogs. Personally, I'm over them doing that here."

Oh. Okay.

I let out a long breath as I counted to ten. There was no need to speak about my family like that.

I was about to respond when Bitsy leaned closer. "Just one more thing, Trina. I hope Mari and her volunteers are more careful than I've heard they are."

"What are you talking about, Bitsy?"

She shrugged. "They go wandering through the dark on land that doesn't belong to them, and the next thing you know, something is blowing up. They'd be safer in Tennessee, I think. Nobody knows them there."

I frowned. "Something is *going* to blow up or something blew up *after* the bomb squad came in to handle it? The two scenarios are very different. And one of them is a very distinct threat."

Bitsy held her hand out as if silencing me. "Don't try to twist my words, Trina."

"I'm not. I'm trying to understand what you're saying." I paused to calm myself. "Are you threatening my niece and the rescue group? Or maybe you're confessing to something? Like a pipe bomb in a field at the Double J?"

Her face colored and she took a step backward, her oversized purse sliding off her shoulder. "Don't be ridiculous."

Not a no, I noticed. But also not a yes.

"If you're mad at anyone, it's me, Bitsy," I said. "Do not misdirect those feelings and take it out on my niece. She has done nothing wrong and, for that matter, neither has my mother. You stay away from them. Do you understand?"

Bitsy gave me a look that said she was done with the conversation and then turned to stalk away. I climbed into my car and started the engine, directing the air-conditioning vent toward my flushed face.

What in the world had just happened?

Maybe there were some good points to living in Nashville instead of Brenham, chief among them the fact that I would never run into Bitsy there.

I placed another call to Mama. "I'm just about to leave. I wanted to check on you one more time."

"Goodness, Trina. You were here an hour ago."

"I know," I said as I watched Bitsy climb into her SUV. "Hey, so I'm curious. In all those casseroles and desserts you've received, did you get anything from Bitsy Decker?"

"The little Realtor who's been chasing Wyatt Chastain for the past month?" Mama said. "I sure did. She sent cookies. Store bought but wrapped pretty and tagged with her business card."

Of course.

"Trust me on this, Mama," I said as tires squealed, indicating Bitsy was driving away. "Throw them away."

My phone beeped with an incoming call. I repeated my warning, made Mama promise to dump Bitsy's treats, and then hung up.

I switched to the other call and said hello without looking to see who the caller might be. "Trina Potter?" an unfamiliar female voice said.

"Yes," I said, glancing at the caller ID.

"I'm Anna Wright." She paused. "Dallas Wright's daughter."

I stifled a groan.

Before I could respond, she continued. "I wondered if I might meet with you."

"Oh," I said slowly, "I'm sorry. I'm catching a flight back to Nashville in a few hours. Maybe another time?"

"Actually," she said slowly, "I'm in Nashville next week for a conference. I just assumed you were too. Do you have any time to see me while I'm there?"

"Look," I said slowly, "if this is about your father selling the family home, I really don't want to get in the middle between the two of you."

She laughed. "It's nothing like that, I promise." Then she paused. "To be completely truthful, it is about my dad but not in the way I expect you're thinking it is. And for the record, I'm glad the property is being sold. It's a relief that I'm not the one having to make that decision."

Not at all what I thought she would say.

"Okay." We settled on a time, and then I gave her the address for my office at the record label.

"Thank you," she said, and I had the feeling she meant it.

CHAPTER 18

The flight back to Nashville was uneventful, but the meeting the next morning was anything but. I prepared to defend myself against a schedule that would require me to spend all my time on the road or in Nashville performing or recording.

I wasn't expecting Sticks to tell me that I had to choose between making records and taking time off. He didn't say it like that, but the ultimatum was implied. I walked out of the meeting not knowing what to do.

My heart told me to toss it all and go home to Brenham. My head, however, said I should at least meet with my accountant to see if I could afford this.

I placed a call to the accounting firm I employed and left a voice mail, then tucked the phone into my purse and drove home. I kicked off my shoes just inside the door and left my suitcases where I'd rolled them. Locking the door, I padded to the kitchen and put some water on to boil. I rarely kept a pitcher of sweet tea in the house, but I was craving one now.

Actually, I was craving some time in one of those rockers on Dallas's front porch. My front porch, I amended. But sweet tea here in Nashville would have to do.

With Patsy and Cline boarded at the pet spa until tomorrow, the house was eerily quiet. I sorted through the mail that my housekeeper had stacked on the counter near the back door, then walked over to the window overlooking the pool and the Cumberland River off in the distance.

Compared to this place—a modern glass and steel with furniture to match—the Wright home was shabby. What I wouldn't give for shabby right now.

My phone buzzed and I groaned. Ever since I returned, the calls and texts had been coming in at regular intervals. Everything I had put off to hurry to Mama's side needed to be done, and everyone wanted it done immediately.

I shut off the ringer and sat the phone on the counter just as it rang again.

"Enough." I walked through the house to the bedroom and tucked the phone into the drawer on the nightstand.

It was ludicrous to be without contact, but I needed this for just a minute. Or an hour. Or who was I kidding? I could use a very large dose of absolutely nothing to do.

The teapot's steamy shrill sound cut through my mental whining. I poured hot water over the teabags in my ancient Revere Ware saucepan, and then I set the timer for five minutes.

Only then did it occur to me that while I was successfully shutting out the professional world I was not ready to reenter yet, I was also unable to receive calls from Mama or Mari. Given the nature and tone of the conversation with Bitsy this morning, I certainly didn't need to be unavailable to them.

Reluctantly, I hurried back to the bedroom, retrieved the phone, and went back into the kitchen to finish making the tea. I removed the tea bags then poured the water over ice in my favorite pitcher. As the ice crackled and snapped, I dumped in a generous scoop of sugar just like Mama always did.

When I was in college, I called this her glucose tea. I was on a health kick back then, too fat because my size 2 jeans weren't as loose as I thought they ought to be. Now I happily poured a glass of the sweet concoction and gave thanks I could still fit in my size 10s.

The liquid slid down as smoothly as I hoped, and I'd finished half of the glass before I realized I hadn't even gone back to the table to sit down with it. I topped off the glass and left the kitchen to slide open the back door and take a seat in the shade.

It seemed hotter here than it was in Brenham. Impossible, of course, but maybe I was just looking for something to complain about.

The phone buzzed again, and I glanced down at the caller ID. US Government.

Well, that was different. I decided to answer.

"This is Agent Mendez with the ATF. Our mutual friend Wyatt Chastain asked me to contact you. He said you had some questions."

I nearly dropped my tea trying to set it down. "Yes," I said. "I do, although right now I don't really know what I don't know." I paused and shook my head. I sounded like an idiot. "What I mean is, I have some concerns about the pipe bomb that you're investigating."

"I understand," he said in clipped tones. "Wyatt told me it was placed near your niece's dog rescue operation."

"Yes," I said. "It's probably too soon, but my main question is, can you tell who could have done this? I really don't like the fact that no one has been charged with building this."

"I don't like that either, ma'am," he said. "And you're right in saying that it is too early to tell. What I can say is that I was able to bring enough of the remaining pieces of the exploded bomb to our lab to have them analyzed."

"That's good news. How long does something like that take?"

"I couldn't say. It all depends on the tests that have to be run." He paused. "Actually, I have some questions for you, if you've got a few minutes."

"Yes, fire away." I paused to groan. "I guess that's not something appropriate to say to an employee of the Federal Bureau of Alcohol, Tobacco, and Firearms."

Silence.

Then he cleared his throat. "Anyway, I've read the reports filed by the folks in Brenham. There were no potential suspects listed. So my question to you is, do you know of anyone who would do this?"

"With any certainty?" I said. "No."

"All right, that's fair. And let's be clear that I am talking about someone who would either want to harm people—say the occupants of the Double J Ranch or the volunteers at the rescue—or property?"

Bitsy's words were running through my mind. I had no proof. She certainly hadn't clarified her statement to the point where it became an actual threat that I could tell Agent Mendez about.

"Can I think about that?" I asked him.

"Of course, but my guess is at least one name came to mind when I asked that question. I understand you don't want to implicate an honest person, but please understand that it's far better to have an honest person exonerated of the crime than to allow a guilty person to offend again."

"But it's been six months," I protested. "Almost seven. There haven't been any more pipe bombs that I've heard about and no threats to Mari or her volunteers."

"But?"

I sighed. "You're really good at this."

"Yes ma'am," he said. "It's my job. So what is it that you left out of your previous statement?"

"Well," I said slowly, "one of the volunteers seems to be afraid to go out with the others now. I've tried to find out why, but she's been evasive."

"But you have an opinion."

"It's just an opinion and not based on facts," I warned him. "But yes, I think the combination of the pipe bomb and other things have frightened her. She's my niece's best friend, but she will not tell me what those other things are. In fact, she denies them. However, I feel like I haven't gotten to the bottom of this."

"And you most likely have not," he said. "I don't suppose she's the one you thought of when I mentioned a suspect, is it?"

"No," I said quickly. "Absolutely not. But I do think that maybe there have been some threats or perhaps something dangerous that has happened that Mari and Parker—he's her main volunteer—aren't telling me about. It's odd because Parker is very protective of Mari, so I would think he would want to tell me if he was worried."

"Unless he's trying to handle this on his own. We guys like to think we can ride in like the Lone Ranger and save everyone, but that's rarely a good idea without backup."

"I hadn't thought of that, but it's certainly a possibility."

"Unfortunately, there are a number of possibilities right now. But after looking at the preliminary data, I'm in agreement with Chastain that a closer look needs to be taken at the evidence."

"Thank you," I said on an exhale of breath.

"I'll let you know if we find anything new, and I'd like you to promise that you will share any pertinent information with me."

He gave me his cell number, and I typed it into my contacts list. I hung up with mixed feelings. On the one hand, it was a relief that the investigation would continue. On the other, it also would have been nice to hear from an expert that the whole situation was no big deal.

I trudged back into the hallway, unable to ignore the unpacked suitcase. An hour later, with the laundry sorted and my suitcase back in the closet, the quiet enveloped me. No wonder Dallas headed for his cabin. My cure for the quiet was just down the road. I grabbed my keys and headed off to the Posh Pooch to pick up my dogs.

On the way there, my phone rang. I activated the hands-free and greeted my niece. As if we hadn't just seen one another this morning, Mari chatted about her newly updated plans for the Second Chance Ranch Dog Rescue, including a future area for kennels.

I listened happily, adding a word of approval here and there until she ran out of words. "I can't wait to see this in person, sweetheart," I said. "Your mama would be so proud."

"Of both of us," Mari said.

"Yes," I said slowly, "I think she would be. Oh, and Mari, get some quotes on those kennels, please."

"Aunt Trina," she said, a warning in her voice. "I couldn't."

"Okay, then I will," I said, using a tone that conveyed the fact that I meant it.

"Seriously," Mari pleaded, "you have done enough. I couldn't possibly ask this of you."

"You're not," I said. "And I haven't told you I was actually going to have them built. However, I would like to know what it would cost. Got it?"

She laughed. "Okay, got it. I love you, Aunt Trina."

"Oh kiddo," I said, "I love you too."

CHAPTER 19

I hadn't heard the word *no* that many times since I was a child. And I was just getting started on my presentation.

"I appreciate the input," I told my team—a group made up of my agent, assistant, publicist, and a few representatives of Styler Records, including Sticks. "But I need to make this work. I broached the subject six months ago, so this is not new information. I need us to figure out how I can cluster my work so that I can spend stretches of time in Brenham. I am my mother's only living child, and she needs me to be there for her at least on a part-time basis."

We were in a private room at the Oaks Steakhouse, a favorite of mine, though I hadn't touched my lunch today. Sticks stood up, glanced around the room, and then returned his attention to me.

"There's only one way to do what you've asked, Trina." He paused a beat too long and then continued. "You will have to quit."

A hush fell over the room. My agent flushed bright red but said nothing. I had asked her to let me do the talking, and so far she was complying with my request.

I stood and matched Sticks's gaze. Then I let out a long breath.

"No, Sticks. I work hard, and I'm not a quitter. You know that. I am only asking to tweak the schedule so I have longer spans of time off in between, that's all. If I can be assured of that, I will sign the contract as is."

His expression was unreadable. My agent's, however, spoke volumes. A waiter walked in but then abruptly turned around and left again.

My phone buzzed on the table in front of me. I ignored it.

"What's in Brenham that's worth losing all of this?" Sticks finally asked me.

"I said I would sign your contract."

He waved away that statement with a sweep of his hand. "With terms," he said. "And by the way, I think you have officially given Olivia an ulcer."

"She and I have the same goal."

"Not true," he said. "She wants you to make records. You cannot do that in Texas. It's one or the other."

So that's how it was going to go. How I was going to go.

Then so be it. I straightened my backbone. "You want to know what's in Brenham that is worth losing all of this. Why don't you come visit me there and see? You might like it."

With that, I snatched up my phone and purse, turned, and walked out.

My agent caught up with me in the parking lot. "Trina," she said slowly, "be very sure you want to drive away from here with things left like they are."

"I'll keep every commitment I've made," I told her. "I always have. I'll listen to offers if they come, but for now I'm going home to Brenham." I paused. "And yes, I am very sure about that."

Twenty minutes later I was fending off the crazed greetings of my enthusiastic Springer Spaniels, Patsy and Cline, as I stepped inside my Nashville home. The two of them had been impossibly hyper ever since I picked them up yesterday evening.

I finally gave up trying to walk with them weaving their way around my legs and sat in the middle of the front hallway. Cline brought a tennis ball and placed it at my feet, which led to a game of catch that eventually tired all three of us out.

With Patsy on one side of me and Cline on the other, we headed to the kitchen. While the two crazy canines sniffed for food on the cabinet and then, finding none, noisily lapped up water from their bowls, I brewed a cup of Earl Grey and sat at the table waiting for it to cool.

Only then did I pause to really consider what I'd done. I should be worried, shouldn't I? I had possibly just walked away from a lucrative career doing something I loved. I waited to feel regret, but it did not come.

Instead, I thought about how much my dogs would love running amok on ten acres of land. How they could chase squirrels and bark at critters and generally be outdoor dogs for once.

I thought about Mari and her rescue and how very happy it made me to know she would have a safe place to bring her dogs while they waited for new homes. I considered what it would be like living so close to Mama—be it in the same city or on the same property—and I decided that I would like that just fine.

I thought about my sister and how very much I wished that I had purchased a place in Brenham ten years ago so that I could have been there when she was healthy. And then when she wasn't.

Most of all, I thought about how very interesting this new life would be. Was Bitsy a pipe bomber? Did Mama's nemesis Donna Sue Speckle-meyer intend to horn in on Mama's new beau and run off with the retired vet? What new flavor of breakfast taco would Smarty's offer next?

These were the mysteries I would face in my future. And I couldn't wait to solve them.

I picked up the phone to call Mari, but the call went to voice mail. I glanced at the time. Of course. She was working at this time of the afternoon. I left a message for her to call me tonight after work.

My next call was to Mama. "How're you feeling?" I asked and then spent twenty minutes hearing the answer along with a stream-of-consciousness discussion of pies, quilting, and the fact that at her age she shouldn't have to fend off men who were intent on taking care of her.

"Hold on, Mama," I said. "Fend off? Explain please."

"Oh, nothing untoward," she said. "I'm just tired of men thinking I need someone to take care of me. Just this morning I had a fellow stop by and ask if he could help me with any kinds of repairs. Said he was sent by a friend of yours. I hope you're not spying on me, Trina. I am perfectly fine. I've got a home health nurse looking in once a week, and Mari is—"

"Okay, Mama. Remember, I was just there yesterday. I know what's happening with your care. So, who was the man, and which of my friends sent him?"

There was a pause. "I wrote it down. Let me go see." Another pause. "Here it is. His name is Blake Perry. He's a friend of that sweet Realtor lady who brought the—"

"Bitsy?" I suppressed a groan. What was she up to?

"Yes, that's the one. I remember when you two cheered together at Brenham High."

"Right," I said, trying to decide what to do about this. "So, what did you tell Blake Perry?"

"Well, I brought him in and served him some pie and thanked him for the generous offer of help. Then I got his phone number and sent him off."

"You fed him pie?" I said. "Mama, that is not what you do when a stranger comes to your door."

"Oh, Blake is no stranger. I've seen him in uniform over at the shopping center. He's a security guard, but apparently that's just a part-time job."

"I see." I let out a long breath and wondered what Bitsy was up to. "Well, Mama, would you promise not to let him or anyone else into the house without letting me know?"

"I will not," she said, her tone indignant. "I am not a helpless old lady, Trina. I can take care of myself, and I will not have my daughter treating me like a child." She paused. "Besides, I don't think he's coming back."

"Why not," I asked, ignoring the rest of her rant.

"Well," she said slowly, "Hector wasn't fond of him."

"And?" I supplied, wondering just how that crazy cat showed his dislike this time.

"I'd rather not go into details, but let's just say that Blake left with a handful of bandages and my last tube of Neosporin. I'll need to add that to my grocery list. Oh, I ought to do that now. Just a minute, Trina."

"No, Mama," I said, but it was too late. Mama Peach had set down her phone and walked off. I could hear the shuffle-thump sound of her walk as she headed toward wherever her grocery list was. In a couple of minutes, I heard the same sound returning.

"All done," she said. "Now where were we?"

"We were saying goodbye," I told her.

"Oh, well, goodbye, sweetheart," Mama said. "And don't you worry about me. I'm just fine."

Thanks to Hector, I thought rather than said.

After I finished the call with Mama, I considered phoning Bitsy to ask her what in the world she thought she was doing sending a stranger to my mother's home, but I decided against it. We hadn't left things on the best of terms, and it wouldn't help if I brought up yet another subject that might add to the disagreement.

The remainder of the week passed in a haze of costume fittings and rehearsals for an upcoming concert at the Ryman. In between work obligations, I managed to speak with Mama at least once a day.

And always, once I'd finished my call with Mama, I'd update Mari. We'd laugh about our shared relative and alternate between irritation and awe that while she refused to sit still, her ankle was healing nicely and without any pain.

Every few days, Wyatt would text me. Sometimes he would give me updates on the process of purchasing the Wright property, while other times he would tell me stories about things that happened that day. One time he sent a picture of Ed with a mouthful of watermelon rinds stolen from the kitchen trash.

THAT DUDE IS ALWAYS GOOD FOR A LAUGH, Wyatt had typed.

SO ARE YOU, I responded.

He answered with three words: I MISS YOU.

I had the whole morning ahead of me with nothing scheduled until my meeting with Anna Wright that afternoon. I had given her the address of my record label without considering that Sticks might have already ordered that my office there—really just a little room where I sometimes went to write songs or meet with industry or media folks—be cleaned out.

Oh well. I'd face that if it happened.

I'd been back in Nashville for a week, and there had been no negative feedback from the meeting I'd called. Silence, yes, but I hadn't been fired yet.

My finger hovered over the keypad for a moment before I called Wyatt. "Hey there, sunshine," he said when he picked it up on the first ring. "How are things in Music City?"

"Things are fine. I sent the packet of documents back signed and notarized," I said.

"Excellent. That should be the last of the details. Dallas has already turned over the keys, and Mari has been working on the outbuilding she chose as her rescue headquarters. It's a nice thing you did for her, Trina."

"It wasn't just for her," I said. "So how's Brenham? Anything exciting happening?"

"I went out on a rescue with your niece and her crew a couple of nights ago. Trina, those guys are impressive."

"No angry old men with pistols this time?"

"Nothing like that," he told me. "Although Cassidy wasn't there the night I went with them, so I'm not sure what's going on with that. Anyway, when are you coming home?"

Home. "Soon," I said and meant it.

"Good."

A thought occurred. "Hey, what do you know about a guy named Blake Perry? Apparently, Bitsy sent him to my mother's house to see if she needed help with anything."

"That was nice of her."

"I suppose." There was no reason yet to tell Wyatt about Bitsy's behavior the last time I saw her, so I said nothing else. "She sent him away. Apparently, Hector didn't approve."

"Poor Blake. And yes, I know him. He's a security guard, and he picks up part-time work on the side," Wyatt said. "That's about all I can say. Want me to check him out?"

"No," I told him. "That won't be necessary. I was just curious."

"Have I mentioned I miss you?" Wyatt said.

I paused only a second before saying, "I miss you too."

"Come get your house key," he said.

"Bring it to me," I countered.

"Watch what you wish for, Trina. I just might show up on your doorstep."

I laughed. He was joking, of course. But it was nice to think of a surprise like that.

"No way," I told him. "I need you there to make sure everything is okay."

"Everything or everyone?" he asked.

"Both?"

"That's what I thought." He paused. "Look, there hasn't been anything weird happening since you left. Mari takes a chance every time she goes out, but Parker is with her. And so far my ATF guy has no news."

"I spoke to him last week," I said. "I needed to be proactive and see if I could contribute anything to his investigation. He's going to contact me if he has news."

"Well, aren't you the busy bee?"

I couldn't tell whether he was teasing or upset. I decided not to try to figure that out. "Yes I am, and I hate that I have to do this from a distance."

"I'll watch your girls," Wyatt said. "Mama Peach has been asking me to come back for pie. I think I'll do that this afternoon."

"Let me know what the situation is there, please. When I left, Dr. Bishop, the retired veterinarian, was taking care of everything. I'd like to know if all is still well."

"Right. Well, I'll let you know what I find out."

"Thank you, Wyatt," I said. "For everything."

"Oh, don't worry," he said. "I'm keeping track. Nobody gets work out of a lawyer without getting billed for it."

"Really?" I said with a chuckle.

"Trina," he said, joining me with his laughter. "Do you honestly think I have the good sense to remember anything like that when I'm with you? Billable hours is the last thing on my mind."

I had no answer for that. "Get back to work, Wyatt," I told him. "And thank you for putting up with me."

"I look forward to doing more of that," he said, "and I don't mean work."

CHAPTER 20

That afternoon, I stepped inside the lobby of Styler Records. After greeting the receptionist with a smile, I hurried toward my office hoping to avoid Sticks or any of his minions.

I unlocked my office door and stepped inside, breathing a sigh of relief that the key still worked. At my request, the furnishings of the office were spare: two overstuffed swivel armchairs upholstered in a soft cream fabric filled the space in front of a window that had a commanding view of the Nashville skyline. On the table between them was a clear glass chessboard that had been paused midgame ages ago.

It remained to be seen whether Sticks's friendship and the chess game would survive given his behavior yesterday. I looked down at the board and sighed.

Ironically, it was his move.

I walked across the multicolored floral rug to take a seat at my desk. With my gold and platinum records framed on the pale gray wall behind me, I glanced across the space to the comfy cream-colored sofa on the opposite wall. It was there that I wrote many of the songs that I'd recorded for Styler Records.

The only evidence that this space was used for songwriting now was my 1954 Martin D-8 guitar that I'd purchased with my first royalty check. I rose from the desk and retrieved the guitar, then settled on the sofa. Eyes closed, I played the first melody that came to mind and the next one and the next until a knock at the door surprised me.

I glanced at my watch. Where had the time gone?

"Come in," I called as I returned my guitar to the stand.

The door opened, and a pretty brunette stepped inside. She wore turquoise trousers and a matching top with gold earrings and heart pendant. From the top of her perfectly styled hair to the turquoise shoes on her feet, Anna Wright's style shouted calm, cool, and professional.

Meanwhile, my faded jeans, white sneakers, and Willie Nelson T-shirt combined with the messy bun I'd twisted my hair into on the way out the door conveyed a whole other vibe. I mustered a smile and braced myself for the confrontation I expected would occur.

"I'm Anna Wright," she said in an accent that was anything but Texan. "But I guess that's obvious."

After dispensing with the greetings, we moved to the chairs by the window and settled in for a conversation. "How can I help you, Anna?" I asked.

Perfectly manicured fingers played with the gold bracelet circling her wrist, and then she looked up at me. Rather than anger, I saw a neutral expression and then a slow smile.

"I wasn't sure you'd be willing to see me." Anna dropped her hands to rest on the purse in her lap. "And honestly, Daddy would be furious if he found out I got your number off his phone. Please don't blame him for me being able to track you down."

"I did wonder how you managed it," I said. "I won't say anything."

Unless you do something to make me change my mind about that.

"Right, well, thank you." She glanced down at her hands then back up at me. "I just came here to thank you."

"Oh." The word came out on an exhale of breath. "Why?"

Anna paused just a moment and then offered a tiny shrug. "I guess it's okay to tell you, but my daddy hasn't been himself for a long time. He misses my mother, I'm sure, but since she's been gone almost thirty years, that can't really be the only reason."

She paused again but didn't look at me as if she expected a response. Rather, she turned her attention to the view out the window.

"I think he's been lonely, and it's mostly my fault. I went away as a child, not of my own choice of course."

"Right," I said, automatically filling in the silence with words. "I was told you'd lived with relatives during some of your childhood."

"I won't ask who told you that," she said. "But it's true. On the one hand, I was grateful to get out of there. Living with my grandparents back East gave me advantages that a life in Brenham, Texas, never would have. But it did separate me from Daddy. The result of that is he missed me terribly, and I mostly just felt guilty because I hated the time I spent in that dreadful house on that dreadful property."

I wasn't able to formulate a response. How could anyone think that home and the lands around it were anything but beautiful? Relief shot through me at the realization that Anna Wright did not mean to acquire the Wright land that I'd purchased.

"So you're not upset that I bought the family property?" I ventured, wanting to hear her confirm it.

Anna returned her attention to me, her expression peaceful. "I don't care one bit for that home. Daddy told me he put the furniture in storage so I could pick through the pieces to see if I want any of it. I can tell you now that I don't." She paused. "I must sound awful. I love my parents and I am proud of my heritage, but a piece of land and some old furniture will not bring Mama back or put my father in his right mind again."

And there it was. Her reason for coming. To disparage Dallas Wright. Again, I determined to ask her a question that would lay it all out.

"Anna," I said carefully. "Why are you here? Is it about your father?"

She gave me a grateful look. "I like you. You go right to the point. Yes, that's exactly why I'm here."

I waited for Anna to continue. Instead of speaking, she looked down at the chessboard on the table between us.

"Daddy taught me how to play chess. I miss that," she said, toying with the handle of her purse.

So much for getting to the point. I nodded but kept silent.

"Anyway, look. I don't want to say anything to make you change your mind about buying the property. It's a relief to have that issue off my plate."

"But?" I offered.

"You may or may not know that I've been trying to get Daddy to move in with me in Austin. So far he's resisting. He even moved out to that old cabin on the property to make a point to me that he'd live anywhere as long as it was within the confines of the Wright property."

"I know he asked to remain in the cabin after I move into the house," I said. "His portion of the land where the cabin stands will revert to me after he's gone. I've agreed to those terms."

"Right. And since I can't get him to budge from that property, I'm grateful that you agreed to allow him to stay put even if it's in that awful cabin that he loves so much."

She paused, and I noticed a shimmer of tears brimming in her eyes. I rose to retrieve a tissue from my desk drawer to hand to her.

"Thank you, Trina," she said, dabbing at her eyes. "I'm selfishly happy that you'll be there to watch over Daddy, but I couldn't forgive myself if something happened again."

I frowned. "Again?"

Now the tears began to flow in earnest. I returned to my desk, snatched up the tissue box, and delivered it to Anna. I understand crying for your daddy like that when he's gone, but I'd never seen someone cry for her daddy so hard while he was still alive and in relationship with her.

Finally, Anna managed to slow her tears. "I'm so sorry," she said, tossing a used tissue into her purse. Once again I rose, this time to fetch the trash can.

"Honey," I said gently as I returned to my chair, "if you're not mad about me buying the house and you're grateful that I'm letting your daddy stay in the cabin, then what is it that has you so upset? What is it you think might happen again?"

Anna tossed the tissue in the trash can. Slowly she met my gaze. "I love my daddy. Really, I do. But he's got a temper."

I thought of the night we rescued Old Blue. The night Dallas Wright brandished a starter pistol and scared us all to death.

"What is it you want to tell me about your dad, Anna? Is he dangerous?"

"I hope not," she said, and then the tears flowed again. After a few minutes, she shook her head, blew her nose, and stood. "I promised myself I wouldn't cry. I'm sorry I've used half a box of tissues breaking that promise."

"Hey, it comes with the office, so I don't pay for it," I said in an attempt to lighten the mood.

Anna nodded. "Again, I really just wanted to meet you and clear the air between us. There's no telling what my father has said about me. He's not happy with me for trying to force the idea of moving in with me. He says there are too many cars and politicians in Austin."

"He's not wrong," I said. "About the cars. But it seems like he doesn't understand your motive for wanting him with you. Have you explained that to him?"

"I love my daddy," she said. "But he doesn't listen to anything I tell him if it has something to do with moving off his land."

"Are you thinking of forcing him to leave?" I asked, not sure why the idea had come to my mind.

Anna's eyes widened. "I hope it never comes to that. Daddy would never forgive me for forcing him to leave his home." Then she sighed. "But if it does, I won't hesitate to do what's best for him. I wonder if I could ask you to let me know if you ever become worried about him."

I thought a minute and decided that if this were Mama we were talking about, I'd be asking the same thing of someone living in close proximity to her. In fact, that's basically what Wyatt and Mari were doing for me.

"Of course," I told her, and she hugged me.

A few minutes later, we said our goodbyes, and she was almost out the door when I stopped her. "Anna, you never answered my question. I know you're concerned about your father, but do you actually think he is dangerous?"

"No," she said quickly. "I mean, he occasionally loses his temper, but it's not like he's going to burn the house down or anything like that."

CHAPTER 21

"Trina, she almost burned the house down."

I stared at Wyatt's face on my computer screen. I'd wondered why he wanted to talk using video calling, but now that I saw the image behind him as he sat in his car, I understood the reason.

There was a black stain above the kitchen windows, and a woman was taking photographs of the side of Mama's house. Firemen were wrapping up their hoses while Mama sat on the porch fanning herself with a paper plate.

"How?" was all I could manage.

"I'll have to get that story from someone at Brenham FD. Your mother's not talking."

"No, I'm not surprised," I said. "My guess is pie was involved."

"Most definitely after," he said. "I personally have had two pieces of her chocolate pecan pie—don't judge, it's the best in town—and I know there are some happy firemen with to-go slices in their truck."

"Tell her I'm on my way," I snapped. "This is completely unacceptable." Then I shook my head. "No. You know what? Don't say a thing. That would just give my mother time to figure out how she's going to explain this."

"Fair enough. Need a ride from the airport in Houston?"

"I'll pick up a rental there, but thanks." A thought occurred. "Where was Dr. Bishop when this happened?"

"Not here," Wyatt said. "That's all I know. I tried to find out, but there are only a few questions you can ask your friend's mom about her love life before it gets weird."

"Point taken. See you soon."

I went online to compare prices for airline tickets. No more free jet rides for me, of this I was certain. I was just about to complete my purchase when Patsy rested her head on my knee and looked at me with those soulful brown eyes of hers.

Cline was snoring on the dog bed I kept in my home office, oblivious to his sister's distress. Patsy, however, was using every bit of her power to sway me to whatever she wanted.

And in that moment, I was certain she wanted to go wherever I was planning to go.

I sighed as I noted the time was straight up three o'clock. It was a twelve-hour drive to Brenham from where I sat, but I could be in Little Rock by bedtime if I hurried. I spent the next hour packing and stuffing everything in the car, not the easiest thing to accomplish with two dogs circling your every move. Then I made a reservation in Little Rock at the dog-friendly hotel where I'd stayed before.

After that, I sent an email to Olivia at Music Talent Today, asking her to fend off anyone who needed to speak with me in the next twenty-four hours. Finally, I wrote a note to my housekeeper and sent a text to Mari to let her know I'd be arriving soon but not to alert her grandmother.

As I stepped into the backyard to let the dogs have one more run to—I hoped—get some of their excitement and bathroom needs handled before we set off, I texted Wyatt: CHANGE OF PLANS. DRIVING WITH THE DOGS TO LITTLE ROCK TONIGHT. ARRIVING THERE TOMORROW AFTERNOON.

Wyatt responded with three words: SAFE TRAVELS, SWEETHEART.

My mind shouldn't have lingered on the word *sweetheart*. But it did. I continued to think about the meaning of that endearment as I corralled the dogs into my SUV and headed south on I-40.

When I arrived in Brenham the next afternoon, I went straight to Mama's house and found it empty. Someone had boarded up the kitchen window but hadn't cleaned the soot from the exterior wall or the muddy boot prints off the porch. The pungent scent of woodsmoke permeated the yard and made me think of someone barbecuing rather than a house fire.

I let the dogs out in the backyard and then sent a text to Mari and Wyatt to let them know I'd arrived. To Mari I also asked if she knew where her grandmother might be.

While I waited for Mari's response, I walked around the perimeter of the house. There was no damage on the back of the home or on the side opposite from the kitchen. I peered into my old bedroom, the space now claimed as the cat's domain, and could see nothing unusual. Unless you find an entire room dedicated to a cat to be unusual—which I do, but I digress.

When the dogs started up a fuss at something in the backyard, I figured they'd treed a squirrel and told them to hush.

Mari called as I was walking toward the noisy dogs. I shushed them and then answered.

"I'm so glad you're home," Mari told me. "We were out on a rescue and only found out about the fire when Parker drove past Grandma's house afterward and saw the trucks. He stopped to see what was happening and then called me. We took her and Hector to your place. Wyatt and Mr. Wright insisted, but Grandma wasn't happy about it."

"I'm glad you got her there, and you were right to involve Wyatt and Dallas. I'm not sure where we are on the transfer of title, so it may not technically be my home just yet. I need to clarify that with Wyatt."

"It was his idea, so I guess it's fine," Mari offered.

"How was Grandma when you got to her house?" I asked, noticing that the dogs were nosing around in the corner of the yard. "I'm guessing she was pretty upset."

"She seemed fine, actually. I mean, flames had been coming out of her kitchen window, and she wasn't thrilled that the firemen weren't wiping their boots on the rug before they went inside, but other than that she was pretty chill about the whole thing."

"Okay," I said. "Well, at least I'll know what to expect when I get home."

"Cassidy and I stayed with her there last night," Mari said. "I hope you don't mind. We didn't want to leave her alone."

"I'm very glad you did. My home is your home, Mari. Don't you ever forget that." I paused. "How is Hector taking the change of location?"

"I convinced Grandma that since the house filled up with smoke and it was a while before anyone could catch him, she ought to take him to the clinic for observation." Mari paused. "Honestly, he looked and acted fine, but Cassidy and I didn't think we could manage them both last night."

"One disaster at a time," I said under my breath. "Did you get Grandma checked out as well?"

"I called her doctor yesterday once I got her settled here. He told us what to watch for and said she didn't need to come in unless we saw any of the signs. So far she's been okay. I just talked to her about twenty minutes ago."

"Good," I said. "So, how did this happen? Wyatt said she refused to tell him."

"I have no idea," Mari told me. "Every time Cassidy or I tried to get anything out of her about that, she clammed up. We just figured it upset her too much to talk about it."

"Could be," I said. "And what about Dr. Bishop?"

Mari giggled. "She said he was only after her for her pie."

"Do you believe that? I thought he was really smitten with her."

"Aunt Trina, I try not to think about my grandmother's love life, okay? But yeah, I do."

A few minutes later, we hung up. I thought about going inside to see the damage for myself but decided that walking through a smoke-filled home on the same day as a fire occurred probably wasn't the best idea, especially given the fact I made my living using a voice that depended on healthy lungs.

Ten minutes later, I walked into my new home unannounced, only to have my mother glare at me like I was an intruder. Mama was seated like a queen on her throne at an oversized antique desk that filled the formal Victorian parlor to the right of the entryway.

Patsy and Cline were barking like crazy and straining at their leashes, but I wasn't about to let the crazed canines loose until I was certain they couldn't break anything that wasn't mine. And looking around at the antique furniture and fancy rugs, it appeared that my poor pups would be spending a lot of time outdoors or safely corralled elsewhere.

I didn't even want to consider what would happen when Hector joined the group.

Mama pointed to the phone at her ear, then gestured for me to move along. I did, but only because I was more interested in getting these dogs back outside where they could bark as much as they liked.

I walked down the hallway and into the big farmhouse kitchen, mentally noting all the changes I would be making. Was it a travesty to knock down hundred-year-old walls? I thought not, especially if it resulted in an open and airy room at the back of the house.

Someone had painted the kitchen walls and cabinets a bright white that had not faded over time. I liked the look of it and would probably keep it that way. The copper farmhouse sink and matching pot rack over the industrial-sized stove would also stay, as would the brick floors under my feet.

Oh, and the fireplace in the corner would make a great pizza oven, although who needed another source of heat in a Texas kitchen? I'd have to think about that one.

I was inspecting the window of the adjoining breakfast room when I realized I'd let Patsy and Cline's leashes slip out of my hand. I retraced my steps, hoping they weren't bothering Mama, only to realize the back door had a doggie door built in.

"Well that's convenient," I muttered as I stepped outside to call the dogs.

Cline turned and ran toward me. Always obedient, at least when he was awake, he was the first to arrive at my side. Patsy wasn't so disobedient that she ignored me altogether, but she took her own sweet time.

Free of their leashes, the dogs set off adventuring. They were bound on all sides by a white picket fence that set the patch of grass apart from the woods and pastureland that surrounded it.

The same brick used on the kitchen floor had been laid out in a herringbone pattern outside to form a generous covered patio. I settled onto an uncomfortable wrought iron bench and watched my pups play as the weariness settled into my bones.

The drive had been long but not so awful. Patsy and Cline were good travel companions who didn't fuss much about bathroom breaks. But the miles I'd traveled since yesterday afternoon had settled like a weight on my shoulders, and I could feel exhaustion clear through to my bones.

It was hot outside but cooler in the shade. It didn't take long for Patsy and Cline to splay themselves out on the cool bricks and fall asleep.

If I didn't have Mama to handle, I would have been hunting for a nice spot to nap too. As if on cue, Peach Potter glided out the back door, wearing a pink sundress with ties at the shoulder and a look that told me I had some explaining to do.

In her hands were two glasses of iced tea. I jumped up to relieve her of the beverages, then watched her walk across the patio as if she weren't wearing a medical boot on one foot.

I placed the glasses on the table and returned to my place on the bench.

Mama settled herself next to me and extended her injured ankle out in front of her while I reached for my tea glass. The sweet liquid was cool going down and most welcome. I pressed the cold glass to my forehead and closed my eyes.

"Why in the world are you here, Trina?"

"Mama," I said, choosing my words carefully as I opened my eyes and returned the glass to the table, "really? You set fire to your home, and you thought I wouldn't show up to make sure you're all right? Or are you just surprised that I found out, since you didn't bother to call me?"

"I am fine," she said demurely, avoiding my steady gaze. "I'm about to pull my hair out trying to deal with the insurance company over the little mishap, but otherwise all is well."

I noticed she hadn't commented on not having informed me of her predicament. I decided to let that go for now.

Instead, I slid her a sideways look. "Just how did this 'little mishap' happen, Mama? People's kitchens don't just catch on fire by themselves. Something had to have happened."

Mama sighed. "Why does everyone want to know that? There was a fire. I tried to put it out. The fire department did it for me." She turned her attention to me. "I'm sorry you had to come all this way for nothing."

"Right, well, I'm here now," I said, fighting the urge to snap at her. "There is a lot to do."

"Like what?" she said, reaching for her tea glass.

"We'll need to get someone out to take care of the damage at your place. And I'm going to need to get the old furniture out of here so we can fill the house with things that actually belong to me. I don't want to be responsible for breaking someone's family heirloom, and between Hector and my two dogs, that is very likely."

Mama appeared to be listening, but I got the impression she wasn't really. So I continued.

"Once we get someone out to assess whether your furniture can be cleaned, we'll decide what will be moved over here and what will be replaced."

I waited for her protest. Waited for her to give me what-for about trying to get her out of her home. Waited for the lecture on the slippery slope that would land her in a nursing home.

Instead, my mother smiled sweetly, took a sip of iced tea, and nodded. "I think you're right, dear."

I'm sure my shock showed on my face. However, Mama said nothing about it. Instead, she calmly sipped her tea and watched the dogs' antics as they played on the lawn.

"You were right," Mama finally said, still not looking at me.

"About what?" I asked, hoping I would hear her admit one of the many things I'd told her was true, correct, or a downright good idea. Goodness knows there were plenty to choose from.

"Those are some lovely industrial-sized ovens. I think I'll bake a pie tomorrow."

"I was right about the ovens?" I couldn't help saying. "Not about being worried that you were staying alone in your home so soon after your time in the hospital? Nothing else but the fact that I have nice ovens?"

Mama reached over and patted my arm, giving me a genuine smile this time. "Trina, honey," she said slowly, "choose your battles."

Then she stood up and walked back inside, ending the conversation and leaving me with the empty tea glasses.

CHAPTER 22

Later that afternoon, Wyatt texted me to say he would be stopping by with a bucket of chicken, a dozen biscuits, and one of every type of side that the Cluck Hut made. I was on the front porch when he arrived.

"Isn't your mama allowing you in the house?" he called as he stepped out of his truck.

"It's more of a preference, actually," I told him as I jumped up and hurried down to help him unload the food. "I could either stay inside and listen to Mama argue with the insurance company folks or come out here and sit in the peace and quiet."

Wyatt appeared to consider the options and then grinned. "Good choice."

Mari drove up just as Wyatt began piling containers of food into my arms. "Let me help," she called. "I've got a wagon that'll get all of that at one time."

Sure enough, my niece had a foldable red wagon in the back of her car. "For pet supplies," she said as she rolled it past me to allow Wyatt access. "Do you have any idea how heavy bags of pet food are?"

"I think it's written right there on the bag," Wyatt said. "That's why I don't try to memorize it."

"Very funny," Mari said, her camaraderie with my friend evident. "You could have used this when we were chasing down that dog in Highland Park Woods last week." She turned to me. "We were told it was a big dog, so I borrowed an extra-large crate from the clinic."

"Turns out she borrowed the two-ton extra-heavy crate and then asked the old man to carry it." He winked at Mari. "Good thing I'm a muscleman."

She laughed. "Good thing you exaggerate." Mari turned to me. "So what really happened was the crate was—"

"Marigold, is that you?" Mama called from the porch. "And which of you ordered chicken delivery? I could have easily fried some up."

"That'd be me, Mrs. Potter," Wyatt said. "I thought it might help if nobody had to cook tonight."

"Plus we have no chicken to fry or much of anything else except the makings of an omelet or a grilled cheese," I commented in a tone that was only loud enough for Mari and Wyatt to hear.

"Tell Wyatt thank you, Grandma," Mari said. "It was his idea."

"Thank you, Wyatt," Mama said. "I didn't recognize you. I thought maybe you were one of those food delivery fellows."

"Well, Mrs. Potter, technically I am today."

I took one end of the wagon and Wyatt the other, and together we maneuvered the food up the steps to the porch. From there we let Mari and Mama roll the feast into the kitchen.

Wyatt watched them go, then turned his attention to me. "How're you holding up?"

"You assume I am," I said.

He laughed. "Well, there's my answer. Want to sit out here until they call us to come in?"

"You're reading my mind," I said, happily choosing a rocker and making myself comfortable.

"Did you get any information out of her about the fire?" Wyatt asked after he'd taken the chair next to me.

I related my conversation to him. "So just about as much as you got," I said. "She's hiding something, but I guess I'll find out what it is eventually."

"Or she'll tell you when she's good and ready."

"Yes, possibly, though I'm not going to hold my breath on that one." We sat in silence for a moment, and then I spoke up again. "I met Dallas's daughter last week."

"You did?"

I nodded. "Anna was at a conference in Nashville and asked if we could get together. She seems nice."

"Did she give you any trouble about buying the place?" Wyatt asked. "Because, as of today, it's yours free and clear. I was actually about to tell you that when Mari drove up."

"That's great news!"

"I'll have all the final papers in hand tomorrow. I can bring them by after work," he said, sliding me a sideways glance.

"Or I can pick them up when I go into town," I offered.

"Yeah, sure." He paused. "So, you and Anna got along okay?"

"We did," I told him. "And I think I understand her." At his surprised look, I continued. "She's worried about her parent who is alone, just like I'm worried about mine."

"The difference is you didn't try to force your mother to move in with you."

I shrugged. "We weren't at that point yet. Her father moved out of a perfectly lovely home into a cabin on the back of the property. Who does that, Wyatt?"

"The man who sold you this property," he said. "Look, I can't speak for anything other than what I know about Dallas Wright. He's a good man who knows exactly what he's doing. He didn't want to live alone with the memories anymore, and that's why he's out there."

"Is he safe out there?" I asked.

"If you mean is the cabin a safe place for Dallas to live at his age, then yes. It's clean, it's air-conditioned in the summer and heated in the winter, and he keeps the place up. No signs he's been neglecting his nutrition, his meds, or his health." He grinned. "Are you surprised that I checked that closely?"

"I am," I told him. "Why would you do that?"

"First off, I like him. Dallas is a good guy. A straight shooter—pardon the reference to an interesting memory we share."

I grimaced. "Anna mentioned he has a temper."

"So would I if I was continually being told I needed to change my way of living." Wyatt let out a long breath. "Look, my best advice is to stay out of Dallas and Anna's family dynamic. Picking sides in that battle is not a good idea."

"I can see that."

He nodded. "And as to how I know so much about Dallas, as an attorney admitted to the bar of the state of Texas, I'm a de facto officer of the court. If I were to have knowledge of an elderly person living in a potentially dangerous situation, I would be obligated to report it. When I heard my daddy's old friend had moved out of a perfectly nice home and into the old shack out back, I knew I'd best see what was what."

"So he's fine," I said. "And he's not going to lose his temper on me?"

"Trina," Wyatt said slowly, "I cannot guarantee that any more than I can guarantee that anyone is going to lose their temper on another person. However, I will make you this promise. If he does, it will be the one and only time. Got it?"

I nodded, smiling. "Got it."

The front door opened, and Mari peered out. "Grandma is setting the table."

Wyatt jumped up first. "I'll go see if I can help her."

Mari moved back to allow him to disappear inside. I followed at a more leisurely pace. As I stepped past my niece, she grasped my arm.

"Is Grandma okay?" The look on Mari's face nearly broke my heart. She'd lost her mama, and now her grandmother had given her a scare. "Yes, sweetheart, Grandma is fine. Sassy as ever. You should have heard what she told me on the patio this afternoon."

I related the story about the ovens, and Mari started laughing. "Yep, Grandma is just fine."

"Of course Grandma is fine," my mother said from the other end of the hall. Now sit yourselves at the table or you'll lose out on first pick of the chicken."

We both knew she would give first pick to Wyatt, so neither of us hurried. Sure enough, by the time we had settled at the massive rosewood table in the formal dining room, Wyatt's plate was full.

"Mama," I said as I beheld the crystal goblets, china plates, and silver serving pieces she had used for the meal, "you went a bit over the top for take-out fried chicken, don't you think?" I hurried to address Wyatt. "Okay, that did not sound like I meant it to sound. This chicken looks and smells amazing."

"No offense taken," he said. "And I do admit I haven't dined in such a fancy situation since I was at my cousin's wedding out at Old Dobbin. You know the place, Mari? Seems like a lot of people your age are getting married in places like that. This one used to be a watering stop for a railroad. I forget which one."

"I know that place," she said. "You wouldn't believe the location where my friend got married."

That sent the conversation off in a different direction. I was thankful for what I knew had to be an intentional diversion. I'd have to tell him that before he went home.

Later, after Wyatt and Mari left, I cleared the table and began the process of washing the dishes. After a few minutes, Mama joined me.

"Sit," I told her. "I'll do this. You need to keep off that ankle or you'll be wearing that boot even longer."

To my surprise, she climbed onto a barstool on the other side of the counter and settled in. "I am fine," she said after a few minutes.

I looked up and found her watching me, her expression worried. "You believe me, don't you?"

"Of course I do," I said. "You've got physical limitations right now thanks to that ankle you broke, but otherwise there's nothing wrong with you. And as long as you follow the doctor's orders, the ankle will heal."

She nodded. "I know."

Then she paused and appeared to be thinking rather than wishing to speak. I went back to work on the dishes.

After a few minutes, she spoke again. "I didn't mean to set that fire."

"I didn't think you did, Mama," I said gently.

"I forgot I'd put a pie in there," she admitted sheepishly. "I made the first two and had them cooling. I'd had enough pecans for a third pie, so I went ahead and mixed that up real quick and stuck it in the oven since it was already hot."

She paused again, her neatly manicured fingers drumming on the countertop. Then she sat up a little straighter.

"I forgot to set the timer. I went in my sewing room to start pulling fabric for that square-of-the-month quilt I'm doing, and I guess I lost track of time." She shifted positions. "One minute I was trying to decide between tropical colors or a red, white, and blue theme, and the next my smoke detectors were squawking and Hector was howling."

"That must have been scary," I offered. "I'm glad you didn't hurt yourself getting out of the house."

"Me too," she said. "I went looking for Hector and couldn't find him. I walked all through the house calling him, and it kept getting smokier.

Then I couldn't hear him howling over the sound of the smoke detectors anymore. I noticed the back door was open, and I figured he'd managed to escape."

"Mama, I don't think Hector could have opened the back door," I said gently.

"But he can," she protested. "I've seen him do it. He gets up on the cabinet and turns the knob with his paws." She illustrated the maneuver. "I didn't mind. It saved me from having to put in a pet door. I'd already spent enough on his cat-io, so I was grateful for some savings."

Hector, the cat who calls 911 and exits the building on his own. I'd have to tell Wyatt about this. Too bad there wasn't a video of it to add to our collection.

"So I figure the Wrights will be coming for their stuff soon," she said out of the blue.

"Anna said she didn't want any of it," I told her. "But I'd feel better if we had our own things here. Do you think you'd be up to a furniture shopping trip if I hired some guys to pack all of this up and put it in storage?"

Mama grinned. "I'm always up for a shopping trip." Then she sobered again. "What are we going to do about Mari?"

"I don't know what you mean," I said. "Mari seems fine to me."

"Oh she is," Mama said. "But I worry. She's living alone in that apartment. She's young and single. It just seems like your sister would want us to watch over her more than we do."

"Mama, she wouldn't want to move in with us any more than you wanted to move out of your home to live with me. Besides, she's got her friend Cassidy living nearby, and she knows she's always welcome here."

My mother seemed to consider this a moment and then nodded. "You're right. I couldn't wait to have my freedom when I was her age. But will you promise me that you'll make the offer?"

"Does that mean you're willing to stay with me permanently, Mama?"

"Only if you're willing to stay here in Brenham permanently," she responded.

"I'm doing my best," I told her. "I've had a few meetings, and I have my agency clearing my schedule. It'll happen, though I will have to do some traveling."

"Which is why it would be nice to have Mari here."

I dried my hands and reached across to grasp hers. "Okay, Mama, I will talk to her. She'll be back tomorrow to meet with the contractor."

CHAPTER 23

The next morning, Mari and I walked through the building where the rescue would be located. Too big to have been a garden shed and too small for a barn, the wooden structure was just the right size to hold kennels and equipment for the rescue.

Plus it was far off the road, reachable by a gravel road or a trek across the pasture from the main house. That made me feel better about anyone trying anything like that horrid pipe bomb. If someone could find the rescue where it would be hidden, then I'd know for sure that they were targeting it. It was not a place where an accidental bomb would show up.

Only minor changes needed to be made, and those should be done quickly. As eager as Mari was to move in, I was even more eager to have her nearby.

We'd already worked out the details with We Build It Contractors. The site foreman, a skinny guy with the name Heavy Duty embroidered on his shirt, had gone off to the local Lumber Mart to get his supplies while the rest of the team took measurements and made notes.

With the addition of windows for a cross-breeze and fans to help in cooling, the building would be perfect for the pups. There was even a heater that could be turned on if the nights got cold, which rarely happened, but the heat would be appreciated when it did.

"Are you sure you don't want to repaint or add your personal stamp to the interior or exterior?" I asked as I ran my hand over the solid doorframe. "Maybe some pretty vinyl for the floors?"

"It's perfect just the way it is," she exclaimed. "And concrete floors are much more practical."

And Mari was nothing if not practical. I smiled. "I'm glad you let me add the built-in kennels. I think that's a much more efficient use of the space."

"I appreciate that, Aunt Trina. But I worry about the cost."

I grinned. "Maybe I'll raise the rent to pay for them."

Mari wrapped me in an impromptu hug. "You're the best, Aunt Trina."

"Well, I am your favorite aunt," I told her.

"And not just because you're my only aunt," she said with a grin.

This banter had been part of her growing-up years, and I was so happy that it had continued into her adulthood. The joke that I was her only aunt and her favorite never got old.

"Okay, so show me where you're going to put the rest of the things besides the kennels," I said.

Mari walked me through her plan and then beamed. "I just can't believe we'll have storage for food and supplies, fresh water for the dogs, and even a little spot where we can clean them up or have a vet look at them, if needed. There's even a place where a few of the volunteers can gather if we need to meet."

"It sounds wonderful. I'm so glad I'll be close by if you need the help."

"Speaking of volunteers, I have a new one."

She gave me a look. "Dr. Bishop. He's going to help us with assessing the rescues."

"That's great."

"It is," she said, "but it's kind of awkward because apparently Grandma dumped him. Does that put me in the middle?"

"Not at all," I said. "He's a vet, and your rescue needs a vet. Embrace the offer and be happy for it."

"You're right. And he is such a nice man."

"Speaking of Peach Potter." I caught Mari up on my conversation with Mama and finished with "I told her you were happy where you were."

"That's so sweet," she said. "No offense, but I love living in my little apartment with Cassidy just three doors down. And you know how I feel about doing things on my own."

"Sweetheart, you're still young and need your freedom. We'll always have a guest room ready if you want to sleep over."

Mari nodded. "I'm sure I will, especially when you're away and Grandma is alone there." Then she paused. "Aunt Trina, it's so weird to think that you'll be living here. I love it," she hurried to say, "but I'm kind of worried that you've given up a lot to do that. Have you?"

I thought a moment. "I don't know," I finally said. "Time will tell."

That's all I was willing to say to her on the matter. Time would tell. I hoped I'd still have something left of what I built, but if I had to choose, I wouldn't miss another minute of however much time my mother had on this earth, if I could help it.

"I'm also worried that Grandma gave up so easily," Mari said.

Mari had said what I'd been thinking. "I know. Me too. That's not like her."

She scrunched up her nose. "It's totally not like her."

"I'm trying to look at the positive and not think about what she might be up to."

"Good plan," Mari said. "And maybe she really has missed you." She paused. "Can I change the subject for a minute?"

"Sure," I told her. "Go ahead. What's up?"

"It's Cassidy," she told me. "I'm worried about her. She's been skipping out on rescues for a while now. I thought maybe she didn't want to do them anymore or maybe I said or did something that made her mad. She says it isn't either one. I don't know what to do."

I thought of my concerns about Cassidy and wondered if I should share them with Mari. I decided to phrase them as questions instead of stating my opinion.

"Have you ever asked her directly if she's maybe afraid of something?"

Mari looked confused. "What would she be afraid of?"

"That's what you would need to ask her," I said. "But you did have that pipe bomb incident. Maybe that has her spooked."

"I hadn't thought of that," Mari said. "I know everyone made a big deal out of it when it happened, but Cassidy wasn't there. I'm the one who almost stepped on it."

Mari covered her mouth and looked away, obvious signs that she'd said more than she intended.

"Mari," I said slowly. "You never told me that."

She let out a long breath. "I never told anyone that. If Parker knew, he would freak out. Maggie too since it was on her land. Well, her husband's family's land, anyway."

"You almost stepped on a pipe bomb." I said the words, unable to process the meaning of them. "I'm going to need the details, sweetheart."

"Okay," she said slowly, "I mean, since I already messed up and told you it happened, I guess I might as well tell you the rest."

"Yes," I said firmly.

"I was at the rescue checking on a Pomeranian we'd brought in the afternoon before. I didn't know Maggie had brought the dog up to her house for the night. Apparently, Maggie's dog and this little guy had struck up a friendship, so she figured it would be fine for them to hang out in the house together. She texted me that there were no dogs in the rescue building, but I didn't see the text. I walked around inside and wondered why the Pom wasn't in a kennel. It was super early, so I didn't want to call Maggie. I wondered if the dog got out."

She paused and looked down at her feet, then back up at me. "So you went looking for the dog."

"Yes," Mari said softly. "I figured she might have run into the exercise area since it was where we let her run a little before we kenneled her. There are some shrubs and trees in the field, so it would have been easy for her to hide out there. I decided to start in the corner of the pasture and search. That's where I nearly stepped on the bomb. It was right there in the corner by the gate. Right where anyone would walk."

I shook my head. Words refused to come as I tried not to imagine the scene she'd just described.

She paused as tears gathered in her eyes. "I was almost blown up, Aunt Trina. My foot was this close."

I moved fast to embrace Mari before the tears flowed. "But you weren't," I said. "Thank the Lord, you weren't."

Mari held tight to me for a minute longer, then stepped out of my embrace. She swiped at her eyes with the backs of her hands. "Anyway, it all turned out fine. I just wonder if maybe Cassidy is afraid because she saw how upset I was. I couldn't bring myself to tell her or Parker what a close call I'd had."

"Maybe you should," I suggested.

"Maybe," she said.

"But the good news is, you don't have to worry about that anymore. You have a space here that's far from the road and definitely not accessible to strangers unless they're able to get inside a locked gate and past a security system."

A smile rose on my niece's face. "And that is exactly why I agreed to this arrangement. I wanted to do it all on my own like I promised Mama I would, but I won't do it at the expense of putting the dogs or my volunteers in danger."

"Or yourself," I urged.

"Well, yeah, or myself."

The sound of car wheels alerted them to a visitor. "That was fast," I said. "There must have been no lines at the Lumber Mart."

I stepped outside to see Dallas climbing out of his truck, quickly followed by a beautiful golden retriever. "Good morning," I called.

Mari followed me out then gasped. "Is that Old Blue?"

Dallas returned the greeting, then beamed at the dog making circles around his feet. "We call her Penny now, but believe it or not, she's the same old girl I tried to catch all that time. She was so full of brambles and matted up, but look at her now."

I knelt and Penny came toward me. After a moment, she let me scratch her behind the ear. It didn't take long before Penny had approved Mari and me for belly-rub duty.

The minute Dallas said, "That's enough, Penny," the sweet pup rolled to her feet, shook her fur back into place, and walked over to him and looked up with adoring eyes.

"Wow, she really likes you," Mari said.

"Penny is a good girl," Dallas said. "She and I get along just fine. I sure appreciate that you kids rescued her. I'd been trying for a long time and may or may not have ever had any success without your help."

"Dallas, you and Penny are proof that Mari's rescue is doing good things." A thought occurred. "Oh! What if I was able to get an article written about the rescue featuring Penny's story? Do you think that might bring in more donations?" I paused. "And Dallas, would you allow it?"

"You bet I would," he said, patting Penny's head.

"Do you think people would really want to read about us?" Mari asked.

"Why wouldn't they? We get enough bad news. Why not some good news?" I said, warming to the idea. "If we hold off until the building is finished, we could incorporate that into the article. Show people what their donations are going toward."

"Well," Mari said thoughtfully, "I think that's great, and I also think I might know just the reporter to speak with. I met her when my rescue of Beau Jangles made the news." She grinned. "Her name is Mollie Kensington. I'll text her and see what she thinks."

Mari retrieved her phone and stepped away. I smiled at Dallas. "You two make quite a pair."

"I think so too," Dallas said. "I'm wondering if we ought to introduce Penny to your Patsy and Cline. Since they're neighbors and all."

"Great idea," I told him.

A few minutes later, I returned with my two. The trio began a dance of sniffing and snorting but quickly became friends and were soon romping around the property.

"Looks like we've created a pack," Dallas quipped.

"If Penny keeps these two out of trouble, I'm happy with it."

He snorted. "I was thinking it might be the other way around. Though my only complaint about Penny is no matter how much food she gets from me, she insists on eating off the grill next door."

"That probably doesn't make your neighbor happy," I said, remembering the delicious scent of grilling I'd smelled when I'd gone out on the rescue hunt for the dog now known as Penny.

Dallas's face went serious. "I never had a beef with Deke. Say, you don't dress your dogs in those clothes your mama makes, do you?"

"Heavens no," I said. "Neither of them would stand for it, even if I wanted to. I think those work better on little dogs with fewer fashion opinions. Mine are more of the fur-only type. By the time I get home from the groomer, they've already managed to pull off their fancy bandannas."

Mari returned to us and grinned. "Mollie loves the idea. We'll chat next week after she's had time to run it by her editor."

After a moment of celebration, Dallas called Penny and she came running. My two followed at a more leisurely pace. Once Penny was loaded in the truck, Dallas followed to drive away.

Mari was still grinning when I turned around to look at her. "So much is happening so quickly. I can't even believe it."

The next morning, work began bright and early on the rescue building. By the time I went down to check out their progress, the crew had most of the framing done for the kennels and were cutting out the rectangles for windows.

I'd brought Patsy and Cline. As I watched them sniffing around and distracting the crew, I realized this was not the best decision. I shooed them away, and they set off running toward the trees while I retraced my steps across the pasture.

I was almost home when I heard the crack of a gunshot.

CHAPTER 24

I called the dogs and then set off in the direction from which the gunshot had come. Then I heard another shot and picked up my pace.

"Hey, stop shooting!" I called. "There are people over here."

"And there are trespassers over here," a male voice echoed across the trees.

I made my way in that direction, following the path through the trees until I began to smell the familiar scent of someone grilling. Uh-oh. Two missing dogs and the scent of meat on a grill did not add up to a good thing.

At least not for the man who was likely missing whatever he'd put on the grill.

My heartbeat sped up as I stepped into the clearing and spied a man standing on the other side of the fence. The dark-haired fellow was of average height and above-average girth. He wore jeans and a T-shirt with a red baseball cap turned backward. In his right hand, he held a rifle, and it was pointed directly at me.

"Put that gun down," I shouted, picking up the pace as I strode toward my fence with my phone now out. "I'm dialing 911, so you'd better do what I say."

"Hold up there," the man said. Then he lowered his weapon. "I wasn't trying to hurt anyone. Just had some marauders out here stealing from me, and I wasn't about to let that happen."

"Marauders?" I said, stopping at the fence with my phone still at the ready.

"Yeah." He gave me a sideways look. "Do I know you?"

"I'm Trina," I said. "Trina Potter."

"The singer?" At my nod, he grinned. "Well, how about that? I have all of your records."

I kept my smile but groaned inwardly. So much for privacy if I'd moved in next door to a fan.

"I'm Deacon King," he said. "Deke 'the BBQ King' King, actually. Looks like we're neighbors."

"I guess so," I told him. "I hope you don't plan on shooting that gun toward my property again. I'm sure you're a nice guy, but I can't have that. Plus it's illegal."

"I know it is," he said. "I watch that game warden show on cable. No shooting across property lines and no hunting from the road. That's fine for hunting, but this was me defending my property."

"From marauders."

"Yeah, marauders. And trespassers. A couple of black and white dogs intent on taking what I'm cooking."

I shifted positions, my phone still in view. "Did they succeed?" I asked, dreading the answer.

"Not completely. I've still got my ribs, but the string of sausages is gone. You wouldn't happen to know who those animals belong to, would you?"

"Yep. They're mine. Send me a bill for what you've lost, and I'll pay it," I told him. "But if you ever shoot that thing across onto my property, I will be calling the law. Got it?"

The BBQ King stared at me, gloved hands on hips. "And to think I just preordered your greatest hits album." Then he turned and walked away.

I sighed as I tucked the phone in my pocket. I'd have to find the two sausage thieves before they got into any more trouble.

"Hey!" my neighbor called.

I stopped and turned back around to face him. "Yes?"

"I won't be responsible for what happens if those dogs come back here. I'll teach them a lesson, and that's a promise."

"Is that a threat, Deke?" I asked, frowning.

"No ma'am," he answered, a menacing tone in his voice. "It's a promise."

I took the long way back through the woods and pasture, trying to find those dogs. When I hadn't located them a half hour later, I stomped into the kitchen, still upset about the confrontation. "You've got a visitor," Mama said. "I put her in the family parlor."

"We have a family parlor?"

"That's what Dallas grew up calling the little living room off the front hall. The one opposite the office."

"Right."

I headed to the room and found a police officer waiting for me. Mama could have been more specific in her description of my visitor. I put on my best smile and greeted him.

Officer Sam Ferguson rose to introduce himself. "We've had a complaint about shots fired. I'm here to investigate."

"Oh, well, then you're at the wrong house," I said. "The guy next door is the one who was doing the shooting. To be precise, he actually aimed his rifle at me. Would you like a description?"

"Interesting." He opened his notebook and glanced at it, then looked up at me. "Is his name Deacon King?"

"Yes, that's the guy," I told him.

He closed the notebook and tucked it back into his uniform pocket. "He's the one who placed the call. Said he'd come upon a set of. . ." He opened his notebook again. "Says here he called them two 'thieves, marauders, and trespassers.' "

"Of all the nerve," I huffed. "I don't have any guns in the house, and Dallas—he's the older gentleman who lives in the cabin at the back of the property—has only a starter pistol that shoots blanks. Why would my neighbor make that accusation?"

"I guess I'll have to pay him a visit and find out." He stood as if to go, then paused. "You wouldn't know what provoked him, if he is the one who was shooting, that is?"

"Oh, he was definitely the one. I should have taken a photo of him. I had my phone in my hand but was thinking of calling 911, not putting out a social media reel."

"Yes ma'am," he said patiently, "but my question was whether you know why he might want to threaten you. Was there a specific reason or threat?"

Before I could respond, the sound of paws thundering across

hardwood floors echoed outside in the hallway. Patsy came barging in with Cline right behind her.

Each of them had a length of sausages in their mouths.

Somehow I managed to keep a straight face as I said, "Yes, Officer, there was, and it involved these marauders and trespassers."

A few minutes later, the officer left. His follow-up call a short while after that included a warning regarding my thieving trespassers and marauders continuing their covert snacking and a promise that he'd have to give them a citation should it continue.

I didn't ask how a dog might be cited for something, but I agreed to everything he said. I also reminded him that I had requested Deke send me a bill for what he'd lost.

"That ought to close the book on this caper then," he said. "To tell you the truth, this isn't the first time we've had reports of a run-in with Deke. When Dallas lived there, his dogs were regularly in trouble."

"So I've heard," I said. "I'll do my best to keep Patsy and Cline on my side of the fence, and I will have a standing agreement with him to pay for whatever my dogs steal. Beyond that, I don't know what I can do."

"Just a piece of advice," Officer Ferguson said. "Deke's got a temper. He's well-known to us and not just because he keeps us supplied with ribs and brisket."

"Great," I said under my breath. "Well, that's good to know. When I moved out here, I had hoped I was getting peace and quiet."

I hung up and tucked the phone in my pocket, then stared down at the not-so-innocent faces of my dogs. "You two are causing a lot of trouble for me," I said. "Getting shot at is not your finest hour."

Someone knocked on the door, and the dogs dropped their stolen snacks and went wild barking. I stepped over the sausages and went to answer the door, but Hector beat me to it. The cat was sitting on the hall table, opening the door just like Mama said he could.

Once again, I didn't think of filming it until it was over.

A man wearing a shirt with the We Build It Contractors logo on it stood on the porch. "Did that cat just open the door?"

I looked him straight in the eyes and said, "Yes. His name is Hector, and that's one of his many skills. May I help you?"

"Um yeah," he said, eyeing the orange tabby as the cat disappeared down the porch steps and out onto the lawn. "I, um, well, I'm Rocky." He pointed to the name embroidered on the pocket above the company logo. I'm supposed to tell you that the supplies will be delivered tomorrow, and we'll get back to work then."

"Okay, thank you." I made to close the door, but he continued.

"So the guys and I, we were wondering. . . That is, we've got a bet, and so I. . ."

I shifted positions. "And that bet is?"

"Some of them think you're that singer who was from here but is famous now." He shifted positions and met my gaze. "The rest think you're not."

Great. For this reason, I'd had Wyatt purchase the house in the name of the trust where I kept my assets.

"Which way did you vote, Rocky?"

"That singer lady fixes herself up fancy. You don't even wear makeup, and well. . ." He ought to have been embarrassed at pointing out the fact I stood in the doorway looking like I'd just come from a hike in the woods.

Because I had.

Patsy and Cline tired of the two of us and went back for their treats, dragging them past Rocky and out onto the porch. Hector ignored the dogs just as he had been doing since their first meeting. And once the dogs understood that Hector would swipe their noses with his claws if they got too close, a truce was born.

Thus far, it still held.

I remained in the doorway for another moment and then offered the young man a smile. "Better luck next time, Rocky." Then I moved to close the door.

"Dude," I heard him exclaim as he walked away, the door still not completely closed, "you're not going to believe this."

I stalled my movements, now interested in what he would tell whoever was on the other end of the phone. I was used to the reactions of people who met me outside of my hometown, but it was rare to have someone so impressed by me here in Brenham.

"So I'm at that lady's house, right?" he said. "And this is the craziest thing ever. I mean like ever, ever."

I grinned. Goodness, he was making me blush with his enthusiasm over meeting me.

"Yeah, dude. So I just watched a cat open a door. Not lying, dude."

My phone rang, and I answered it without looking.

"Hey there," Wyatt said. "How's your day going?"

"Oh, fine," I told him, moving from the doorway to my favorite rocker on the porch. "So far I've been shot at, threatened by Brenham PD with citations on behalf of a pair of thieving marauders and trespassers, and I just lost out to Hector in impressing a guy named Rocky. How's your day going?"

CHAPTER 25

There was nothing but silence on the other end of the phone. "Wyatt?" I finally said.

"Yeah, sorry. I'm here. I'm just trying to figure out the subtext in everything you said."

"There is no subtext," I told him. "Those things have actually happened. To me. Today."

"I see." I heard his office chair squeak and knew he was at work. "Well then, I guess you've had a busy day."

"It's been an interesting day. I'll say that."

He chuckled. "I was calling to see if you and your mama wanted to grab some dinner with me."

"Oh, that's sweet, Wyatt, but if we do, I would need to be home early. I've got an early meeting tomorrow morning to go over the plans for a concert coming up in the fall."

"No problem. I'm in trial prep all week, so an early night works best for me."

"Okay great," I told him. "Can I check with Mama and let you know?"

"Sure," he said and hung up.

I rose and went looking for Mama. I found her in the little sunroom off her bedroom that she'd set apart for Hector.

"What are you doing in here?" I asked when I spied her peering into the bottom floor of a multistory cat-climbing contraption.

"I was looking for Hector." I helped her stand. "Have you seen him?"

"He's out front with Patsy and Cline," I said. "He opened the door himself."

"And the dogs aren't bothering him?"

"Nope."

She smiled. "See, I told you he was a smart cat."

"Right. Anyway, Wyatt just called. He wants to take the two of us to dinner."

Mama waved away the idea. "You two go ahead. I've got plans."

"Plans?" I gave her a sideways look. "What kind of plans?"

"Stargazing," she told me. "With Howard."

"Howard?" I shook my head, then it came to me. "Howard Nelson? The pastor?"

Mama grinned. "Apparently, he got a little worried about where I stood with him when he heard I was seeing Elvin. He asked me to go with him tonight to look at the stars in a field away from the city lights."

"Mama, do you have any idea how that sounds?"

"Oh, hush," she said. "There's a meteor shower tonight, and Howard is an amateur astronomer."

"Right. Just like that boy who kept asking me out senior year. He always had a quilt in the back of his car because he loved to show the cheerleaders the falling stars. Because what could happen with a girl and a guy lying on a quilt out in the middle of nowhere?"

"Trina, really," Mama said. "You assume way too much."

"Do I?"

"Yes, you do. There's no way Howard or I could possibly get up off a quilt if we were to lie down on it, especially in the middle of nowhere. Maybe if we were twenty years younger, but there's not a man alive who's worth breaking a hip for when the nearest ambulance is miles away."

"Right," I said as I headed out of Hector's lair.

"It'll be chaise lounges in the back of his pickup truck, if you really want to know," Mama called to my retreating back.

"I do not, but thank you, Mama."

Returning to my bedroom, a sunny space on the back corner of the house that looked out over the pastures, I retrieved my phone. This was the first room that saw the furniture removed and stored and then newly purchased antiques brought in from the shops in Round Top.

Neither Dallas nor Anna wanted anything in the home. This felt like a sad commentary on what the past meant to them.

I thought of the old car that Wyatt drove us to prom in as I dialed his number. That old thing had rust on top of its rust, and yet it held a place of honor in his garage. Sentimental value meant something to my old friend.

I liked that about him. But then I liked a lot of things about Wyatt Chastain.

"Sorry, Wyatt. It's going to be just the two of us tonight. Mama has plans."

He made a joke about my mama's popularity, then went off on a tangent about pies that had me laughing loud enough to cause Mama to appear in my doorway. Seeing it was just me on the phone, she shook her head and walked on by.

"So around six, then?" he said. "I'd like to have a look at the progress on that rescue building before we go anywhere."

"I can tell you the progress."

"Okay," he said. "But I still want to see the space."

"All right." I paused. "Is there something wrong?"

"I'm not sure," he said. "We can talk more about it tonight."

I hung up and walked over to the small desk I'd placed in the corner where the light from the windows was best. I hadn't checked my emails since yesterday, mostly because I knew there would be something there that might cause me to have to leave town.

A fitting, a reminder about a rehearsal, a meeting.

There were any number of reasons I might be pulled away from here. It was only the fact that I promised when I left Nashville that I would not let my life in Brenham detract from my career in Music City that had me opening the app and waiting for the emails to load.

Sure enough, there was a fitting and a rehearsal for a television special I'd promised to do, and there was a meet-and-greet for a charity event I'd committed to ages ago. All three were clustered together in the middle of next week. This made me smile.

"Thank you, Olivia," I whispered.

I transferred the information to my calendar, then went shopping for airfare. I set up a flight that got me there in time for the first event and back home the morning after the last one, and then I messaged Mari to let her know when I would be gone.

I spent the remainder of the afternoon with Mama, shopping for furniture online and poring over the catalogs that my mother had collected. Between the two of us, we managed to agree on furniture for several rooms and the back patio.

That accomplished, I dressed for dinner then waited on the porch for Wyatt to pick me up. Mama slid the door open, her expression horrified.

"Why are you sitting out there?"

"Because it's nice out here," I told her.

"My mama told me never to look like I was waiting for a man," she said. "And she was right. Come on inside, and Wyatt can come to the door for you when he gets here."

"Mama, don't be silly," I said, laughing. "I am waiting for a man, and there he is now."

I gestured to Wyatt's truck coming up the driveway. I was still laughing when I climbed inside the vehicle.

"Care to share the joke?" he asked.

"My mother is afraid I look too anxious because I'm sitting on the porch waiting for you," I said as I buckled up.

I slid him a sideways look. He wasn't smiling.

"What?" I said.

"Aren't you? Anxious to see me, I mean."

"Well, of course, but. . ." My words trailed off. "Actually, yes. Very much so."

"Me too," he said with a grin. "In fact, if I had a porch, I would be sitting on it the next time I knew you'd be showing up."

"Thank you, Wyatt," I said in mock seriousness as we turned onto the downtown square. Then I saw a familiar face climbing out of an Uber in front of the Ant Street Inn. "Wait. Stop the truck. Pull over."

He did as I asked and then threw the truck into gear. "What's wrong?" he called as I jumped out of the truck and dodged traffic to hurry toward the inn.

"I don't know yet," I called over my shoulder.

Wyatt caught up at the curb and fell into step beside me as I practically ran toward the Ant Street Inn. "Where are we going exactly?"

"I saw someone I know. He was going that way," I told him. "And that someone should not be in Brenham."

"Is he an escaped prisoner or something?" Wyatt asked. "If that's the case, we ought to call the law instead of trying to apprehend him ourselves, don't you think?"

Ignoring the questions, I stopped at the inn and then opened the double doors and stepped inside. Pausing only for a moment to look both directions, I headed across the polished wooden floor toward the reception desk hidden behind the stairway wall.

I followed the hallway down to the empty ballroom then back again past the empty gift shop and back to peek in the busy Brenham Grill that shared a lobby with the hotel. Determining that he wasn't there, I went to the reception desk and rang the bell. It was better to ask than to try to find his room.

"Trina, you need to tell me what's going on. You're acting kind of crazy right now."

I was, so I didn't bother to deny it. A moment later, a woman stepped out from a back room. "I'm looking for someone who is staying here," I said. "He's a friend, and I just saw him come in. Would you be able to tell me his room number if I give you his name?"

She looked past me to Wyatt. "Are you her lawyer, Wyatt?"

"If need be," he said. "But mostly just a good friend."

The woman returned her attention to me. I'd spoken to her a dozen times when I last stayed here, but at the moment I couldn't remember her name to save my life.

"Okay, what's his name?" she asked me.

"Styler is his last name. First name is Gilbert. Or Sticks."

"Sticks?" Wyatt said. "Really?"

"He used to be a drummer," I told him.

"Right," Wyatt said, shrugging. "Of course."

"He's about this tall." I indicated a height slightly above my own. "And he'll be wearing his hair in a platinum ponytail."

Wyatt's brows went up, but he said nothing. I returned my attention to the woman on the other side of the reception desk.

She looked up from her computer screen and met my gaze. "Styler, you said?"

"Yes, Gilbert Styler. That's Styler with a y."

She shook her head. "I don't have a record of him checking in here."

"But I saw him come in," I protested.

"Maybe to eat at the restaurant?" she offered. "It's right there, and people use our lobby for access."

"I checked," I said on an exhale of breath. "He wasn't in there."

"Thank you," Wyatt told the woman. Then he grasped my elbow and moved me away from the desk. "Come on, Trina. Let's go."

I wriggled out of his grasp. "Not until I check upstairs."

"Is that all right?" Wyatt asked the woman, but I was already heading that way.

Apparently, she didn't mind, because he bounded up behind me a moment later. The wide center hallway was more ornately decorated than the lobby down below.

Elegant groupings of comfortable furniture were situated along the carpeted space while chandeliers glittered overhead, and beautifully framed art shone beneath spotlights on the walls. I heard Wyatt's low whistle.

"Wow," he said. "This is something."

"You've never been up here?" I asked him over my shoulder.

"No, just downstairs on my way to the ballroom or the restaurant. This is fancy."

"It's beautiful," I said. "I've stayed here a few times."

Though I was tempted to knock on every door, I didn't. Instead, I sagged onto one of the overstuffed sofas and rested my chin in my hands. Wyatt settled beside me.

"Okay," he said gently, turning my face toward him. "Tell me what's going on, Trina. Who is Gilbert the Stick Styler?"

"Sticks," I corrected. "And he's my producer."

"Why would your producer come to Brenham?" he asked.

"I have no idea," I told him, "which is why I wanted to find him. See, he was vocal that he wanted me to keep my home base in Nashville."

"And just who is he that he gets to determine where you live?" Wyatt demanded.

"He's the one who put me on stage and recorded me when I was a nobody. I owe him loyalty," I said, "but not to the point where my family is neglected."

Wyatt nodded but otherwise kept quiet as he gently settled me against him. I leaned in, resting my head on his shoulder, suddenly feeling very tired.

"Twice I tried to get my team on board with the idea of me moving here. The first time around, it was a total bust. After Mama fell, I knew things had to change, and if it meant my career suffered, so be it. That's when I bought the house."

"That turned out to be a better idea than you expected when your mama burned her kitchen up," he offered.

"It did," I said. "When you called, I went into panic mode. The only person I notified about my plan to drive to Texas to see to Mama was my agent, Olivia. She said she'd handle everyone else. I thought she had."

"But seeing your producer here makes you think she hasn't?"

I let out a long breath. "I don't know, Wyatt. I really have no idea what him being here means. If that was him. I'm having my doubts now. I mean, I could have sworn it was him. But why would he check in under any name but his own? It's not like people here would know him and swarm the hotel or anything."

I sat very still, pondering all the reasons why I shouldn't be concerned about Sticks coming to Brenham. Then I began ticking off the reasons why I should. Before I realized it, I had nuzzled against Wyatt's neck and was enveloped in his arms.

Where I felt safe.

And it felt wonderful.

I looked up at him and caught him looking down at me.

And then he kissed me.

CHAPTER 26

We left the inn a few minutes—and a few kisses—later. Out on the sidewalk, Wyatt grasped my hand, and I smiled up at him.

Somehow we'd left my house as friends, and after just one kiss everything had changed. Not really, of course. Honestly, I'd been contemplating what a kiss from him would be like ever since he called me sweetheart on that text that day in Nashville.

Now I knew. And I absolutely was not sorry that I knew.

We walked without speaking until we got to the truck. Ever the gentleman, Wyatt opened my door for me and waited until I got in. Then he turned me toward him and kissed me again.

"I just had to see if it was real," he said.

"Nothing inside counted?" I said.

"All of it counted," was his response. "But there's something about a kiss in the moonlight."

I looked around. It wasn't even dark yet.

"Um, Wyatt," I said.

"I know," he responded with a grin. "But a guy can imagine. Maybe I'll get one before I take you home?"

"Maybe," I said, matching his grin. "But right now I'm starving. I'm guessing you had plans to go somewhere nice, but would it hurt your feelings if I suggested somewhere else?"

"Like where?" he said warily.

"Dairy Bar?"

"If I hadn't already kissed you, I would now. Dairy Bar it is." He ran around the truck and got into the driver's seat, then closed the door. "Just one caveat. You need to understand this important fact."

"Okay," I said, laughing at his silly attempt at seriousness. "What's that?"

"I do not share my fries. If you want fries, you're going to have to get your own. That's a rule," he said as he started the truck. "So if you can't abide by that rule, tell me now."

When I stopped laughing, I said, "I promise to abide by the rule. But I have one that you're going to have to abide by."

He made a face as he shifted into Drive. "Do tell."

"I never kiss a guy who's had onions on his burger."

Wyatt shot me a glorious smile. "Duly noted. There will be no onions on my burger tonight, and that is a promise."

We had a great time at the Dairy Bar. True to his word, Wyatt did not order the onions on his burger. Unfortunately, I couldn't help stealing one or two of his fries, although he was a good sport about it.

The sun was just teasing the horizon when we headed back toward my place. The crew had been busy working at the rescue site when we left for dinner, so I asked him if he would like to see it now.

"Sure," he said, and bypassed my driveway to head toward the gravel road that led to the rescue building.

We stopped with the headlights still on and illuminating the future headquarters of Mari's rescue. Stacks of building materials were situated on one side of the structure, and tools were on the other.

Wyatt walked the site, occasionally pausing to study something more closely. Then he came back to where I stood leaning against the truck.

"What do you think?" I asked.

"That you're even more beautiful by truck light." He leaned down to kiss me just as something crashed inside the building. I jumped and so did Wyatt.

He snatched up a flashlight from the door of his truck and went looking for the cause of the noise. I followed at a safe distance.

Wyatt was almost to the door when the figure of a man stepped into view. "King?" Wyatt said. "What are you doing here?"

Deke King held his hands up as if he was about to be arrested. "Just looking around, I swear," he said. "I was at the feed store this morning and heard there was going to be a dog rescue built here. I figured I'd see it for myself."

"Now you have," Wyatt said.

"And you've trespassed," I told him sternly. "I certainly hope you haven't thieved or marauded."

Wyatt looked at me like I was crazy. In that moment, I sort of was. How dare this man who'd only just this morning pointed a gun at me show up at my niece's rescue building?

"Leave," I told him, my voice shaking. "Just go now."

"And don't let anyone catch you back here," Wyatt said. "I know you've shot at a dog before, so you being here on the premises is suspicious."

"I didn't mean anything by it, I swear." He inched his way past Wyatt to address me. "I was wrong to aim that rifle at you."

"What?" Wyatt snapped.

"It's okay," I told Wyatt. "I handled it."

"Well, anyway, I'll just walk back home now," Deke said to Wyatt before turning back to me. "And we'll forget that you owe me for sausages."

"Send me the bill anyway," I told him.

"And close the lid on that grill, man," Wyatt said. "There's no need to be offering that kind of temptation. Those dogs don't understand that what's smelling so good isn't theirs for the taking."

"That's no excuse," I said. "But Wyatt is right. If it's an ongoing problem, and not just from my dogs, then maybe there's more than one solution."

Deke shook his head. "Closing the lid impedes the smoking process. It's a technical thing that you two amateurs probably wouldn't understand, but the bottom line is a closed lid makes for an inferior product."

"And an open lid makes for missing product," Wyatt said. "I don't blame the animals." He paused. "Weren't you just leaving?"

"I was," Deke said, heading off down the road.

"Come on," Wyatt said, helping me into the truck.

He pulled the vehicle onto the road, shining his lights on Deke King's retreating back. When the neighbor had disappeared into the woods that edged the fence line, Wyatt drove me home.

"He pulled a rifle on you, Trina? A rifle?" Wyatt said when he'd brought the truck to a stop in front of the house.

"Just the one time," I told him. "And to be fair, I told you I'd been shot at this morning. It was just wedged in there between the Brenham PD threat of citations and the guy who thought I wasn't fancy enough to be the real Trina Potter. That guy will be back with his buddies tomorrow to do the work on the rescue building, by the way, if you want to go yell at him too."

Wyatt slid me a sideways glance. "You really did tell me that? About the rifle?"

"I really did," I said as I slid my hand across the distance between us to touch his shoulder. "I say brilliant things, Wyatt. You should hang on my very word."

He grinned. "Okay, now you're just messing with me."

"Yes, I am."

He unbuckled his seat belt and climbed out. I did the same, and we walked toward the front door together.

This time when he kissed me, it wasn't a surprise. We were still kissing when someone turned on the porch light.

"Mama?" I said as my mother's face peered out of the partially open door. "You were supposed to be out looking at stars."

"And I will be," she said. "But apparently the best viewing time is the middle of the night. Howard will be here soon." She looked from me to Wyatt then back to me again. "What?"

"You turned on the porch light, Mama."

"I sure did. Reminds me of back when you were in high school."

"I'm getting a little of that vibe now," Wyatt whispered in my ear. "Thinking it's past your curfew. I'll call you tomorrow." He looked toward Mama. "Good to see you again, Mrs. Potter."

And off he went to his truck while I was left to wander back inside and wonder what in the world happened tonight. Did we just fall in love, or had that been simmering since senior year?

I had no idea. But I planned to find out.

The next day, I spent the morning at my computer working on the business side of my music career. Mama was on hold with the insurance company again, so I made a sandwich and poured some iced tea and called it lunch.

After lunch, I took my sheet music out onto the porch to practice the new music I needed to learn for an upcoming awards show. Hector let himself out. Crossing the patio, he settled in a patch of sunlight and promptly fell asleep.

I hadn't been sitting long before I spied three dogs making their way across the pasture. Two were mine and the other was unmistakably Penny, formerly known as Old Blue.

I watched as the dogs played a bit and then parted ways, with my two picking up speed as they neared the open gate of the backyard. A gate I doubted my mother had opened. And I knew I had not.

Patsy arrived first, as usual, but when I looked up again, Cline was nowhere to be found. I called him twice before he showed up.

Curious, because it was usually his sister who ignored me to do what she pleased. Cline finally arrived. In his jowls was a bone.

"What do you have?"

After a brief battle, I retrieved the bone from him and examined it. The unmistakable scent of barbecue smoke clung to the thing, as did enough evidence of meat to allow me to determine that this had recently been on the grill.

"Cline," I said with a groan. "You're going to cost me a fortune."

Patsy sat quietly as if indicating she was the good sibling. I figured she was probably just the smarter one and had buried her bone out in the pasture.

The next day was a repeat of the one before, minus Penny. Two dogs enjoying themselves in the pasture and then my two returning home with evidence they had once again raided Deke King's grill.

I left the scoundrels inside and went into town to the hardware store to buy locks. I had no proof, but if neither Mama nor I were leaving the gate open, that cat was the likely culprit. I resisted the urge to ask for something cat-proof and selected a few that looked like they might be.

It was there that I met up with Rocky from the contracting crew. He had a big paper sack in his arms and didn't appear too happy to see me.

"Hello, Rocky," I said genially. "Did they run out of something at the jobsite?"

"Something like that," he said, then tossed a twenty-dollar bill onto the counter and hurried out without collecting his change.

"I'll bring it to him," I told the clerk. "His crew is working on my property today."

I paid for my purchases, then walked out into the afternoon sunshine. I'd just climbed into my car when I spied Rocky hurrying across the parking lot with the bag tucked under his arm. Intent on saving myself a trip to the jobsite, I snatched up the cash that belonged to Rocky and climbed out of my car.

"You forgot your change," I said, catching up to him.

"Oh, right. Thanks." Rocky looked over his shoulder, then back at me. "I need to go now."

"Sure," I said, following the direction of his gaze.

After Rocky left, I walked over to the car that sat at the end of the parking area. A man with white hair pulled back into a ponytail sat in the driver's seat looking down at something, possibly a paper sack.

I was just about to turn and walk away when the driver looked up and spied me. "Sticks?"

CHAPTER 27

My producer looked at me like he'd seen a ghost. It took him a full minute of staring at me through the glass before he reacted and lowered the window.

"Hello, Trina," Sticks Styler said casually, tucking the paper sack under the seat beside him.

The car, a generic white sedan, was obviously a rental. Sticks would never be seen in anything other than his very British Range Rover or one of his sports cars.

"What are you doing here?" I demanded.

"If I said I came to Texas to try to convince you to come back with me to Nashville, would you believe me?"

I gave him a sideways look. "Normally, I would. But because you've phrased it as a question, now I'm wondering if that's the truth."

"Good catch." He grinned. "Okay, well, maybe I've found another Trina Potter and I'm going to make her a star."

"Not likely," I said. "I'd vote for the first one over the second. Look, you had to know you were going to run into me eventually. Brenham is a small town. Why all the cloak-and-dagger stuff? And don't tell me that wasn't you hiding in the Ant Street Inn when I spied you the other night."

He drummed his fingers on the steering wheel. "I don't know what you're talking about."

"You saw me and ran," I said.

Sticks sighed. "Okay, I did see you, and yes, I wasn't ready to speak to you just yet. Oh, and by the way, you were getting quite chummy with that Texan fellow in the upstairs lobby."

Wonderful. My sweet first kiss with Wyatt happened with this guy somehow watching.

"Sticks, everyone here is a Texan," I said, hoping to derail the direction the conversation appeared to be going.

"Well, maybe I'm here because I wanted to see what kind of place Texas was. I mean, if you're so attracted to it, then maybe it's worth a look."

I waited for Sticks to crack a smile. He did not.

"Okay," I finally said. "Well, you've seen me, and you've seen Texas. You've had your look."

"I have." He paused. "You need to go back to Nashville, Trina."

"Okay, now we're getting somewhere," I said. "That is why you're here. Admit it."

"I have. The logistics just work better when you're at hand, Trina. Just the other day I had a session free up, and I thought I'd get you in to do some recordings. Nope. Cannot do that. Trina is in Texas with her cowboy."

"Wyatt is not a cowboy," I said tersely. "He's an attorney."

Sticks threw up his hands. "Brilliant. Another lawyer. Just what I need."

My phone buzzed, and I retrieved it to glance at the screen. My messages indicated I had a text from the ATF agent.

I tucked the phone back into my pocket and returned my attention to Sticks. "I understand that you would like me close by so you can arrange impromptu studio sessions and generally have me on your short list of singers to call on."

"The arrangement has worked nicely for you in the past too."

It had. On more than one occasion, being close by had secured gigs for me that I might never have gotten otherwise. And more than one of those studio sessions had resulted in a gold record.

Essentially, I owed Sticks a debt of gratitude for his belief in my talents. I wouldn't have the career I had without him.

But I did not owe him my soul.

"Sticks, I appreciate you more than I can say. You're the best. Truly.

You made my career, and I plan to keep my promise to be where I need to be when I need to be there. I've just spent the morning in meetings, and I've got more set for tomorrow."

He tucked a platinum strand of hair behind his ear. "I'm glad to hear it."

"I'm keeping my promise to you, but I'm also keeping a bigger promise to my daddy to look after my mama," I told him. "As much as you've done for me, you cannot trump that one."

Sticks inhaled deeply and then exhaled, all while staring straight ahead through the windshield, presumably at the cars passing on the street. Without looking back at me, he nodded.

"I get it," he told me. "But I also think the solution is to move the whole family to Nashville." Then he turned my way. "Is it bigger percentages you need? Have Olivia call me. We can talk about that."

"I've told you, Sticks," I said. "Even if I could get my mother to leave Texas, which I am 99.999 percent certain she will never do, I have my niece to consider. Her late mother was my sister, and I'm her only family. She's got roots here, and she's started this amazing dog rescue that she's passionate about. And she's really good at what she does. I'm not going to mess that up for her."

"No, I heard you were actually encouraging her," he muttered.

"I am," I said firmly.

"Fine. You want something nice for your niece to use for her dog thing? No problem." He was gesturing wildly, a true sign that I'd gotten him riled up. "We can do the Taj Mahal of doggie palaces if that gets you back to Nashville. I'll find stray dogs myself and send them to your niece for care, if that makes her happy. I just need this madness to end."

"Sticks, stop." I paused. "It's not madness. It's Texas."

His expression hardened. "Right at this moment, Trina, it's all the same."

"Look, why don't you stop by while you're here? Come and see where I'm living. Mama will bake a pie for you. I'll introduce you to Mari and her volunteers."

He shook his head. "I'm not going to change my mind. Nashville is where it's at, and you need to be there."

"Tell that to Willie Nelson," I said with a grin. "He lives an hour and a half from here down Highway 290, and he seems to be doing okay."

Sticks glanced around and then back at me. "This isn't Austin, and you're not Willie Nelson."

"I'm not going to argue with you," I told him. "I respect everything about you except for your taste in cars and your opinions about Texas." I retrieved my phone and sent him a text with my Brenham address on it. "I hope you'll stop by while you're here."

"And I hope you'll come to your senses," Sticks said.

"I think I have," I told him.

"Right." Sticks shrugged. "Okay then. If you change your mind, I am, as you know, staying at the Ant Street Inn." He shook his head. "And I thought London had odd street names. Anyway, I'm in the Galveston suite. If you need to know which one that is, it's the one with the excellent view of the sofa where you were snuggling with your lawyer."

"Fine," I said, giving him a look that told him this Texan wasn't budging. Nor was I happy about his comment on my snuggling.

"Fine," he responded. A moment later, he backed out of the parking spot and drove away.

It was only after he'd gone that I realized I hadn't asked him what was in the paper sack or why it appeared he knew Rocky from the construction crew.

I returned to my car and started the engine. The afternoon was hot, and standing in the sun in the parking lot talking to Sticks had improved neither my mood nor my temperature.

With the cold air blowing on my face, I read the text from Agent Mendez.

NEW INFO. CALL ME.

I placed the call on the hands-free, then sat back and waited for it to connect. "Mendez."

"This is Trina Potter. You told me to call."

"Potter, right." He paused, and I could hear paper shuffling in the background. "So there's new findings. Something odd that might be an anomaly or even contamination from the crime scene."

"Okay. What's that?"

"I'll skip the technical names and summarize," he said. "We found traces of several chemicals that, when added together, are only present in one thing: hair dye."

"Interesting," I said.

"More specifically," he continued. "Platinum hair dye."

"So let me see if I understand. There were traces of these chemicals on the bomb? Could it be what set it off?"

"No," he said. "There was another combination of chemicals used for detonation. The chemicals I'm talking about were strictly outliers. Essentially, they did not belong there. I went back to the records and contacted anyone who was in the chain of possession in case there might have been contamination from that source, but I came up with nothing."

"How would this stuff get on the bomb?"

"That's the mystery. The only way that I can see it happening is if the person handling the bomb or its parts allowed it to come into direct contact with platinum hair dye. And I'm talking about the professional grade dye, not the box stuff from the drugstore."

"So we're looking for a beautician with a grudge."

"Essentially," Agent Mendez said. "Know anyone like that?"

"I don't," I said, though at least two platinum blondes came to mind, and neither of them liked the fact that I had returned to Brenham, Texas.

"Is there any way to know when the bomb was built or how long it had been in the field?"

"Impossible to determine time frame with just fragments we have. However, the reports say the bomb was in thick grass, so we can assume it was well hidden both from the road and from the structure where the dogs were kept nearby. The choice of chemicals used meant that the bomb was relatively stable."

"So it wouldn't have exploded if someone stepped on it."

"Oh, it probably would have," he said, "but it wouldn't have just gone off with no one around or if someone just moved it. Basically, it could bounce some, say in a car or in a padded container, but the metal used will bend. As soon as pressure is applied, like stepping on it or hitting it with something, the bomb goes off. It's not sophisticated, but it works most of the time."

"Okay," I said, trying not to recall Mari's admission to me that she'd almost stepped on the thing.

"Is that all?" I asked.

"For now," he said. "Though frankly I don't know that we'll get anything else from the tests we're doing. I'm surprised we got what we did. The discovery of residue of platinum hair dye gives us something specific that we didn't have before."

"One more thing, just so I'm clear. The dye would have to be transferred directly to the metal or something inside the bomb, right?"

"Yes."

"Does the dye have to be fresh? Could you have your hair dyed at the beauty shop, come home and make a bomb, and somehow transfer the chemicals to the bomb because you, oh, I don't know, ran your hand through freshly dyed hair?"

"Unlikely," he said. "I'm only reading the report, and I'm certainly not the chemist doing the analysis, but my understanding is there would have to be actual hair dye on the hands or splattered on the device. And it would have to be in sufficient quantities to coat some of the pieces enough to where traces would remain after the device was detonated."

"Okay."

"You're thinking of someone."

"More than one person," I admitted.

"And you'll share the names when you're more certain they are suspects?"

I agreed that I would, and then we hung up. I sat there in the parking lot of the hardware store, digesting these new facts. What did they mean?

Wyatt's office was nearby, so I headed there in hopes he might share a legal pad and pen so I could work all of this out. He was in court, but Desmond handed me the supplies I requested and led me into the conference room. I took a place at the large granite-topped table and went to work. By the time Wyatt joined me, I had several pages of scribbling but nothing that made sense.

"Okay," he said as he gave me a quick kiss on the cheek and then sat next to me. "What's going on? Desmond said you were in the middle of something important."

I filled him in on the conversation with Agent Mendez and then showed him my work. "I've got two suspects: Bitsy and Sticks."

Wyatt chuckled.

"What?" I said.

"Come on, Trina. Neither of these sounds like a bomber. Bitsy and Sticks? Sounds like a girl band from the nineties."

"Be that as it may," I continued, "those are my suspects. Neither of them wants me here."

I told him about the conversation I'd had with Sticks a short while ago.

"So you were right about seeing the drummer guy. He was in town."

I nodded, choosing not to tell him what the "drummer guy" saw while we were upstairs. "And he's vocal about me returning to Nashville."

"Why? You're keeping up on your end of the commitments, aren't you?"

"I am."

He loosened his tie. "Then he needs to chill. It doesn't take a lawyer to know you cannot require someone to do more than they are contracted to do."

"I get it, but family comes first. I'll leave the music industry before I abandon Mama and Mari. It's not like it was when Vanessa was alive. She took care of things, and I checked in when I got a chance." I paused, determined not to let the tears gather. "I missed a lot. I won't make that mistake again."

Wyatt swiveled his chair toward me and grasped me gently by the shoulders. "Trina, do not do this to yourself. Your sister, rest her soul, sent you off to be a star while she was her own kind of star here in Brenham, taking care of your mama and her daughter."

"Yes, she was," I managed.

"All right, so we're going to start over with a clean sheet of paper and see what we can figure out with what you've just learned, okay?"

Together we drafted a timeline of the incidents that happened from the time the bomb was detonated until now. Then we sat back and stared at the results.

"The bomb went off three days before the Christmas parade," I said. "Bitsy was obviously in town, but Sticks wasn't."

"No," Wyatt said, "but he knew you would be here, didn't he?"

"Definitely."

"You said his goal is to get you to bring your mother and niece to Nashville. Why not do something to convince you that someone you love was involved in something dangerous? That would get you convinced that she needs to move her work elsewhere, wouldn't it?"

I gave that some thought. "In theory, yes, but if his intent was to frighten us, why is it he has never mentioned the bomb? Wouldn't it make more sense if he was bringing that fact up to me regularly? We just had a heated argument, and he never once said anything about it."

"Yeah, I agree. Doesn't rule him out, but it makes me wonder. He's got motive, but did he have opportunity?"

"He's got money and a private jet," I offered.

"That's easy to check on," he said. "Isn't that how you got here for the parade?" When I nodded, he continued. "I'll check the flight records for the days before you used the jet. It should be easy to see if the same plane you flew in on had been here before."

"And if it hasn't?"

"Then we're pretty close to ruling him out. It's already a stretch, Trina. I mean, you're expecting someone to have wet hair dye on their hands and handle a bomb? Who does that?"

"I know, but that's the clue we've got." I paused. "Okay, so Bitsy. Thoughts?"

He cringed. "Yeah, Bitsy stays on the list."

"Because you two were together while I was in town for the parade?"

"We were not together in the way you're meaning it. She's an old friend. I'd just done her divorce, so we'd spent time together on a professional basis, but that's all."

"I believe you, but would Bitsy characterize the relationship the same way? She wants me gone so she's got a clear shot at you. Why are you smiling?"

"Sorry." He affected a serious expression, but it only lasted a moment. "Oh, come on, Trina. Let me have my moment. Back in high school when I was an awkward band nerd, I would never have believed that one day I would have two cheerleaders fighting over me."

CHAPTER 28

I gave Wyatt a look. "Really, that's what you get out of this conversation about who might have planted a bomb?"

"Right." His expression sobered. "Back to the facts. The bomb was found three days before the parade."

"Mari almost stepped on it," I said softly. "She admitted that to me recently."

"I didn't know that," he said slowly. "And I guarantee she didn't tell Parker, or he wouldn't have skipped it when he was telling me about the dangers they've faced. Maybe that's why Cassidy is reluctant to go with them."

"Because Mari told her?" At his nod, I continued. "Maybe so. But back to Bitsy. We've got motive. But honestly, Wyatt, do you see her making a bomb on her own?"

"Maybe her stylist doubles as a bomb maker," he said, then waved away his own comment with a sweep of his hand. "Forget I said that. It was a terrible joke. This is serious."

"It is, but seriously, I think she would have to have had help somewhere if it's her." I paused. "You know her better than me. Is there something you learned about her during her divorce that makes all of this make sense?"

He met my gaze. "Well, her ex is a hairstylist, so there's that."

"Wait. What?"

Wyatt retrieved his phone and opened a social media app to show me Bitsy's ex. "The details are protected by attorney-client privilege, but part of the arrangements involved who got custody of the hair extensions. Not kidding."

The man on Wyatt's screen did not look anything like a hairstylist. Rather, he appeared to be one of those outdoorsy types who loved to hunt, fish, play golf, and generally look more manly than the average guy. He also had a preference for tank tops and, upon closer inspection, tanning and tattoos.

"He's a hairstylist?" I said.

"Yes, and one whose haircuts start at $350 and go up depending on the service." He paused. "It was those extra services that ended him up in trouble with his wife, if you know what I mean."

"Gross," I said.

"But apparently he's got his own line of extensions and fake-hair products under the name of Joey Bananas Enterprises. He was about to hit it big when he was served with divorce papers. Everything got put off, per Bitsy, until the divorce was over. She claims he did this so he didn't have to share any profits with her."

"That's dirty," I said. "But not a reason for her to plant that bomb. Or him to, for that matter."

"And I negotiated a settlement that addresses that situation, so it ended up handled favorably for Bitsy but not so much for Joe."

"Okay, so we've got Bitsy and her husband on the list, but Bitsy is mad at me, and Joe is mad at Bitsy. Why would he work with her to do this?" I asked, and then I had the answer. "Of course. He agreed to help her scare me out of town so that the way would be clear for the two of you, and in return she gives up her interest in his hair stuff."

"Maybe," Wyatt said, "but how do you explain that the bomb went off before you were here? It's one thing to hear it happened. Wouldn't it have been a stronger incentive to be affected by it if you'd been here and actually seen the crime scene?"

"True," I said. "But this is Bitsy, so who knows?"

"Do you want me to talk to her about this?" Wyatt asked.

"What would you say? Hey, did you or your ex ever plant a bomb? And to be more specific, did you do this while you had platinum hair dye on your hands?"

"Basically, yeah." Wyatt shook his head. "Do not underestimate the legal training, Trina. I cross-examine people for a living. I could get an answer to that question, no problem."

In that moment, I had no doubt Wyatt believed he could. However, I couldn't resist taking a dig when it was so easily offered to me.

"How many of them have you in their sights as their next husband?" I asked, trying not to laugh when his expression changed to shock.

"Well, when you put it like that," he finally said. "That would narrow it down a bit. But I could still get some information."

"Okay," I said. "I'll let you decide how you're going to handle that. For now, we have a list of two viable suspects and one with motive but who may not have been in town when it happened."

"Yeah," he said. "That's what it looks like to me."

"Okay, I've never researched plane records. Do you know how it's done?"

"I do," he said. "I just make a call to the airport and ask." He shrugged. "I've done some legal work for just about everyone in town."

"Including someone at the airport who can answer the question about whether the record company jet made more than one appearance in the area?"

"Exactly."

"He might have flown into Houston or Austin," I challenged.

"Not a problem," he told me. "I'll find out. It's all about the IFF number. The FAA keeps track of those things."

"Okay then," I said as my phone rang.

"Go ahead and take the call," Wyatt said. "I'll be in my office checking on this IFF number. Just come on back when you're finished."

I answered the phone and was greeted by someone speaking so rapidly that I couldn't understand him. "Slow down," I commanded. "I don't know what you're saying."

"Okay," a man said, "I am at your jobsite. That little dog office that's going up?"

"The rescue operation location," I offered. "Has something happened?"

"Yes, right. So we were working on the roof, and Rocky was in his truck, and then out of nowhere a tree. . ." His voice tapered off.

"What happened with a tree?"

"It fell," the man said. "On Rocky. The ambulance is on its way, and the cops are coming. I figured you'd want to know."

"I'm on my way." I snatched up my purse and headed down the hall to Wyatt's office. He looked up as I opened the door. "There's been an accident at the rescue."

In a matter of seconds, we were out the back door to the spot behind the office where Wyatt parked his truck. Desmond followed us out.

"What about your appointments?" he called.

"Reschedule them," he said. "There's been an emergency."

I hung on tight while Wyatt drove. We arrived just as the ambulance was leaving. I jumped out as soon as the truck came to a stop and headed for the first police officer I could find.

It was Officer Ferguson. "I didn't think I'd see you again so soon," Sam told me as we both surveyed the damage.

A huge tree lay half-buried in the cab of a red pickup truck. I could see from the damage to the vehicle that someone had pried the door open enough to remove Rocky.

"I just saw him at the hardware store a few hours ago," I said. "If that long."

"What was he doing?" he asked.

The question took me aback. "Buying. . ." I realized I didn't know what was in his bag. "Well, buying something. He was in a hurry to leave and went off without the change from his purchase. I offered to take it to him since I knew where he was working."

"Do you still have it?"

"No," I said as I watched what appeared to be a crime scene team marking the ground around the crushed truck. "I saw him in the parking lot a few minutes later and gave it to him there."

Sam wrote all of this down in his notebook. I turned to watch the crime scene officers move from the truck to the tree, walking the length of it until they reached its base.

"Ferguson," one of them called. "Come look at this."

Wyatt moved to stand beside me. "That tree was cut," he said.

"How do you know?"

"While you were talking to the cop, I went and looked at the base of that tree. From a distance, mind you. I don't do much criminal law, but I know enough to be respectful of a crime scene." He lifted his phone to show me a photo of the base of the tree. "Look at that."

Clearly someone had cut that tree precisely to cause it to fall on the jobsite. If poor Rocky's truck hadn't been there, the tree would have split the rescue building in half.

But who? And why?

Sam Ferguson was back with his notepad open again. After a nod and greeting to Wyatt, he turned his attention to me. "Miss Potter—"

"Trina," I corrected.

He nodded. "Trina, do you own a chain saw?"

"Me personally? No. However, I've only lived here a short while, and I inherited a lot of things from the previous owner. It's possible that you would find at least one in one of the outbuildings. Probable actually. You're welcome to search."

"Okay." Sam made a note.

"As Trina's lawyer," Wyatt said, "she's giving you permission to do a search of her property because she has no knowledge of any use of a chain saw or any other type of saw on trees on this property."

"Yes," I said. "That's right. In fact, I have no knowledge about most of the things in regard to this property."

"What about Dallas Wright?" Sam said. "Would he know?"

"I'm sure he would," I said. "He grew up here."

"And still lives on the property?" Sam said.

"Yes, the cabin in the back is his for as long as he is alive," Wyatt interjected. "And for the record, Dallas is my client as well, so I will need to confer with him if you're going to want to search his portion of the property."

Sam smiled. "Then you might want to go speak with him, because these guys are looking to build a case against whoever placed a cut in that tree such that it fell on that man's truck."

"Well, I guarantee it wasn't either of us," I told him. "And my guess is it was my niece's dog rescue building that was the intended target, not Rocky's truck."

"Agreed," he said. "But who would want to ruin an empty dog rescue building?"

Wyatt and I exchanged glances. "How much time do you have?" I said to Sam.

We made arrangements to meet back at my home after Wyatt was given time to speak with Dallas about the search. I climbed back in the truck with him, and we headed off in that direction.

"I'll drop you off and then go see him," Wyatt said. "As your lawyer, I need to remind you not to say anything that might incriminate you."

"There's no danger of that," I snapped. "I certainly didn't cause that accident today."

He pulled the truck over in the driveway and leaned across to give me a kiss. "Not what I meant," he said. "Just answer whatever questions they ask to the best of your ability. Don't guess and don't embellish."

"Wyatt, you act like they are going to suspect me."

"No, I act like a lawyer because I am one. Of course they're not going to suspect you. What purpose would you have to pay someone to renovate a building and then turn around and smash it?"

"Okay," I said. "Duly noted."

"Exactly." He grasped my hand and brought it to his lips. "I'll be back as soon as I can. Go tell your mama to get busy baking pies. Apparently, that's what she does when first responders show up."

"Hush," I said with a laugh, knowing that was exactly what she would do once I told her what was going on down at the rescue site. "I need to call Mari first. Then I'll go in and break the news to Mama."

I made the phone call to my niece, telling her gently that while her building was fine, a man was in the hospital and his truck crushed. Then I waited for her reaction.

"Oh wow," she said. "That's awful. And all from a tree just randomly falling. I guess that's a hazard of being in the woods."

I had a choice in that moment of correcting Mari or allowing her to think, at least for now, that this was an accident. Without any proof to the contrary just yet, I elected to choose the easier path for Mari.

"Yes, who could have predicted it?" I managed. "I just wanted you to know. There's no need to come down here. In fact, the police have it taped off for now, so I don't think you'd be allowed in anyway."

We spoke for a few more minutes, and then I went inside to tell Mama the news. As Wyatt had predicted, she hurried to the kitchen.

A half hour later, Wyatt returned. His expression told me something was wrong.

"The police have confiscated a chain saw," he said.

"Why the long face? We figured they would find one somewhere on the property. Why wouldn't we have one given the acreage?" I said.

"Agreed," he said, "but the one they found was under Dallas's bed."

"So?" I said. "Let the man keep his things where he wants."

Wyatt nodded. "Normally, I would agree with you, but the police found it suspicious. So they confiscated the saw to test the blade and see if it matches the cut marks on the tree." He paused. "And they took Dallas in for questioning."

"Oh no. Shouldn't you be with him?" I asked.

"I'm going, but I wanted to let you know what's happening."

"Okay," I said. "But did he give you any reason for why he hid a chain saw under his bed?"

Wyatt frowned. "He said he didn't put it there." He paused. "But there's more."

"What else?" I said, dreading the answer.

"Remember when he complained that his daughter had taken his guns away?" At my nod, he continued. "Apparently, they were also under his bed."

I let out a long breath. "What do you make of this?"

"I don't know," Wyatt said, sadness in his eyes. "It's still my belief that Dallas is as sharp as a tack, but he cannot explain how a stash of guns ended up in his cabin, and when you combine that with a chain saw that might have been used to cut down that tree, well, it doesn't look good."

CHAPTER 29

The contractors returned to work the next morning, minus Rocky, who was still in the hospital but expected to make a full recovery. Wyatt spent most of the evening and into the night at the police station, but ultimately Dallas had been allowed to go with him under instructions not to leave town.

"Where would I go?" he asked me as he sat on our patio enjoying a slice of Mama's apple pie.

"What do you think happened with those guns, Dallas?" my mother asked as she sat on the bench sewing sequins on a dog tutu.

"I wish I knew, Peach. Anna took them away from me several months ago. It was our last big fight before I moved permanently into the cabin. I'd been staying there off and on before, but when she took all my guns and said I wasn't stable enough to have them in the house? Well, that was the last straw."

"Couldn't you have just gone and bought more?" I asked him.

"Why would I do that? These were heirlooms. My daddy's guns and his daddy's guns that were used to provide food for the family back in their times. I'm not much of a hunter now, what with the H-E-B just down the road. But I'm not going to let somebody tell me I can't keep them, especially not my daughter."

"That's right," Mama said, sliding a sideways glance at me. "Sometimes these children of ours treat us like we are the children."

"I do not do that, Mama," I said.

"No, of course not," she responded, though I could have sworn a look passed between her and Dallas.

"I'm just glad they let me go," Dallas continued as he took a sip of sweet tea. "I like sleeping in my own bed, and those cells are not the most hospitable."

"No, they're not," Mama said.

"How would you know?" I asked my mother.

Her brows rose. "It was just a little misunderstanding and nothing I intend to discuss with my daughter." She turned her attention to Dallas. "Why did they let you go? Did Wyatt convince them they had the wrong man?"

"He told them what I've just told you. That these were valuable family heirlooms. Then he told them to send a man back to my cabin and see if they could find the bullets that went with them."

"And did they?" I asked.

"They did not," Dallas told me. "Because those firearms haven't been shot since John F. Kennedy was president. Maybe even before that."

"And the chain saw?" Mama asked before I could.

"When a man doesn't have any weapons that will fire, what do you think he will do if he's threatened by an intruder?"

"Call 911?" Mama said.

"Threaten them with a starter pistol?" I put in.

Dallas grinned at me, then shook his head. "Neither. I find a chain saw can sound big and bad without being dangerous at all. But when you're in my cabin in the middle of the night, I'd rather the intruder think it's going to be the end of him."

"Why wouldn't it be?" Mama asked.

"Because I keep the guard on the thing unless I'm cutting a tree," Dallas answered. "Everything works and it's loud as can be, but the blade doesn't spin. All the bark without any bite."

"Speaking of," Mama said, nodding toward the pasture and the three dogs—two black and white and one cream-colored—racing toward us with Deke King running behind them. "I can't see that far. Does that fool have his rifle out? If he does, I'm going to be the one calling 911." She looked at Dallas. "Since your chain saw has been confiscated, that is."

"No," I told her. "He's just running. No weapons visible."

Mama sighed. "Then you'd better go get your checkbook, Trina. My guess is they got into sausage again, but it could be steaks. I don't see bones, so that rules out ribs."

Dallas stood and retrieved his wallet. "Let me."

I shook my head. "No, it's my turn. You paid last time."

"I'm beginning to think this is a money-making scheme," Mama said.

"I'm beginning to think we should stop buying dog food," I told her.

Just before they reached the yard, my two dogs veered off toward the front of the house. Only Penny returned.

"Must be someone out front," Mama said. "Probably more delivery boxes. At least I hope so. I'm almost out of tulle, and I've got a big order of extra-large doggie bridal wear to get out by the end of next week."

"I'll go see." I got up and went through the house just as the doorbell rang. I opened the door, and there stood my producer. "Hello, Sticks," I said as my dogs danced around him, begging for his attention.

"May I come in?" was his response.

I opened the door wider and gestured for Sticks to enter.

He glanced around as he walked inside, then looked back at me. "Kind of sparse decor," he said.

"I'm working on it gradually," I said. "As you can see, I've left everything back in Nashville. There never was a plan to completely move away from there, Sticks. I've told you that."

Another look around the entry hall, and then he returned his attention to me. "I need to confess something, but I'd rather not do it in a hall. Is there a place we can sit?"

The last thing I wanted my mother to hear was another recitation of all the reasons why my career would be ruined if I stayed here with her. I wasn't about to give her any reason to go back to her own home and pretend she was fine alone.

I considered the choices available to me, all of which would be rooms that my mama could easily come visit. However, if I took Sticks out on the porch, she'd assume I was conversing with the UPS guy and leave us alone.

I motioned for him to follow. We settled on porch rockers and then sat quietly for a moment. I watched the dogs play and then eventually wander off.

"I have to admit this is peaceful," Sticks said. "And it would be easy to get used to."

Silence fell between us again. Finally, I'd had enough.

"I doubt you've come here to enjoy the peace and quiet, Sticks. Why are you here?"

He gave me a sideways look. "Because I figured you wouldn't come to me."

"I just talked to you yesterday," I said. "But you're right. I wouldn't."

"Look, I'm going to level with you. You and I worked great together. There was a chemistry there that was magic. You sing like an angel, Trina, and I knew how to get the best out of your voice."

"I notice you're speaking in past tense."

"I am." He paused. "Because all of that happened spontaneously. Remember, you'd text me at all hours and say I've got an idea and I'd meet you at the studio, whatever time it was. We made magic in those sessions, Trina. Just you and me while everyone else was asleep."

I smiled. "We did. And we still can."

"We can't," he said. "It doesn't work like that. I can't schedule a meeting with you a week or a month ahead of time and expect that the muse will show up then too."

"I think it can."

Sticks balled his fists and pressed them hard against the arms of the rocker. "Just move back to Nashville and end this madness. I'll get with Olivia and sign whatever she puts in front of me. Just come home. Bring half this town if you want, but come home. You're the face of my record label. My muse and my friend, Trina. I don't want to make music without you."

I settled my thoughts. "This is my home, Sticks," came out on an exhale of breath. "Find a building here in Brenham, put in your dream studio, and we'll keep making records together at all hours of the day and night. And maybe we will finally finish that chess game."

"I can't do that," he snapped.

"You can," I said calmly. "You just refuse to try it."

Sticks stood and stared out across the property in front of him. Then he turned to face me. "Nashville has everything that this little town has and more."

"It doesn't have the Second Chance Ranch Dog Rescue team, Sticks. Or my mother, or my crazy neighbor who is making a fortune off my dogs stealing whatever he's grilling. It doesn't have a lighted Christmas parade or the Round Top Antiques Weeks or the Royer's Pie Haven, now does it?"

"You're not making sense, Trina."

"I'm making perfect sense, Sticks. Yes, I miss texting you in the middle of the night when song lyrics occur or watching you mix sounds to produce something that sounds even better than what I had in mind. But I don't miss Nashville." I paused. "I'm serious. Give Brenham a chance."

I hoped he might soften, but as I watched his face, I could see his mind was made up.

"Sit down," I told him. "I'll get some sweet tea and a slice of Mama's pie, and we can talk about a song idea I've had for a while."

"Sorry, Trina," Sticks said. "I'm not signing any new contract with you while you live here."

"You cannot dictate where I live. You know that."

"Not directly," he said. "You're right about that. But I know what works best for you and me, and if it's the last thing I do, I will show you that you'll never be as happy here as you were in Nashville."

I laughed. "How are you going to do that?"

He stared down at me, anger flashing in his eyes. But he said nothing.

"You've felt this way for a while."

"So what?" he snapped.

My anger rose. "So I'm wondering if that 'last thing you do' thing includes putting a pipe bomb outside of the rescue shelter, Sticks. Do you know anything about that?"

His anger faded, replaced by confusion. "What are you talking about?"

I told him. "Did you do that? Because I've got an ATF guy who tells me that traces of platinum hair dye were found on the remains of the exploded bomb."

His eyes narrowed. "Hold on. A bomb exploded near your niece's rescue shelter? Was anyone hurt?"

"No," I said, "though Mari almost stepped on it." I told him the details, including when it happened and how the device was found.

Sticks sat back down. "Oh, Trina. I'm sorry."

His reaction surprised me. Then he swiveled to face me.

"You said platinum hair dye was found." At my nod, he continued. "So the combination of that and the way I've been blustering about like a madman trying to get you to do what I want you to do. . ."

"Has me thinking exactly what do you mean by 'the last thing you'd do'?"

"I'm an idiot," Sticks said, "but I would never harm you or any of your family. You have my word on that. You didn't tell me you wanted to move until you came back from here. And if it's platinum hair dye that you're thinking is the connection to me, then you're wrong." He reached around to tug on his ponytail. "This is all natural. I started turning gray in my teens. People in Nashville think I do this because I'm making some sort of statement or want to stand out, but actually it's just the hair I was stuck with. So if you're looking for someone with hair dye, it's not me. Although I have considered a nice honey blond or maybe blue black like Batman."

"Oh please don't," I said, laughing. "I like you just the way you are."

And as I sat there watching him watch me, I realized I believed him. I told him so, and he smiled.

"Come on, Sticks," I cajoled. "Come to the dark side. Get some property in Brenham. We'll make music together. But I warn you that my niece is very persuasive. She'll have you helping her with her dog rescue or, at the least, convincing you to adopt a dog."

"I've never had a dog," he said. "I think that would be nice." He stood again. "I should go."

A thought occurred. "Do you have plans for the rest of the day?"

"There are meetings scheduled. Why?"

I grinned. "I can't show you the lighted Christmas parade because it's summertime, but I can give you the guided tour of Brenham. What do you say?"

Sticks matched my grin. "Considering I'm the boss and can cancel any meeting I called, I guess I do have some time this afternoon. But don't think you're going to convince me to move here. It's a tiny, ridiculous little town that reminds me of the village where my gran lived. Nothing to do, nothing to see, and more cows than people. Well, in Gran's case it was sheep, but the point still stands."

I spent the remainder of the afternoon giving my English record producer the grand tour of Washington County, Texas. When he complained of hunger, I called Wyatt to meet us at the Dairy Bar.

We'd just settled at a table—the guys with their cheeseburgers and fries and me with my chili pie—when my phone rang. It was Mari.

"Hey, sweetheart," I said. "We were just digging in at the Dairy Bar.

How about I order you something and you can join us? Parker too if he's with you. I would love to introduce you to Sticks. He's my—"

"Aunt Trina," she said, her voice laced with panic, "it's Cline. He's been hurt. Parker and I are rushing him to the vet clinic now."

CHAPTER 30

"What happened?" I said as we all piled into Wyatt's truck.

"Parker and I decided to drive out to see the progress on the building. When we got there, there was no one working. I didn't think that was weird, but Parker did. Anyway, we got out and walked around, and that's when we found Cline."

"He was in the building?"

"Behind it," Mari said. "In a trap."

"What kind of trap?" I said, dreading the answer.

"The kind that trap animals," she said. "It only caught him on one leg. I'm pretty sure the doc is going to say it's broken. We've got him, and Tyler knows we're on our way. He'll be in good hands. But you can thank Dr. Bishop for getting him out of the trap."

"Dr. Bishop?"

"He was here when we got there," Mari told me. "He said he was there to visit Grandma but heard a dog in distress and went looking for the sound."

We arrived at Lone Star Vet Clinic at the same time as Mari and Parker. I flew out of the truck to help the kids get my precious Cline inside and settled on the exam table. Then Tyler announced we were to wait in the waiting room.

Mari and Parker both stayed with the vet to assist in surgery, but Mari hugged me before letting me go out of the room to wait. "Cline is in good hands, Aunt Trina. He'll be fine."

Cassidy joined us with cups of coffee for everyone. "This is Cassidy.

She's the office manager here and also a member of the rescue team."

When Sticks responded with a greeting and thanks for the coffee, she grinned. "I love your accent."

"I love your accent," he said in return.

"Are you new to Brenham?" Cassidy asked.

"Just visiting," Sticks told her, "although Trina is waging a campaign to get me to stay awhile."

"If I had to choose between England and Brenham, I'd take England." She looked at me. "No offense."

"None taken," I said. "It's a great place to visit. Unless your gran lives in a place with more sheep than people."

Cassidy gave me a confused look.

"Actually, I live in Nashville," Sticks told her, ignoring me. "Have you ever been?"

As those two fell into conversation, I leaned against Wyatt. Together we prayed for Cline and for the doctor's hands as he put my sweet dog back together.

When the waiting room clock struck six and the door to the doctor's surgery hadn't opened, Cassidy excused herself from the conversation and went to lock the clinic doors and close up. After she'd completed her closing procedures, the office manager returned to the waiting room.

"So I need to go feed and exercise the dogs," Cassidy said. "Else I'd stay. I noticed you all came in together. Do any of you need a ride home?"

I looked over at my producer to tell her he likely was ready to go. However, Cassidy was already smiling in his direction.

"I can drop you off, Gilbert," she said. "Where are you staying?"

"I'm at the Ant Street Inn," he said, "but I'm in no hurry. I would love to meet your dogs and perhaps have a bite to eat with you after the canines have their dinner?"

Cassidy flushed. "Sure. That sounds great. Let me get my purse."

I looked over at Sticks and grinned. "You two have fun."

"Hush," he said. "I'm still not moving here."

"If I were a betting man," Wyatt said, "I would wager that not only are you moving here, but you're going to end up with one of those dogs. I know for a fact she's trying to rehome one of them, and it's a cutie."

"She is a cutie," I said to Sticks. "But seriously, you behave with

Cassidy, or you'll have me to answer to. I will not have her heart broken by you."

"I am wounded," he said dramatically. "I am not that type."

And he wasn't. I knew that. If he had been, I certainly wouldn't have let Cassidy leave with him.

"There goes the best chance you have of your record producer moving to town," Wyatt said. "They seem to have hit it off."

I snuggled against him, and he wrapped his hand in mine. We were still sitting like this when Tyler came out flanked by Mari, Parker, and Dr. Bishop.

We both stood. "How is he?" I demanded. "Can I see him?"

"He's going to be fine," Tyler said. "We had to do some work on his leg, but thanks to the quick thinking of Dr. Bishop, he won't lose the leg."

I offered the elder veterinarian a hug. "Thank you." Then I went down the line hugging all of them: Parker, Mari, and finally Tyler.

"You can peek in on him for just a second," Tyler said. "But he's sedated, so he won't know you're here."

He nodded to Mari, who grasped my arm. Together we stepped inside. Smells of antiseptic assaulted my nose as I held Mari's hand and tiptoed toward my sleeping pup. Cline was hooked up to all sorts of tubes, and one of his back legs was bandaged.

Tyler and Dr. Bishop came in to stand behind me. "Prognosis is good," Tyler said. "He will limp for a while, maybe always, but he will be up and running again."

"When?" I asked.

Tyler deferred to Dr. Bishop. "Hard to say. I don't know how long he was trapped, but from the wound I would guess not long."

"And there was no one at that jobsite?" I asked, confused.

"Just him," Dr. Bishop said.

"Okay," Wyatt said, linking arms with me. "Let's get out of here. When can Trina visit again?" he asked.

"First thing in the morning," Tyler said. "Kristin is taking the early shift, but I'll brief her on Cline's condition before I leave."

"And I will keep them both updated overnight," Parker said.

"You're staying with him?" I asked as gratitude flooded my heart. "Thank you."

He grinned. "It's what I do."

"And he's sending me home," Mari told her, "because it was my turn last night, and we had several in here. Not much sleep was had by animal or human."

We piled out of the operating suite and into the lobby. "Thank you all so much," I said again as Wyatt led me out of the clinic. I didn't fall apart or cry until I was safely buckled in and on my way home.

"Take me to where it happened," I demanded when we arrived at my home.

Wyatt complied, and a few minutes later we were standing at an empty construction site. The fallen tree had been cut down, and the timber was stacked neatly at the edge of the clearing. A glance into the rescue building showed that there had been progress despite the fact that no one was there this afternoon.

What made no sense, as I scanned the scene before me, was why a trap had been set here. And worse, who had done it?

We returned to the house to find Mama in tears. I explained that Cline would be fine, but that didn't calm her.

"It's not just that sweet dog," she said. "It's Dallas. They've gone and arrested him."

"For what?" Wyatt said.

"Acts of vandalism meant to cause harm," Mama recited from the note in her hand. "The chain saw was a match to the one used to smash that truck, and the old trap that hurt Cline had Dallas's fingerprints all over it."

I sank down on the nearest chair and rested my head in my hands. "Why would he do all of this?"

"He wouldn't," Wyatt said. "He's being framed."

I looked up at Wyatt. Sweet Wyatt who was Dallas Wright's friend and lawyer.

"You would have to say that. He's your client. But the evidence doesn't lie." I paused. "I was warned that he had a temper. I saw it for myself on that rescue."

"You saw a scared old man confronted with strangers on his property after dark," Wyatt said firmly.

"Anna told me she didn't think he was dangerous, but now I'm not so sure."

"Anna." Wyatt said the name with disgust. "She's behind this. Mark my words."

"Why would Anna do any of this? There's no reason for it. You said yourself that the money I paid for this property was put into trust for her. She can access it at any time. The only thing she can't do is remove Dallas from the property, and that is my fault."

"What?" Wyatt said. "Are you now thinking that you've made a mistake giving him the life estate? You wouldn't have this land without it."

"Rocky and Cline wouldn't be hurt without him being here. And who knows? Maybe he built the bomb too. Was he just a rancher all his life, or did he do anything else?"

Wyatt looked reluctant to speak. Then he fixed me with a look that told me he wasn't happy about the answer he was about to give.

"No, Trina," he said, jaw clenched. "He specialized in oil field explosives and ran a custom gun shop on the side. The old gun shop is what was in the building you're renovating."

I gave him an I-can't-believe-you stare. "Explosives and guns," I said evenly. "That explains everything except the bear trap."

"That was likely left over from the days when we had brown bears here," Mama interjected. "My granny would tell tales of the bears getting into mischief. They didn't actively trap them. Mostly they would shoot into the air, hoping they'd move along. But sometimes, especially if an animal was sick or rabid, those things were used."

I sat very still, taking all of this in. Then I looked up at Wyatt. "I know you're Dallas's attorney, so this is a huge conflict of interest for you. But I want to know if it's too late to reverse this purchase I've made."

"It is," he said tersely.

"But I can sell," I said.

"You could," he agreed, "but what about the dog rescue? Are you willing to leave it now that you've almost got it up and running?"

"You mean the rescue that has almost been smashed by a tree? The place that caused my dog to be lying in a hospital right now?" I paused to calm down. "There are other places. I just need to find someone who will buy this one with Dallas on the property. Or, failing that, I need Dallas to sell and move out."

"He's not going to move. I can guarantee that."

"It's not going to work any other way," I said. "I lost a sister. I refuse to lose anyone else. Not on my watch."

Wyatt seemed to be considering his response. Then he shook his head. "I need to go see about bailing Dallas out."

"I wish you wouldn't," I told him. "Leave him there where he can't hurt anyone else."

He stood very still, and I thought he might respond. Instead, Wyatt turned and walked out.

CHAPTER 31

Mama moved over to sit beside me, placing her hand on my shoulder. At the sound of the door closing, Patsy bounded in from who knows where. She stared up at me for a moment, then pressed her head to my knee. I scratched her ears and tried not to cry.

"I know this looks bad," Mama finally said, "but I cannot imagine Dallas doing the things that they claim he has done." She paused. "And if you think of the man we've come to know, I don't see how you can believe it either. What would Dallas have against Mari's rescue? Thanks to her, he has Penny."

"I know, Mama, but the facts are the facts. You heard what was said. How can you come to any other conclusion?"

The question of the platinum hair dye niggled at my mind, but I pushed it way. Despite that one outlier of a fact, everything fit nicely into place. With further investigation, surely that could be explained as well.

"Time will tell," Mama said. "Meanwhile, don't you think you should call his daughter? She ought to know what's going on with her daddy, and I guarantee Dallas isn't going to call her."

I glanced at the clock. "It's late. Maybe I should wait until morning."

"If it was your daddy, wouldn't you want to know now instead of in the morning?" she asked.

I nodded in agreement. "What's your impression of that feud?" I asked, an idea forming.

"My impression is you've got two stubborn people who are a lot alike. Neither of them can see the other one's point of view."

"Did you know Anna's mother?" I asked.

"Not well, but we were cordial. She was much younger than Dallas, so it was a shock when she took sick and died while Anna was just a little girl. Dallas was lost, and I expect so was his daughter. It's been all these years, and neither of them have found their way back to the other yet."

"Maybe it's time they did," I said, picking up my phone.

"What are you up to, Trina?"

"Just calling Dallas's daughter like you suggested."

She waited a minute, then moved toward the door. "I'll go check and see if Penny needs food or water. I don't know that Dallas got to either of those things before the police came for him."

"Take a flashlight and use the golf cart, please."

Just a few days ago, Wyatt had shown up with a golf cart for Mama. He'd claimed he was worried that her pies wouldn't travel as well by hand as they would on that cart. Where they would travel other than over to Dallas's cabin or the rescue, I hadn't a clue.

But my mother was thrilled with the gift, and I was grateful. She was still in the boot from her fall and still arguing with the insurance company over how and when her house would be repaired. With this cart came one more incentive to stay where she was, here with me.

Anna picked up just as the door was closing behind Mama. I greeted her, apologized for the late hour, and briefly told her what had happened, carefully leaving out my anger at what had been done.

"Oh, Trina," Anna said, tears in her voice. "I'm so sorry. I could have prevented all of this, and I didn't. You have every right to be furious at me."

"No," I said quickly. "I'm not furious at you. I just thought you ought to know what was happening here. His lawyer is headed to the jail now, intent on bailing him out."

"I wish he wouldn't," she said. "I don't see that he's safe to return home. I knew I should have pressed for that guardianship, but Daddy seemed like he was all right. I promise you that if I'd had any inkling of this, I would have told you that day we met in Nashville. I would have warned you."

"You've been nothing but honest," I said. "And we did talk about your father's anger. I made this decision on my own, and now I'm the one who has to figure out how to fix it."

"What are you going to do?"

"I'm not sure," I said. "My lawyer says the contract I made with your father cannot be undone. This is all really new. It just happened. But my first thought is to put the place up for sale."

"I understand," she said. "Though you may have trouble finding another buyer with my father living back there."

"I might," I said, "but I'm willing to risk that. I lost my sister last year, and I won't let the family I have left be harmed."

"I'm so sorry. I've tried for years to convince him to stay with me. As you know, that effort has failed miserably." She paused. "But maybe there is another way."

"What would that be?"

"My attorneys have told me that I either need to get Daddy into a guardianship or I need a power of attorney to be able to handle his business affairs. As of now, I don't have either."

"I'm not sure how I can help with that."

"If he was given a choice of remaining where he is but with me in charge of him, would that make you feel any better?"

I thought a moment. "Right now, no. Sorry."

"Okay, I see your point," she said. "Then really there's nothing other than selling that will work for you."

"Yeah," I said. "And I really don't want to do that because I love it here. But I don't have any choice, do I?"

"I'm the wrong one to ask. I never wanted to live there."

"Right."

"Thank you for letting me know about this. I'll see what avenues are open to me on my end, but I doubt my attorneys will have any advice that they haven't already given me." She paused. "And I'll be praying that if you do sell, the right buyer comes along."

"Thank you," I said and hung up.

Now what? I went into my room and retrieved the notes that Wyatt and I had put together. After scratching my producer's name off the list of potential suspects, I wrote another below it: Dallas Wright.

Then I sighed. The facts did not lie, but I sure did like that man. Well, I liked him once he'd sat on my patio sipping sweet tea and complimenting my mama on her pie-baking skills. I hadn't liked him at all when he was pointing a pistol at us.

A starter pistol, I reminded myself. After we'd shown up in the dark of night unannounced and with flashlights shining in his face. When I thought of it that way, I had a hard time thinking I wouldn't react the same way.

Beside Dallas's name I added a note about him being an oil field explosives expert and gun shop owner. Then I sat back and looked at our work.

There were two suspects on this list: Dallas and Bitsy. With this new development in regard to the rescue building, Bitsy was almost ruled out. She did have a connection to the residue on the bomb that was undeniable, but nothing that had happened since then could be tied to her.

Were they in this together? And if they were, what was the goal? To run me out of town and Mari and Mama with me? I could see Bitsy thinking she'd benefit from that by having Wyatt all to herself, but what was Dallas's benefit?

He had what he wanted right now. The cabin and adjoining property were his for the rest of his life. There was no one bothering him back there. No one who had any kind of interest in what he was doing.

Well, not completely true. Anna cared, or at least I got the impression she did. But she cared from a distance, figuring out her plans through her lawyers without wanting to actually do anything in person or by herself.

I wasn't judging her. Taking care of a family member who didn't think he or she needed care wasn't for wimps. And if you add in being busy with work, traveling for your job, and living in a city an hour and a half away, that complicated things even more.

Plus she'd never lost a sister or made a vow that she wouldn't lose anyone else.

I stopped myself. "She lost her mama, idiot," I whispered. "So maybe this is just her way of playing the hand she was dealt."

I took another look at the list and considered Bitsy's place in all of this. I couldn't imagine her building a bomb, but anyone could find instructions online for just about anything. I couldn't rule that out. And now that she didn't have her hairstylist husband to do her hair, did she do her own? I had no idea nor any thought of how to find out.

Oh. Of course.

The next morning, I picked up the phone and called Bitsy. "Trina. What do you want?"

I ignored the terse greeting and plowed forward. "I know we didn't end our last conversation in the best way, but I have a problem and I figured you were the one to go to about it. See, I need a hairstylist here in Brenham, and since you always look so good, I thought you could give me the name of the person you use."

Silence.

"Bitsy?"

"I'm here."

More silence.

"I really need a cut, and I'm considering a new color. Where do you get yours done?"

"Sorry, I can't help you," she snapped. Then she hung up.

"Okay."

Either Bitsy didn't have a stylist to recommend, or she didn't want me going there. Time to get creative.

It took a full half hour to call every hair salon in Washington County, but when I was done, I knew one thing for certain. Bitsy Decker did not get her hair done anywhere nearby.

I added that to the list and then scanned the rest of the page. Wyatt was going to check whether the record label's jet had been in the area before it brought me here for the Christmas parade, but with Sticks no longer a viable suspect, I scratched out that action item.

What else stood out in all of this? Then I had it. If the crew had been working on the rescue building when Cline wandered through, that accident wouldn't have happened. Surely someone would have removed the trap if they'd seen it.

Mama was at her hair appointment, so I secured Patsy inside to keep her safe and took the key to the golf cart. Before I closed the door behind me, I stared at the tabby cat staring at me from his perch atop the cabinet over the sink.

"And don't you let her out, Hector."

A few minutes later, I pulled up on the jobsite. Because the golf cart was silent, none of the workers realized I was there until I announced myself.

To my surprise, I spied Rocky wearing a neck brace and hammering shingles on the new roof that was going in. He sat his hammer aside and climbed down to greet me while the others continued working.

"It's good to see you," I told him. "How are you feeling?"

"I'm okay," he said. "My neck's a little stiff, but it'll heal."

"I'm terribly sorry that happened to you," I told him. "A man has been arrested for cutting that tree, you know."

"Oh, yes, I know." He looked around then leaned close. "But he didn't do it."

"What? Why would you say that?"

He gave me a sly smile. "Because I hear things and I see things."

Like you heard that tree that fell on you? I wanted to ask. Instead, I said, "Like what?"

"Okay, it's fuzzy because, well, I've had a head injury. But I can tell you that there's this guy who doesn't want you to live here." He shrugged. "Something about it being inconvenient."

"Late thirties with white hair? Just a little taller than me? British accent?"

"I don't know." He shook his head, then winced as if the action had hurt. "Maybe. Why?"

"Because he's a friend of mine. We worked all of that out."

"Right." He shrugged. "Then I guess it's all okay."

"Seems to be." I paused. "So, that day in the hardware store, what were you buying? You seemed to be in a hurry."

He gave me a confused look. "I don't know."

"You don't remember what you bought? You left so fast that you forgot your change. I gave it to you in the parking lot."

Another confused look, this one slightly less believable than the previous one. "You know, it's funny. I don't remember anything that happened leading up to the accident. My only recollections that day are getting up and getting ready for work and then waking up in a hospital bed with some nurse apologizing because whatever she was about to do was going to hurt."

"Nothing at all?"

"Nope." He paused. "Well, fuzzy things. Like that conversation I told you about. It's in here somewhere, but I can't make it come into focus."

He pointed to his forehead.

I went over that interaction in my mind then tried again. "Do you know a man named Gilbert Styler? He also goes by Sticks."

"Sure," he said. "My wife had a crush on him when he was in that boy band back in the day. Played a mean set of drums, but I thought the long white hair was kind of silly."

"Would you remember if you saw him that day at the hardware store?"

Rocky gave me an incredulous look. "Sticks Styler in Brenham at the hardware store? That's as crazy as a cat named Hector that can open doors."

I walked away from the conversation more confused than ever. I'd ruled out Sticks, but was he truly out?

Basically yes. Though it was possible he could have paid Dallas to do what he'd done. But how did Bitsy and her platinum hair dye fit in?

It was all so confusing.

Then I recalled the real reason for showing up here. "Rocky," I called. "Who would have been in charge here while you were recuperating?"

He shrugged. "You'd have to call the office. I don't know, other than it wouldn't be any of these clowns."

I made a mental note to place that call when I got back home. First, however, I completed my tour of the jobsite, noting that the renovations were nearly done.

The interior smelled like wet paint, so I kept my hands close by my side as I walked to the back of the space, then made an attempt to open the door to check on the kennels. It stuck, so I had to yank hard before I could get it open.

That's when I spied the bomb.

CHAPTER 32

I backed out slowly, my phone in my hand. Then, realizing I didn't have a photo of the thing, I took just enough steps forward to capture a shot of it before backing out of the building.

"Everyone needs to leave now," I said, my voice as calm as I could manage. "Pick up your tools carefully and move out of the area."

Rocky stormed up and waved away the men who were obeying my command. "Do not listen to her. I'm the foreman on this jobsite, and it's not near quitting time." He turned to look at me. "No offense, ma'am, but there's work to be done here."

"Right," I said. "But there's just one problem. There's a bomb in there."

At the word bomb, the crew scattered to pile into their van and flee. It was only after Rocky and I stood there alone that I thought I very well might have allowed the person responsible to get away.

"That's not funny," he said. "I needed them here to finish the trim work. Now I have to do it myself."

I looked up from dialing 911. "Rocky, I think that head injury has made your thinking a little slow. There is a *bomb* in there. It is in the back of the building where the kennels are. I don't know how much of that you're understanding right now, but nod if you get the fact that this place could blow up."

"Oh, I get it," he said with a nod. "But nobody's been back there in a long time. Last man I caught in there was—"

"Hold that thought," I said as the 911 operator answered. I gave her the information and held on until she made arrangements for first responders. "If Sam Ferguson is available, he's been out here and knows where the building is. Otherwise, I'll send someone out to the road to meet the officers."

"Ferguson is available, so I'll send him," she said. "Meanwhile, evacuate the area, please, but be in a place where officers can find you."

"Already done," I said. "It's just the construction foreman and me, but we're moving to safety now. Tell Officer Ferguson he can find us up at the house that's on the property. He'll know where I mean."

After I hung up with the operator, Rocky and I drove up to the house and settled onto the porch. After declining my offer of a glass of tea, Rocky turned toward me.

"So that bomb," he said. "Are you sure it's a live one? I mean, just because it looks like a bomb, that doesn't mean it is one."

"I hope it's not," I said. "But let's go back to what you were telling me about having caught someone in the building. Do you remember who it was?"

"Yeah, that barbecue guy," he said.

"Deke King?" I said, recalling when Wyatt and I had also caught him in there.

"Yeah, that's the guy. Deke 'the BBQ King' King."

"When was that?"

"A couple of days ago," he said. "We'd finished that part of the building and had the door closed so we wouldn't get paint in there. It sticks, but it's on the punch list to fix."

"I noticed," I said.

"Well, anyway, we got to the jobsite and there was someone stuck inside there. I had to let him out."

"Did he have a reason for being there?"

Rocky lifted a shoulder in a half-hearted shrug. "He said he was just looking around to see the progress. Then he left."

That's what he'd told us too.

"Did you notice whether anything was missing?"

He shook his head. "There was nothing to go missing. It was just a room with kennels in it. What would he take?"

Good point.

My phone rang just as I spied Sam Ferguson walking up the driveway.

I glanced down at the screen and saw it was Wyatt. "I can't talk right now," I said when I answered.

"So you're still mad at me." A statement, not a question.

"Actually, I'm about to speak to a policeman about the bomb I just found at the rescue building, Wyatt. It's not a good time."

"I'm on my way."

"No," I said, but he'd already hung up.

I stood and welcomed the police officer. Rocky gave Sam a more reluctant greeting.

"We keep meeting like this," Sam Ferguson said to me. "Tell me what happened this time."

"I drove over on the golf cart to see the progress on the renovations. When I got there, I talked to Rocky and then went inside. The door stuck, so I had to yank on it. When it opened, the bomb was there on the floor."

"That's all?"

"Should there be more?" I said.

"She's telling it just like it happened," Rocky said. "We were talking, and then she sent my crew away and told me there was a bomb."

"About that," he said to Rocky. "I'll need a list of the names of your crew."

"Sure," he said. "I'll call the office and get that for you."

"While you're at it," I told him, "ask who was filling in for you on the day the bear trap hurt my dog."

"Right." Rocky stood up and moved to the far end of the porch to make his call.

"I'm starting to think you've made someone really angry, Trina," Sam said. "The question is who?"

"That's a question I've been trying to figure out," I told him.

"I saw that Dallas Wright made bail. Do you think he's responsible for this?" he asked.

"I think it's possible," I said. "It would fit with what's happened and what his skill set is."

"You mean the old gun shop that was here?" Sam shook his head. "Not seeing a connection. He sold guns but no ammunition. Said he'd worked too long in the oil field to have anything that would blow up around him."

"Really?" I said softly.

"Yeah, he's deaf in one ear from an explosion that almost killed him. Didn't you know that? Being his neighbor and all."

"I did not," I said. "He shows no signs of that."

"Implant," Sam said. "I only know this because my pop used to bring me to the gun shop. He was a collector of old guns and said that nobody could restore a weapon like Mr. Wright." He paused. "That's another thing. All Dallas worked on back then was the old stuff. Historic rifles and pistols were his specialty. I'll get my dad's guns someday when he's gone, but I'm in no hurry to inherit them, you know?"

"Right," I said, though my mind was churning through the facts at a high rate of speed.

Dallas Wright would only work on historical weapons and refused to have ammunition on site because of his hatred of explosives.

"I was surprised when they got him for vandalizing this site and nearly killing that guy."

"Apparently, he'll be fine," I said. "But yes, I was shocked that he was charged."

I didn't mention that since then my shock had been reduced to something akin to sadness. Because as much as this new information might take Dallas off the list for planting bombs, it still left him there in regard to the tree and the bear trap. Unfortunately, that meant he must remain on the list.

Rocky turned around and called my name. When I answered, he said, "Blake Perry."

"What about him?" I asked, vaguely recalling the name.

"That's who was in charge while I was gone. Apparently, he was just a temporary hire. The guy is—"

"A security guard at the shopping center," I said, my memory of him returning. "And a friend of Bitsy Decker."

I stood to address Sam. "Do you need anything else from me? I need to run an errand."

"No, I think I've got everything. I'll call you if I come up with anything else."

"Okay great." I paused at the door and spied my mother driving up. "This is where you and the guys have a choice to make. Either I can tell

Mama that there are a whole bunch of first responders at the rescue site, or I can skip that part and let you leave before she sees you. You know what happens either way, right?"

Sam laughed. "What flavors does she have today?"

"Last I saw she was pulling a chocolate pecan and an apple out of the oven." I paused. "She just came back from the beauty shop. If you work that into the conversation, she'll probably offer you a scoop of Blue Bell on the side."

Sam stepped into the driveway and waved at my mother. "Hey, Mrs. Potter. How're you doing today? Your hair looks lovely."

I slipped inside and grabbed my purse and keys. By the time I returned to the porch, Mama had finished chatting up the officer and was offering Rocky a slice of pie.

"I'll be back soon," I told them and drove away.

I found Bitsy at her office on the square. She looked up from her computer screen and frowned. "What do you want?"

"Hello to you too," I said, making myself at home by settling onto the chair across from her.

I glanced around the office, done up in shades of white and cream with rose gold accents on the lamps and pillows, and then returned my attention to her. "Nice place you've got here."

"Right. So again, what do you want?"

"Okay, well, I'll get to the point, then. How long have you been dating Deke King?"

Bitsy's eyes widened, and then she laughed. "Did he tell you that?"

"No."

"Good, because it isn't true." She tucked a platinum strand behind her ear and sighed. "He's persistent, but I'm just not interested in a man who smells like smoked meats all the time. What kind of relationship would that be for a vegetarian like me?"

"I can see your point, but—"

"Besides, he already has a girlfriend, though why he's in a relationship with her, I cannot imagine."

"With who?"

"Anna Wright."

I sucked in a sharp breath, then forced myself not to react any further.

Of all the names I could come up with, hers was not one I would have expected.

"Have you met her?" At my nod, she continued. "She's just not his type. Can you imagine a corporate type like her spending time with a guy like Deke? I just can't see it, but it mostly works for them, I guess."

"How long has this been going on?"

"Ages, I guess. I think she and Deke had plans to merge their properties into one big old happy family farm or something like that. Then her daddy decided otherwise. I don't know if that's why Deke has started coming around and crying to me about how he misses me."

She looked at me as if I would know the answer. When I said nothing, she continued.

"I always send him home with a firm no and then diffuse my essential oils to cover the barbecue scent. Eventually, he'll figure out I'm serious."

Bitsy looked at me as if it was my turn to speak. It took me a minute to realize it was. I'd been too busy adding these facts to the list in my brain.

"So, okay, do you know why Deke would keep going to the rescue building? He's been caught there twice recently."

I left out the part about the bomb. That would come out soon enough.

"I have no idea, but if he shows up again, I can ask him."

"Right, okay." I paused trying to get my thoughts back on track. "So tell me about Blake Perry. He's a friend of yours, right?"

She nodded. "Such a nice guy. When he heard your mother had been injured, he offered to help with repairs. He told me later that she was waiting for her insurance company to pay out and not doing anything yet."

"Yes, that's right." I paused. "Did you know he was working construction? Specifically at the rescue building?"

Bitsy shook her head. "I know he takes odd jobs, but I have no idea if he was working there. Ask him."

"Okay, do you have his number?"

She gave me a look. "I have everyone's number, Trina."

A moment later, my phone buzzed with a text. I glanced at the screen to see that Bitsy had sent me the contact information for Blake.

"Anyone else you'd like to call?" she asked.

"Your ex-husband?" I said before I could stop myself.

Her eyes narrowed. "Which one?"

"Joey Bananas," I said.

Bitsy stood, slamming the lid of her laptop closed. "Out."

"Look, I need to ask him something. It's for—"

"Out, Trina. Just get out."

Was it my imagination, or had her bitter tone gone slightly soft? "Bitsy," I said gently. "I'm sorry. You told me at the Christmas party that you were glad for the divorce, so I didn't expect that asking for his contact information would be hurtful. Please forgive me."

She landed back on her chair with a soft thud. "Trina, why are you still here? I asked you to go."

I picked up my phone and tucked it into my purse and then rose. I was halfway to the door when a thought occurred. I turned around to face Bitsy. "What is he holding over you? Maybe I can help."

Ten minutes later, I left with everything I needed to put the pieces together and solve this puzzle. Well, almost everything. I still needed to speak to Blake Perry.

CHAPTER 33

I walked out of the real estate office door and ran right into Wyatt. Literally.

He grabbed me to keep me from teetering backward, then held me close. I quickly stepped out of his embrace to gather up the two purses I'd been carrying.

"Trina, I have been looking for you. I told you I was on my way to your place, but when I got there I found a bunch of Brenham PD's finest having pie along with the bomb squad, but you were gone."

"Oh, that's right," I said. "You did tell me you were on your way."

I was about to apologize when I remembered I was mad at him.

"Look, I bailed Dallas out last night, and I know you didn't want me to. But he's old and I believe he's innocent. However, I understand how you feel about this, so I took him to my place. He'll stay there until everything is settled."

"Thank you, Wyatt," I said. "You're a nice guy."

He gave me a confused look. "You didn't think so last night."

"I've learned a few things since then."

Wyatt looked past me to Bitsy's door. Then he returned his attention to me. "Okay, want to tell me what you've learned?"

"Can we go back to your office?" I said. "It's kind of complicated, and I still have one more phone call to make."

As we walked around the square to Wyatt's office, he nodded toward the purses I carried. "Two handbags? Is that a new fashion statement?"

"Better than that. I'll explain after we make that call."

Blake Perry picked up on the first ring. I let Wyatt do the talking since he had a friendship with the guy.

"Just one question for you, buddy," Wyatt said. "I understand you've been taking some night school classes. Is that true?"

"Yeah, at Blinn," he told us. "Why?"

"Humor me. It's for something I'm working on. What classes are you taking?"

"Art," he said.

"Specifically, what kind?"

"Sculpture and metalworking," he said. "Would you like to see some pictures?"

"I would love that," Wyatt said. "Would you mind sending me the ones of the metal stuff? That's what I'm most interested in."

"Sure. Hang on a sec." He paused. "Okay, done. What's this about, Wyatt? Is Bitsy in trouble?"

"Not anymore," Wyatt said, scrolling through the pictures Blake had just sent. "I'll fill you in on the details, but just one more question about the last photo. Do you know where that piece is?"

"It sold at a charity auction and barbecue last weekend over in Fayetteville."

Wyatt looked up at me and grinned. "Thanks, buddy. If you've got documentation on that, hang on to it. You'll probably need it later."

"Wyatt, what's going on?"

"Gotta go, Blake," he said, then hung up and made a call to Sam Ferguson. "Exactly what we thought," he said when that brief call ended. "The bomb in the rescue building was a fake." He met my gaze and grinned. "We've got 'em."

"We do," I agreed. "Now how do I finish this?"

Wyatt grinned. "We'll have a party."

"Be serious," I told him.

"I am," he said. "I'll throw a barbecue at my place. We'll invite all the major players and see what happens."

"It'll never work."

"Trust me," he said. "I've done a lot of legal work for a lot of people in this town, including most of the folks on our guest list. None of them is going to suspect."

"But it's short notice," I said. "People will be busy."

"Trust me," he said. "And I think we ought to leave the evidence in the safe at my office, don't you?"

One week later, I was standing in the kitchen of Wyatt's home, looking out onto his back deck. The expansive space was filled with guests, including more than one undercover police officer.

Agent Trent Mendez was dressed as a waiter, ferrying sodas and waters to the guests in between stops at the grill to assist Brenham's BBQ King as sous chef. Three other members of the ATF team were doing a fabulous job as a Miranda Lambert tribute band.

"I cannot believe you managed this," I told him. "It's as if you blackmailed them all to be here."

"*Blackmail* is such an ugly word, Trina," he said with a chuckle. "For most of them, all I said was I needed guests at a party, and I would waive the remaining fees they owe me if they would show up."

I laughed. "I can see that would be a strong incentive."

"Incentive," he repeated. "I like that. Now, let's get out there and have some fun. I'm starved."

"Are we really going to serve dinner before we make arrests?"

"It would be cruel not to, don't you think? I mean, it's not like they'll get anything decent to eat in jail. Might as well get thrown in the slammer with a full stomach."

"I don't see Bitsy out there," I said. "I figured she would want to be here."

"She'll be here," he told me. "But for obvious reasons, she didn't want to show up before the main event."

"I guess that makes sense," I told him. "How did you get her ex here? Surely he wasn't a client."

"Hardly. I told him that I was hosting a group that had heard of him and wanted to hear more about investment opportunities in his company. He couldn't get the address fast enough."

"Of course."

"Okay, showtime," he said. "Let's do this."

Wyatt stepped out into the late evening sunshine. I followed a step behind. Deke had finished grilling and was chatting with Joe Bonnano about investments. Anna Wright was making polite conversation with

Mama and Pastor Nelson about piecrust over by the appetizer table.

Meanwhile, Mari, Parker, and Cassidy were being entertained with stories of Sticks's boy band days. Rocky and Blake had gone to the edge of the deck to examine the construction of the benches there. Reporter Mollie Kensington was asking questions of Tyler, Kristin, and Dr. Bishop while her photographer talked to Maggie about camera angles and shutter speeds.

The remainder of the guest list, all law enforcement, appeared to be having the time of their lives, dancing to the country trio or chatting in small groups on the edges of the deck.

As Wyatt and I planned, I took the lead in ushering our guests over to the table set with place cards for each of the guests. Once everyone had been seated, Wyatt motioned for our waiter, aka Agent Mendez, to begin food service.

When the last plate of pie was cleared, Wyatt stood to get his guests' attention. "Thank you all for coming," he told the group. "Trina, would you join me, please?"

I rose and stood beside Wyatt.

"Some of you know why you're here, but most of you do not," Wyatt said. "I'll let Trina take it from here."

I smiled as I addressed the guests. "First, to the band, you guys rock. See Sticks Styler afterward to talk about a contract."

The band members whooped and high-fived, generally doing an excellent job of convincing everyone they were excited about a possible record contract. Who knew undercover officers were such good actors?

"Okay, so now for the rest of you. I'm just going to start at the beginning. You probably weren't warned that this will also be a fundraiser for my niece's dog rescue, but that's on the agenda for tonight. Feel free to write a check to the charity, and remember, guys, she's a 501(c)3 organization. Mari or Parker will take your donations afterward."

"Or now if you want," Wyatt said. "Joe, since you're the businessman here, how about you start us off?"

Joe Bonnano laughed and held up his phone. "Do they take PayPal or Venmo?"

"Both," Parker said, then called out the payment information for both.

"You're terrible," I whispered to Wyatt.

He leaned toward me. "Let the man do something good for once."

I shook my head and pushed him away. "Okay," I said. "So we wanted you all here because Wyatt and I have been trying to solve a puzzle, and you're part of the solution." I paused. "Well, some of you are, anyway."

CHAPTER 34

"Oh, fun and games," Joey called out. "I like puzzles."

"Right," I said. "This puzzle is probably not one you're going to like, Mr. Bonnano, but I'm getting ahead of myself. I'll start with you, Deke."

"Me?" the BBQ King said.

"You and Anna were going to combine your neighboring properties to form one big plot of land. You just needed Anna's father to cooperate. Failing that, Anna needed to get his power of attorney. Your father messed that up when he sold his property to me. He thought he was doing the right thing since you weren't interested in living there. She told you that, didn't she, Dallas?"

"She did," he said, his expression sober as he turned to her. "Sweetheart, if you'd just told me you wanted the land, I would have deeded it over to you. Why did you take the hard way?"

Anna's face flushed, but she ignored her father's question. Deke remained silent.

"But why would the two of them want to put their lands together?" Wyatt asked, obviously unable to control himself. "Trina is going to tell you."

"We'll get back to that," I said. "See, I went back and did some checking as to why Anna was at a conference in Nashville while I was there. Turns out she's a geologist. Isn't that right, Anna?"

"That's right," her father said for her. "And she's a good one too. I'm proud of that girl."

"Don't be too proud, Dallas," Wyatt said. "She got you arrested."

"That's a ridiculous accusation," Anna said.

"It was you and Deke who planted the evidence that got him put in the slammer," Wyatt said evenly.

"Hey now," Deke said. "I'm innocent here."

"No, you're not," I told him. "You're the one who had the chain saw the whole time. Dallas told us you borrow his to cut wood for your grill when your chain saw isn't working, so it wouldn't be unusual for you to have it, would it? But that's not the answer you gave, Deke. You're also the one who cut the tree and then hid the chain saw under Dallas's bed."

"And the creep who caught Trina's dog in a bear trap."

"If I did all that, wouldn't I have left fingerprints? How do you explain that?"

"Look in your pocket," I told him. "What are those?"

"Gloves," he said sheepishly.

"Which I have seen you wear on more than one occasion."

"We all know you wear them when you're cooking and when you're cutting wood," Dallas added. "I'm the only one who uses that thing with hands that don't have gloves on them." He looked over at Wyatt. "Didn't I tell you that was the case?"

"You did," Wyatt said. "And that was an essential piece of the puzzle. Thank you, Dallas. It also helped that you knew the bear trap would have had to be oiled and repaired before it would work. That's where Rocky comes in."

Rocky stood and turned to Deke. "I'm not taking the fall for you, man. I don't care how much free barbecue I get." He returned his attention to me. "Yes, I bought the supplies to get that stupid trap from the Wrights' barn working, but if I'd known what he was up to, I would never have done it. He never told me a dog was going to get hurt."

"He wasn't supposed to," Wyatt said. "Was he, Deke?"

"Don't answer him," Anna said.

"He doesn't have to," I told her. "When you couldn't get control of this property by legal means, you had a backup plan to put your father into a guardianship. But first you had to show that he was a danger to himself and others. That's where the trap and the second bomb come in."

"Second bomb?" Rocky said. "I thought it was—"

"A fake," Wyatt supplied. "Yes, it was, and Deke knew it. Anna had been trying to convince him to get rid of the rescue building in hopes of running the Potter ladies off the land. It almost worked too."

"I was ready to sell," I admitted. "Anna knew that, which is why she pushed Deke so hard to send me over the edge with a bomb that would close the rescue down before it ever opened."

Anna rose. "I don't have to listen to this. I'm leaving. Deke, come on. Let's go."

"I suggest you stay," Wyatt said. "You'll want to hear the rest of this."

"I really don't," she told him.

I walked over to Anna and leaned close. "There are police officers everywhere," I whispered. "And Mollie over there is with the local newspaper. If you want to make headlines complete with photographs, go ahead and make a fuss and get arrested right now."

Anna gave me a glare but sat back down. She'd be arrested anyway, but not just yet.

"So Deke decided rather than actually plant a bomb, he'd just get one from an art student who was taking a scripture and metal works class. Isn't that right, Deke?"

"No comment," he said.

"This is great," Joe Bonnano said. "Dinner and a play. It's a whodunit mystery game, right?"

Wyatt grinned at me, then nodded toward Joe. "You could say that. Just hang with me a minute, and I'll get to your part."

"Awesome," he responded.

"So we've covered the bear trap, the falling tree, and the fake bomb," I said. "What else is left?"

"The reason for it all?" Wyatt supplied. "And for that, we need both Anna and Joe up here."

Joe jumped from his seat to come and stand beside Wyatt. Apparently, he was embracing what he thought was a mystery party theme with great enthusiasm.

"The reason is mineral deposits," I said. "Isn't that right?"

Deke stood. "That's preposterous. I don't have anything under my land worth drilling for, so I doubt the Wrights do."

"That's where you're wrong," I said. "Anna ran some tests to see what was there. Am I right, Anna? When you do a test, you test in a wide circle around your designated area. Fifty miles or so? You're looking for anomalies. Hills and valleys and such."

"No comment," Anna said, borrowing Deke's line.

"Right," Wyatt said. "Well, Deke, you'll be happy to know that the report included sizable mineral deposits under your land and Wright land."

"That's Potter land," I corrected.

"And that's the problem," Wyatt said. "Your plan didn't work, Anna. The land and the mineral rights belong to Trina and her family. And Deke isn't going to be able to spend his royalties where he's going."

"Where am I going?" he demanded.

Two members of the tribute band rose to move on either side of him. "Jail," the one who looked like Miranda said. The third member of the band tapped Anna on the shoulder. "And you're going with them, sweetheart," she said.

"You're not cops," Deke said. "You're girl singers."

The Miranda character laughed. "We're both, honey. Want me to do a little 'Folsom Prison Blues' for you after we read you your rights?"

Mollie grinned at me, then nodded for her photographer to snap some pictures of the arrest. *So much for not being a headline, Anna.*

"So let me understand this," my mother announced, standing. "You mean to tell me that Dallas's daughter and that idiot next door were willing to sell this nice man down the river just to get at some mineral rights?"

"It looks that way," Wyatt said.

"For that, my daughter's dog was hurt?" Mama continued, her temper obviously rising. "And bombs were planted?"

"Funny you should mention that, Mama Peach," Wyatt said. "See, we've explained everything that has happened, from the falling tree to the bear trap, but there's one bomb that doesn't fit the pattern."

"That's the one that was planted at the Double J," Parker said. "I never understood that one. It wasn't close enough to do any harm to the building that Maggie had loaned to us, but it was definitely live and could have caused a lot of damage if it had gone off."

Mari met my gaze but said nothing. I exhaled a long breath and nodded in agreement with the blue-eyed vet tech who'd stolen my niece's heart.

"And that is where Joe Bonnano comes in."

Joe whooped. "All right. Now this party is getting fun. What's my part?"

On cue, Bitsy Decker stepped out of the kitchen onto the deck. At her arrival, the ATF squad moved into place behind Joe.

"Your part is as the angry ex-husband looking to keep from paying his ex-wife her half of the business," Bitsy said.

Joe's eyes widened as he realized this was no game after all. "What's she doing here?" he demanded.

"She's going to explain your part in the bomb at the dog rescue," I told him.

"I didn't plant a bomb anywhere near a dog rescue." He made a move to leave, but two agents held him in place.

"He's not wrong," I said. "Is he Bitsy?"

"Nope." Wyatt reached under the table in front of him to retrieve Bitsy's purse and then held it up.

"I didn't put it in there either."

"No, you didn't," Bitsy said. "You put it in my garage."

Instantly, Joe's defiant expression soured, and his shoulders sunk. His bluster was gone, and he made no comment.

"I thought it was something that had fallen off my car," she said. "I stuck it in my purse, thinking I would bring it to the dealer to get it put back on."

"You're joking, right?" my mother said. "That is absolutely the dumbest—"

"Mama," I interrupted, "that's enough."

"Anyway," Bitsy continued, "the short version is that when I heard Mari and her group were keeping dogs on the Double J, I went out to investigate. I've been trying to get an option on the property across the street, and I figured if there was a big dog kennel right there at the road, that would affect the price."

She paused. Wyatt nodded toward her. "Go on."

"So I was tired of this heavy thing in my purse. It kept clanking around and making noises while I was driving, so while I was out there in the country, I took a picture of it for the dealer's service people and then tossed it over the fence."

A collective gasp went up. I gave my mother a warning look lest she say anything.

"I only found out it was a bomb when I saw the news. Goodness, I was carrying a bomb around all that time?"

"For the ATF guys in the room," Wyatt said, "explain the platinum hair dye, please."

"Oh right," she said. "I was doing my hair when my purse fell off the counter."

Another gasp went up.

"The car part thingie fell out and rolled across to my feet. My hands were covered in dye, but I didn't want to trip over it, so I did the safe thing and put it back in my purse."

"Honey, the safe thing would have been not to have a bomb in your purse," Mama said.

I glared at her. She shrugged.

"So, to recap," Wyatt said. "The first bomb was Joey Bananas trying not to cut Bitsy in on his business."

"What about the report of the white van?" one of the officers asked.

"I really did see one," Bitsy said. "But since I didn't want to be in trouble for littering a bomb, I didn't leave my name. I only found out later it was the white van that Mari's rescue uses."

"Right," Wyatt said. "And everything else can be traced back to Anna and her accomplice, Deke." He paused. "Have I missed anything?"

"Just one thing." Pastor Nelson stood. "Might I have the floor? If you're finished highlighting the felonies and misdemeanors, that is."

Mama looked up at him, shaking her head. "What is this about, Howard?"

"It's about you. Us. Oh, just hold on. This could take a minute."

With great effort, the elderly pastor managed to go down on one knee. "Peach, you are the most interesting woman I know. No one else makes dog clothes and pie like you do. And no matter what you think, you have always had my heart."

"I object," Dr. Bishop said.

"To what?" Wyatt asked.

"Whatever he's about to ask."

"You can't object, Elvin," Mama said, "you're a veterinarian, not a lawyer. You were saying, Howard?"

"I was saying what I've wanted to say for a long time. Will you marry me, Peach Potter?"

"Give me another chance," Dr. Bishop pleaded.

Mama gave him a look. "I told you before, if Hector doesn't like you, then I can't possibly consider a life with you."

"But Hector dislikes almost everyone," the veterinarian protested.

"Not me," Pastor Nelson said.

Later I might tell Mama that the reason the pastor was so popular with her cat was the treats he fed Hector when Mama wasn't looking. Or maybe I'd just let her think that Hector actually liked someone.

CHAPTER 35

Three weeks flew by. Mama's engagement was almost as big a news story in Brenham as the arrest of Anna Wright, Deke King, and Joe Bonnano. Wyatt suggested we hold another party—this time to celebrate the opening of the Second Chance Ranch Dog Rescue facility.

With barbecue no longer a menu choice, Wyatt took over the catering duties with Mama tapped for dessert, of course. Mari requested that we make it family and the original volunteer group only, so that's what we did, with one exception.

Sticks.

He called to make a special request that he attend. Something about big news.

He was practically family anyway, so we all agreed.

And, of course, all the dogs were specially invited guests with their own menu. Hector, however, had to stay at home. He didn't travel well anyway.

That evening we were back on the deck with the sun setting in a glorious riot of purples, golds, and pinks behind us. Mari and Cassidy had strung lights over the tables, giving the dining spot a festive look.

I walked out to see what they were up to, and Cassidy pulled me aside. "I've been needing to have a conversation with you. I haven't been completely truthful."

"Oh?"

She glanced around, then returned her attention to me. "See, I've mostly stopped going out on these rescues where it's just Mari and Parker for a good reason." She paused. "It's not being too busy or anything else. It's because I am trying to throw them together, okay? I know they like each other, and I feel like if they go on more rescues, just the two of them, then that will draw them closer together."

I smiled. "That makes perfect sense, Cassidy. However, I think you need to be honest with them. They're worried about you."

"Oh. I didn't think about that. Them being worried and all. Yes, I should." She paused. "Does it have to be tonight?"

"It should be soon," I said. "Maybe the next time you're asked to go out when it would just be the three of you?"

Cassidy grinned. "Right, yes. Good idea." Then she went off to help Mari with the decorating.

Later, after a delicious Mexican food dinner from Smarty's under the stars, Sticks clinked his fork against his glass and called us to attention. "Thank you all for having me tonight. I just want to let you all know first that I've taken Trina's advice."

"My advice?" I asked.

"Yes, thanks to Bitsy Decker, I am the owner of the property across the road from the Double J Ranch. I'll have a recording studio up and going by October, according to my architect. The house will take longer, but it should be done by spring. I'll still keep the business headquartered in Nashville, but I'll be back and forth."

"That's wonderful," I told him, resisting the urge to say "I told you so." "Welcome to Brenham."

"Thank you. Maybe now we'll finish that chess game."

"I'd like that," I told him.

"That's not all." He nodded to Mari, who stood and went over to the area where the shelter dogs were playing. "I'm the proud pet dad of this cutie."

Mari held up a very familiar-looking dog. "That's Honey," I exclaimed.

"She was recently returned to us," Mari said. "Her new owners were transferred overseas and couldn't take her. Sticks has been her temporary foster. They hit it off."

"Cue the happy ending," Sticks said.

The family applauded, and Parker even whistled. Sticks motioned for them to be quiet again.

"One more thing," Sticks said. "The record label is honored to be the first to have an ongoing endowment to the Second Chance Ranch Dog Rescue. We'll figure out the details, but I'd like to make sure there's funds for the rescue to continue its good works."

A short while later, the guests began to leave. Mari and Parker corralled the dogs into the van. Then Mari called to Cassidy to join them.

She looked at me and smiled. "No time like the present," she said as she walked toward her fellow rescuers.

I walked inside to help Wyatt wash dishes. When we were done, we walked back outside. Everything was quiet and still now. Patsy and Cline were snoring next to Ed, fast friends who'd worn each other out racing around the property like the crazy dogs they were.

Wyatt settled onto the outdoor sofa, and I curled up next to him. I was happy and tired, but the good kind of tired. He grasped my hand then stood.

"Wait right here. I've got something for you." He hurried back with two mugs, and after he returned to the seat beside me, he offered me one of them.

"What is this?"

"It's a froufrou latte with the works, including sprinkles and edible glitter." Wyatt shrugged. "I love you, Trina Potter. I keep my promises."

"I love you too, Wyatt Chastain."

"Yeah?" His grin was immediate and adorable. "How about that?"

I took a sip and smiled. "It's perfect." Then I sighed. "Everything about this evening has been perfect."

Wyatt took the mug from me and placed it on the table and then covered my lips with his. "Now it's really perfect," I whispered, settling once again beside him.

"So Trina," Wyatt said, "I wasn't exactly truthful about something."

My heart sunk. So much for being perfect.

"You know how I had your birthday on my calendar, and I told you it was the day I bought the place?" At my nod, he continued. "Well, that part was right. But there's more. See, I planted my pecans on that date so I would have a reason to have your birthday on my calendar. Before I had those trees, I didn't have a reason. Well, except that I hoped that one day I'd get to tell you happy birthday on that date."

Tears shimmered in my eyes. "Wyatt, really? All those years you thought of me? I mean, it's not like we did much talking to one another except at the odd event here and there."

"A guy doesn't forget his first cheerleader, popular girl prom date."

"Is that all I am to you, Wyatt Chastain? Your first cheerleader, popular girl prom date?" I said playfully.

"Nope." He leaned in for another kiss. This time when he pulled away, he slid off the sofa and onto one knee. "I want you to be not only the first but also the last. Will you marry me, Trina?"

"What?" I said much louder than I intended.

All three dogs awoke and barked in unison.

"Not you three," Wyatt grumbled. "I'm talking to the lady."

I smiled. "And the lady says yes."

Kathleen Y'Barbo is a multiple Carol Award and RITA nominee and bestselling author of more than one hundred books with over two million copies of her books in print in the US and abroad. A tenth-generation Texan and certified paralegal, she is a member of the Texas Bar Association Paralegal Division, Texas A&M Association of Former Students and the Texas A&M Women Former Students (Aggie Women), Texas Historical Society, Novelists Inc., and a member of the executive board of American Christian Fiction Writers. She would also be a member of the Daughters of the American Republic, Daughters of the Republic of Texas, and a few others if she would just remember to fill out the paperwork that Great-Aunt Mary Beth has sent her more than once.

When she's not spinning modern-day tales about her wacky Southern relatives, Kathleen inserts an ancestor or two into her historical and mystery novels as well. Recent book releases include the bestseller *The Pirate Bride*, set in 1700s New Orleans and Galveston, and its sequel, *The Alamo Bride*, set in 1836 Texas, which feature a few well-placed folks from history and a family tale of adventure on the high seas and on the coast of Texas. She also writes (mostly) relative-free cozy mystery novels for Guideposts Books.

Kathleen and her hero-in-combat-boots husband have their own surprise love story that unfolded on social media a few years back. They make their home just north of Houston, Texas, and are the parents and in-laws of a blended family of Texans, Okies, and a trio of very adorable Londoners.

To find out more about Kathleen or to connect with her through social media, check out her website at www.kathleenybarbo.com.

GONE *to the* DOGS
Book 3

Releasing January 2023

BARKING UP the WRONG TREE
BY JANICE THOMPSON

Inquisitive, detail-oriented veterinarian Kristin Keller prides herself on winning over any dog. But has this self-proclaimed dog whisperer finally met her match in a Sheltie named Remington who has just won the Texas state agility course competition? The champion pooch is acting out of sorts—almost as if he is not the same dog. Has he, by chance, been switched out with another dog just before the next big competition? Kristin and the other Lone Star employees will do anything to help the Atkinson family figure out this mystery surrounding their beloved Remington.

Paperback / 978-1-63609-451-9